TEAR TIME

First Published in the USA by

Kissaki-Kai
55E Route 70,
Marlton,
NJ 08053

Paperback edition. 2009

ISBN 978-161623804-9

Cover Image 'At Gunpoint' © Imagecom | Dreamstime.com

Cover artwork: alliesloan@everlookmarketing.co.uk

The author can be contacted at:

info@kissaki-kai.com
International website: www.kissakikarate.com

Author's Note

This has been a difficult book to write, conscious as I am of the yet unhealed wounds in that lovely country of Ireland. I also empathise with those who are regretful of the past, but who hold to the view that the consensus of local opinion should be acknowledged. I am not alone in considering the problem practically insoluble unless boundless forgiveness is employed by both sides.

I am against the indiscriminate taking of life in whatever cause.

I do not profess to offer any answers here, merely to write a novel which has taken facts in the public domain and altered them, sometimes slightly, sometimes significantly, in order to weave the fabric of the tale. My intention was to write an adventure story which also shed just a little light on the warp and weft of politics, society and human ambitions which drive men to both heroism and despicable acts! Of course, we all know of the 'Intentionalist fallacy.'

My thanks are due to many, but not in the least to my partner in life, Eva, who has patiently read and re-read this work, and gently calmed my protestations when she proved correct over matters of grammar, logic...

Thanks also to Jon and Allie Sloan and their sterling work with the artwork for the cover design.

This is a work of fiction, but, as noted, any references to real people, either living or dead, real events, organisations and localities are used only to give a sense of verisimilitude to the fiction.

The story is the product of the author's imagination, and the words and thoughts expressed by the characters are solely of his invention. Nothing should be imputed from the story to words and thoughts of any real person

Unfortunately, as I write, I find this work to have been prophetic in that even this week in October 2009 brings news of continuing violence in

Ireland with the killings of both soldiers and police. Also ETA terrorist bombers have recently been active in the beautiful island of Mallorca!

On the larger stage, terrorist acts are currently causing the deaths of US and European soldiers who are committed to serving what they deem to be the best interests of us all, peace and freedom.

The tragedy continues and will continue to do so until society refuses to give aid and succour to the purveyors of death and sorrow!

Vince Morris New Jersey 2009.

For Eva

CHAPTER ONE

ITALY

Outside Bologna railway station, the street was still busy. It was 10.20 am. The first rush of commuter traffic was over, but the taxis were still coming and going, weaving their way between the cyclists, pedestrians and kamikaze scooter drivers who had been lured out by the glorious weather.

Small groups of back-packing teenage tourists huddled over street maps and a small congregation of street dwellers in the grimy little alley opposite the station taxi ranks eased their aching joints beneath their rags, grateful for the gentle warmth.

Spurning the acrid tobacco fumes of the platform waiting room, Marcello smiled fondly down at his lovely wife. How beautiful she was, he thought, her ash-blonde hair tumbling and dancing in the warm breeze as she bent over the pushchair to fussily adjust little Giorgio's brightly coloured woollen jacket.

The sun beamed down, and even here on the railway station platform the air was thick with all the scents of early summer. Marcello's heart surged with joy as he looked at the chortling, gurgling infant, all wide eyes and clutching fists as the smiling face of his mother filled his universe. How could he be happier? A gorgeous wife, a fine strong baby boy, an interview for a new job, and all under balmy, Michelangelo blue skies! His spirits danced!

The train stood waiting; the mail and parcels had been loaded and most of the passengers had climbed aboard and claimed their seats.

Almost the last ones remaining on the platform, impulsively he pulled his startled wife fiercely to him, smelling the warm-bread musky smell of all young mothers intermingled with the slightest hint of perfume, smothering her giggled protests with urgent lips.

She had made a special effort, he knew, to send him off in high spirits. This job was important to him, to them, to all three of them.

A last hug and a lingering embrace, then he was aboard, leaning through an open window as the chortling infant was lifted up for a final kiss.

With an iron screech of wheels and a sudden lurch, the train began to pull away.

It was 10.24am.

Adrienne held the baby high, waving Giorgio's tiny arm in farewell.

It was 10.25am.

A blinding flashing fireball of an explosion ripped horrendously through the station. A shattering roar, almost incomprehensible in its intensity, battered and dazed the senses, hammering eardrums into a shocking silence.

To Marcello on the train, it was as if time had ceased to flow.

In a slow-motion nightmare he watched helplessly as the expanding eruption cut down his wife and baby, hurling them around in a swirling, body-smashing maelstrom of bricks, dust and debris.

The train had stopped, and time had stopped. The rictus of Marcello's tormented scream was frozen on his face.

Almost before his stunned brain could even register the deaths of his family, a jagged splinter of glass punched savagely into his left eye. Not a large splinter really, no more than 10 centimetres long, but big enough to tear away the optic nerve and slice deep into the frontal portion of his brain.

Death was instantaneous. Marcello never even felt it. Neither did he see the crumpled remains of the pushchair, nor his wife's broken and bloody arm, sticking up from the dust-hazed debris of the fallen platform canopy that had killed her and his son in the same fatal instant.

Outside the station the traffic was frozen into shocked immobility. For heartbeats the only sound to permeate the unnatural silence was the unnerving shriek of a jammed train whistle. Then, like starting a video from pause, sound and movement returned. The street came to life. The silence was now torn with the panic-stricken screams of the injured and maimed.

Maps and Bicycles clattered to the ground and lay forgotten; doors of abandoned cars gaped open as horrified passers-by ran to help

All except one, that is.

At the far end of the street, leaning casually against the side of a silver-grey BMW 7, a tall, slim, athletic man in an obviously expensive grey pin-stripe suit enlivened by a multi-coloured silk tie, brushed a fleck from one lapel. After a moment spent surveying the ensuing chaos, he briskly pulled open the driver's door and slid behind the wheel.

He looked thoughtfully into the rear-view mirror at the scene of panic and devastation behind him, then, satisfied with what he saw, he eased the car smoothly from the kerb, and accelerated quickly away.

CHAPTER TWO

DUBLIN, 65 YEARS EARLIER

From beneath the dark and stifling fabric of the hood he could feel the gritty roughness of the wall grinding into his forehead.

The spread-eagled position of his body - legs wide astride, arms open at shoulder level, with the fingertips of each hand flat against the brickwork, his feet pulled away from the wall - forced him to lean at an angle with all his weight supported by his aching fingers and brick-scraped forehead.

"Christ!" "How much longer?" He knew he couldn't take much more!

First the hot passion of his rage had seen him through, forcing adrenaline into his system, blunting the pain.

Then eventually the anger had seeped away, leaving in its place a cold hate, which hardened his body against the wicked strength-sapping blows which sporadically and unannounced thudded into his unprotected kidneys.

Later, when hate slid into despair, he tried to conjure pictures of his baby son Sean into his mind to remind him of what he was fighting for, and the smiling face of his wife as she shouted up to him through the hastily erected barricades around the Dublin Post Office, almost lost in the crowds jostling to listen to Patrick Pearse' rebellious speeches as if on an Easter holiday.

Eventually, however, as his captors had known it would, the torture began to take effect.

The minutes merged into hours; every muscle of his body cramped and ached fiercely from maintaining its unnatural position. His ankles and knees began to swell, each joint on fire from the stress and the sporadically administered brutal kicks to calf or shin from a heavy army boot every time he shifted his weight.

Tendrils of white-hot agony played along every trembling muscle.

Shaking with fatigue, he eased his fingers away from the wall for a moment's relief.
Immediately yet another vicious unannounced blow thudded savagely into the small of his back, stopping his breath and spreading fierce waves of paralysing fire up and down his spine and into the pit of his stomach.

As his whole being throbbed in agonised counterpoint to his pounding heart, only by surreptitiously taking most of the weight on his forehead could his fingers gain some relief, but this was at the expense of grinding the roughly woven fabric of the hood deeper into the half-congealed bloody scab above his eyes, re-opening the wound which trickled blood thickly down over the bridge of his nose and into his eyes.

He had no idea how long he had stood there, it could have been hours or even days, all sense of time had gone, lost in a claustrophobic, pain-filled, gagging darkness. Neither could he tell if his fellow rebels who had been frog-marched into the empty room with him were still there or not.
Initially he had been aware of their muffled curses as they struggled against the soldiers, but then the deafening music from a wind-up gramophone had begun and his surroundings

dissolved into a pain-centred universe punctuated only by his own stertorous ragged breathing and the sudden unexpected agony of savage but carefully aimed punches.

The continuous playing of the scratchy dance music only served to further distance him from reality as it wore away at him unceasingly until it dissolved into a meaningless cacophony, gyrating round and around in his pounding head.

Michael Kennedy knew that he couldn't hold out much longer, no matter how he tried. He would soon admit to anything at all, if only they would ask him!

He had finally broken when his swollen bladder had released its pent up urine, first in tiny trickles and then in a sudden flood until the warmth suffusing his groin matched the hotness of the furious tears squeezing from under his tightly clenched eyelids.

His soul protested the degradation of it all.

Aeons passed and the hot liquid staining his trousers grew cold and clammy, and then in time warm again as his body heat dried out the stiffening cloth.

The silent watcher saw it all. He knew when it was done!

He had seen it so many times before. Not torture, exactly; after all, the British army couldn't be seen to be involved in such barbarity, but this "softening-up", well, that was different.
Isolate a man from all sensations except those of his own body for long enough to disorientate him, deprive him of food and sleep, keep him in a fixed and uncomfortable position, with perhaps the occasional little dig from time to time to wake him up, and even the strongest man would crack.

Captain Barton knew that the swaying, sobbing rebel almost hanging between the supporting and restraining arms of the two soldiers on either side of him had reached that point.

He ground the stub of his cigarette under his heel, and nodded to the door.

Why they had to keep this up was beyond him, he thought wearily to himself as he followed the two soldiers and their hooded victim, as they dragged him unceremoniously out of the room and down the corridor.

For all he cared, if they wanted Ireland, then by God they could have it! Bogtrotters, each and every one of them. Shifty bastards, totally untrustworthy, not even capable of keeping the peace even amongst themselves! What on earth was there in this godforsaken country of even the remotest interest for a man of culture and breeding? Certainly nothing worth fomenting a rebellion over!

No, he reflected, best let the buggers have their country and be well rid of it!

He closed the door behind him as he followed the stumbling prisoner into the tiny bare room with its whitewashed walls and single chair. He nodded again. There was no need to issue orders, they had all done this many times before.

The corporal twisted Kennedy around and steadied him so that his back was against the wall; releasing his grip, he reached up and roughly dragged the hood from his head.

Blinking through screwed-up eyes, the haggard figure swayed and almost fell.

"Stand up you bastard!" The corporal's bellow hit him like a blow.

He staggered, his eyes, unused to the light, streamed and burned with tears, blurring his vision. He raised a hand to wipe them.

"Keep your hands by your side!" The voice barked angrily into his ear. "Move when you are told to, not before."

His arm was jerked roughly down to his side.

The immaculate Captain Barton sat down and brushing at a wayward speck with an annoyed flick of his fingers as he crossed his legs. He studied the wreckage of the man that stood swaying before him.

A big, broad-shouldered bruiser of a boyo, six foot four if he was an inch. Couldn't be more than in his early twenties though. His tangled black hair hung limp with sweat over his ears and across his bruised forehead, sticking in places to the half-congealed scab that had leaked rivulets of blood down deeply furrowed cheeks until they had congealed in the great drooping moustache like the dribbles of an old man's meal.

From experience he knew that after the four days that had been spent softening the big man up he now had probably got between two to three hours of relative lucidity in which to tease information from the disorientated mind, before it collapsed altogether.

With a mental sigh he reached into his uniform pocket and withdrew a tortoiseshell Parker and studiously unscrewed the top. He took the clipboard which had been clamped firmly under one arm and balanced it upon his knee.

Quietly, he began:

"Right, let's start at the beginning shall we? He looked up from his pristine notepad: "Name?"

CHAPTER THREE

"FROM LITTLE ACORNS.........."

Michael Kennedy wasn't alone. In similar rooms down the corridor similar scenes were being enacted. Many of his compatriots had already confessed, it didn't matter to what, anything actually, just to end the torture. They had been bundled roughly into military trucks and were even now on the way from the Richmond Barracks to the docks, from there to be shipped across the sea to the English mainland and from there straight to Stafford Military Jail.

Kennedy would soon be reunited with them, and with his erstwhile leader and conspirator, Michael Collins, the 'Big Fellow' himself, who would use this period of incarceration to further his reputation and plot yet more rebellions against the English invaders.

Collins had already noted the name of the bombastic English officer who, in a towering rage, had forced the captured rebels to be paraded along O'Connell Street between two long lines of jeering soldiers to the Rotunda Hospital, and who had then proceeded to beat them.

This same officer who, later, in a gin-heightened red-faced apoplexy, had ordered that one of the leaders - frail bespectacled old Tom Clarke - be strip-searched mother naked in the street, in front of everyone, not fifty yards from his little tobacconist's shop on the corner of Parnell Street where so much of the planning for the ill-fated uprising had taken place.

That first night of the surrender had been spent out in the open by the Rotunda. It had been cold and damp, and no food nor drink was given to any of the prisoners, nor were they issued blankets or any kind of protection. To heap indignities upon the rebels even lavatories were denied them. All bodily functions had to be carried out where they stood, in the open, men and women, huddled together.

That shameful night was by the order of the same English officer, now much the worse for drink; and oh yes, the Big Fellow had his name, and Captain Lee Wilson's fatal appointment in a peaceful lane in County Wexford was already made and noted down, even if he himself did not yet know it!

The same citizens who had originally gathered outside the 'liberated' Post Office building to jeer and mock the rebels were soon to react to the barbarity of the torments which they saw inflicted on their fellow countrymen, and pouring the dregs of humanity wearing British uniforms into Dublin was to be no answer; that would only serve to exacerbate the tension and the loathing of these now confirmed Irish patriots for their foreign overlords.

Michael, like his fellow-prisoner, mentor and namesake Michael Collins, was one of the lucky ones, not deemed important enough to be selected along with the other leaders: old Tom Clarke, the oratorical dreamer of a schoolteacher Patrick Pearse, the mysterious Sean MacDermott, the stereotypical Irish would-be poet Thomas MacDonagh and his fellow scribbler Joe Plunkett.

These never made it to the boat, but were stood up in front of an English firing squad and shot to death. First to have the tiny targets of scrap paper pinned to their breasts were Clarke,

MacDonagh and Pearse, with Plunkett following barely a day later.

The stout little Scottish-born socialist leader of the rag-bag Citizens Army, James Connelly, even though now wasted, sick and badly wounded in the ankle by a ricocheting sniper's bullet and heavily sedated with morphine, was also shown no mercy. Unable even to sit upright in his sick bed, he was manhandled into clean pyjamas and, eight days after the first of his colleagues to face the firing squads, was brought in the dead of night by ambulance from the Castle to Kilmainham Jail.

Then, in the grey, early light of dawn, the sick, semi-conscious man was tied to a chair to prevent him from falling over, blindfolded and then shot to death; being finished off in the usual manner with a pistol bullet in the head.

It was three weeks before the lucky ones, now internees in England, discovered the fate of their companions, and nine months before their general release.

But this was a vital period for the fledgling republican movements, the Volunteers and the Republican Brotherhood, who fed on and thrived upon the hatred whipped up by the savage and barbaric treatment meted out to their leaders, and they used the time well to organise and plot revenge.

The months in prison also provided opportunity for 'The Big Fellow' to increase in reputation and stature and for Michael Kennedy to learn to share his hero's implacable hatred of the British.

Back in Dublin, however, young Kate Kennedy was struggling to keep their little home together by taking in washing from the very same army barracks where her husband

Michael and the other rebels had first been taken. Life had to go on, and Kate, with a tiny undernourished son to feed had no choice, she knew that Michael would understand when he came home.

She wrapped her shawl closer around her thin shoulders and cuddled Sean to her breast, rocking gently in front of the meagre fire, occasionally wiping away a wayward teardrop that threatened to splash upon the baby's head.

Was she crying for her husband, her child, herself, or Ireland?

She couldn't tell you, of course, but this was the beginning of the time of tears - the merry-go-round of death.

CHAPTER FOUR

"......MIGHTY OAKS DO GROW"

The interior of Madrid airport, was much like that of any major airport anywhere in the world at eight o'clock in the morning. Already the long lines of luggage-laden families had formed at the check-in desks, each flustered trolley-pusher edging imperceptibly closer to the one in front to ensure that no-one else pushed in.

Children, bored with waiting, ran about, impatient to be off. Harassed parents checked the flight information screens for explanations of delays.

At one end of the concourse the snack bar was jammed to overflowing. The designers had obviously made a mistake here, for the seats were actually quite comfortable. More so, in fact, than most of those out in the main hall; consequently they were full of leg-weary travellers, stretched out amongst their piles of baggage, to the chagrin of the hungry, the thirsty and the management.

Clasping an undrinkable plastic cup of coffee in one hand and a slim brown leather briefcase in the other, Liam Kennedy manoeuvred his way carefully between bags and around outstretched legs, finally slipping quickly into a seat, almost before the previous occupant's backside had cleared it.

A good-looking man, nose a little too long for his face, slim with dark brown hair and a mouth that seemed eager to smile, Kennedy sat at ease, sipping the evil brew and casually surveying the scene.

With his forefinger, he shot back the cuff of his Cerruti lightweight and checked the gold Rolex Oyster on his wrist, almost eight minutes past eight. Kennedy put the plastic cup down amongst the other empties on the table and got to his feet. As he did so his right foot nudged the briefcase further under the table until it joined the jumbled belongings of another family group.

Murmuring his apologies, smiling disarmingly in the face of the baleful glares of the sprawlers, he pushed his way through the throng, and quickly made his way to the main exit, through the automatic doors and out into the street. Nimbly dodging the stream of taxis and coaches, he crossed the road and climbed into the parked grey BMW.

Checking his mirrors and flicking on the indicator, he slipped the car into gear and edged out into the flow of traffic. He checked his watch again, practically eight-fifteen. He stopped, oblivious to the angry hooting from the vehicles behind.

Sitting there, calmly ignoring the crescendoing anger from the stalled traffic, he watched the second hand on his watch tick irrevocably towards the Rolex symbol at the top of the dial...tick..tick..tick..

With a tremendous roar the airport terminal glass doors vanished in a powdered spray, slammed outwards into the busy road by the force of the explosion.

With just a hint of a satisfied smile Kennedy leaned forward and pushed home the cassette in the player on the dashboard, and to 50 watts of Elton John he engaged 'Drive' and pulled unhurriedly away, leaving in his rear-view mirror an inferno of burning foam-filled seating and melting plastic adding their poison to the hell-like smoking ruin of bodies and baggage.

CHAPTER FIVE

LONDON

"Now come on ladies and gentleman, what can I say for this? I can start on the books at £1500. A very nice Gresley." The porter in the front of the room lifted up the picture and slowly rotated it to give the potential buyers a better look.

"A Country landscape at Little Eaton, fourteen inches by ten, a lovely watercolour, typical of Frank's style, in the original frame..."

The sound of the auctioneer extolling the virtues of the Victorian Derbyshire painter's watercolour did not reach the office on the fourth floor where Charles Grey sat.

In his middle fifties, Grey's name admirably suited his image: medium build, a lined but somehow delicate face, quiet but expensive clothes, greying hair and wearing slightly old-fashioned heavy-rimmed glasses, he gave the impression of a successful but unassuming businessman. It wasn't until you held his gaze that that you noticed its unsettling coldness.

The office was quiet and uncluttered, a plain pale carpet off-setting the richness of the deep mahogany panelling. The afternoon sunlight streaming in from one large window fell across Grey seated at the imposing mahogany partners desk in the large bay. It was exactly how you would imagine the office of successful West End Fine Art auctioneers to be.

It would also be incorrect.

Charles Grey was the deputy director of MI6., The chief overseas security arm of British Intelligence.

The auction business was legitimate, of course, and a very reputable - not to say profitable - business it was, with a world-wide reputation, and offices is many of the major European and American cities.

A far cry from Century House, MI6's prominent new central London headquarters, it had long ago been accepted that certain activities would need an impenetrable cover, completely divorced from the observable day-to-day business of the centre's general intelligence activity.

The special Cabinet sub-committee, originally appointed to deal with national emergency situations such as the Miner's Strike in 1974, but which had soon assumed a much larger remit, had authorised the establishment of an undercover department known as SIG, the Security and Intelligence Group, drawn from the elite personnel of both MI5 and MI6.

Headed by Charles Grey, on secondment from regular MI6 duties, the Security and Intelligence Group had, over a period of ten years or so, completely penetrated a number of reputable businesses which they had continued to use as fronts for their covert activities.

To the regular staff of the Auction House, Grey was one of the directors brought in to the business on the strength of his many and varied contacts in high places all over the world, as well as for his remarkable knowledge of the minor Victorian watercolourists. Never interfering, always a model of politeness, he was well liked, if thought a little 'stand-offish', preferring to keep himself to himself in his fourth-floor office.

Not that he wasn't busy! No, throughout the day he would receive innumerable visits from clients and potential clients, and people seeking his expert advice. Altogether a valuable asset to the company. The unexpected and sudden death of his wife of some thirty years to a particularly malignant cancer of the stomach had had seen Grey plunge even deeper into the secret world that filled his every waking moment.

Of course, some of the visitors to his office were just what they appeared to be. Then again, some were altogether different.

Today, sunk in the depths of a large brown leather armchair in front of the desk and a little to one side, lounged a tall distinguished, somewhat flamboyant character, almost a stereotype of the career diplomat who would never dream of wearing anything but Saville Row suits and the old school tie, unless of course it were the regimental one.

Head of the Foreign and Commonwealth Office, Sir Hector Bainbridge, legs crossed, sat sideways in his chair, smoking a Benson and Hedges and languidly swinging one foot. Looking somewhat bored, he gazed out of the large bay window behind Grey as if fascinated by the London skyline.

In sharp contrast to Bainbridge's smooth urbanity, the third figure in the room sat plainly ill at ease, perched right on the edge his chair, as if he didn't really trust it.

Chief Inspector Malcolm Phillips, ex-Special Branch, now seconded to the FCO, MI5 and MI6 liaison group, in regulation grey crumple, gave the distinct impression that he would be happier standing up. Even happier if it could be at attention!

Close to retiring age, Phillips had spent most of his post-army career at GCHQ, the information gathering centre of British Intelligence, and latterly at the Foreign Office as co-ordinating officer overseeing the protection of foreign diplomats.

The closest he ever got to Saville Row was when he drove along it, and it showed!

Other than the swaying of Bainbridge's foot and the thin plume of smoke from his cigarette that curled up towards the ceiling and the movement of the French carriage clock on the mantel of the Adams fireplace, the room was still.

At last, Grey looked up from the report to the security officer and spoke dryly: "So, in spite of the obvious need for our own diplomatic staff to be adequately protected on foreign duty, it comes down, in the end, simply to money; is that it?"

Phillips cleared his throat nervously: "Well, I wouldn't put it quite like that Sir." He paused for a moment then continued apologetically as Grey stared at him in silence.

"We're quite aware that there is a lot of unrest in certain circles at the moment, and in a perfect world we would be able to provide our embassies and officials with as much protection as necessary but..."

Bainbridge, without removing his gaze from the world outside the window, interrupted, the mellow mellifluousness of his baritone drawl matching the image exactly:

"In a perfect world, dear chap, we wouldn't need a protection section at all, and in a perfect world we wouldn't have a PM having fits over the next allocations budget for the security of her Britannic Majesty's elected government, never mind that of we poor Civil Service full-timers!"

With a deep sigh Bainbridge stood up, eased the creases from his trousers, and began to pace the room. Apparently directing his attention to the small collection of Augustus John etchings on the wall, he blew a small stream of smoke up towards the ceiling and continued, the bitterness of experience detectable in his cultured tones:

"We are only too aware of the realities of politics today. The bomb and the bullet are now just everyday tools given as much - if not more - credence than the mere spoken word." He gave an eloquent shrug: "After all, the effect seems more immediate, and more obvious!"

Defensively Phillips appealed to Grey: "We have done some things Sir. We've beefed up security as much as we can. We've exchanged the Royal Protection Squad's Walther PPK's for Smith and Wesson .38 specials..."

"Oho yes indeed!" Bainbridge's snorted interjection dripped with sarcasm.

"The PPK that was so unreliable that it almost cost Princess Anne's life in that attempted abduction in The Mall, finally withdrawn from Royal Protection service, and what do the higher intellects of HMG decide to do with them - in the interests of economy? ....They issue them to the Northern Ireland Prison Office!" He raised a cynical eyebrow, then continued in softer tones: "Ah well, they are mostly Irish I suppose..!"

"But the bottom line is that we will not be forming our own section?" Grey sat unmoving, staring at the uncomfortable Phillips.

"Well, you see Sir, we've no problem with volunteers; we've ex-SAS, retired Special branch, invalided SBS, and former RMP's, but the trouble is...."

Turning from the etchings, Bainbridge turned his attention to Grey and brusquely finished the faltering sentence: "The trouble is that they'd all have to go on full-time Civil Service pay and allowances, and the Treasury will oppose this absolutely!"

Grey looked quietly at Bainbridge for a moment, then turned to his intercom.

"Mrs Hemmings."

"Yes Sir?" The voice came tinnily through the little speaker on his desk.

Grey clicked the transmit switch again: "Bring in the 'Total Security' file please." He looked up at Bainbridge: "It's as well that we've considered alternatives then isn't it?"

A brisk knock and the door opened. Grey's secretary entered and placed a grey folder with a diagonal red stripe on the desk in front of him. He gave a brief nod of thanks and stood up as the door closed behind her.

"Take a look." He handed the folder to Bainbridge then turned and resumed his seat.

The FCO head stared at him for a moment, then sat down again and began to read as Grey steepled his fingers and continued in his crisp matter-of-fact manner:

"We are not entirely unaware of the priorities of our masters, and there is a way in which we can meet our commitments and at perhaps achieve a little more." He shrugged, adding dryly: "With only minimal expenditure."

As Bainbridge continued to read, Grey pushed back his chair, got up and walked around to the front of his desk and perched himself on the corner, then continued:

"There are actually occasions when it just might suit our purposes to be......let us say a little distant from affairs.."

Bainbridge laughed sardonically: "If the excreta ever hits the fan, you mean!"

Grey smiled: "As you so succinctly put it! Yes. We have investigated the possibility of having one of these new private security firms under contract to us for certain jobs from time to time. Naturally we would help with the training and so on, and it would be much more economic than maintaining our own full-time unit..but..."

Bainbridge looked thoughtful, as if seeing the merits of the idea, then: "But they'd have to be - well, 'Sound'."

Grey and Bainbridge looked meaningfully at each other for a moment, in silence.

Phillips coughed apologetically: "I'm sorry Sir, but I'm not sure I understand..."

"Come, come!" Bainbridge turned on him brusquely. "You were in Special Branch. You must be as aware as all of us that occasionally matters need to be settled in a.." He hesitated momentarily, looking for the right phrase..." in a 'conclusive' fashion!"

Phillips cleared his throat, looking vaguely embarrassed.

Bainbridge turned his attention back to Grey. "Can this be achieved satisfactorily?"

Grey got up from the corner of the desk, walked across to Bainbridge and relieved him of the folder. Returning to his seat, he sat down, placing the file on the desk in front of him.

"I think so! We've had a bit of luck actually; one of our 'acquaintances' has recently retired from active service with 22 regiment of the SAS, a Lt. Colonel actually, who has set up his own private security company - Total Security Inc., it's called." "He's approached us for permission to contract some of his chaps out as bodyguards to some small Arabian potentate who can't seem to bring himself to trust his own people!"

"And he will 'play ball' Even with the.." Bainbridge's mouth twisted expressively..." 'wet' work?"

Grey smiled, but without warmth, a cold, chilling, professional smile: he motioned to Bainbridge's tie:

"Well, he is an Eton chap, after all! And isn't that where a tradition of picking up balls and running with them all began?"

Bainbridge nodded affably and stood up, crushing the remainder of his cigarette into the ashtray. "Best sound him out then."

The meeting was over.

CHAPTER SIX

BELFAST 25 YEARS EARLIER

It was a non-descript front parlour really, nothing out of the ordinary to draw your eye, basically shabby but clean.

Even the house itself in 'Little India' that enclave of streets whose names eloquently underlined a former age of British Imperialism – Bombay Street, Cawporne Street, Kashmir Road and circumnavigated by the Shankhill Road, was simply a basic red-bricked Victorian end-terrace semi-detached - not one element jarred or seemed out of place amongst the rows of its fellows; perhaps the paint on the window sills was a little fresher than some, but the wooden front gate still hung lopsidedly from its top hinge so that visitors tracing the short path of the front garden to the door would invariably announce their presence with a grating squeak.

Nothing except the black Ferguson television in one corner of the room appeared to have been purchased in the last twenty years. Everything exuded an aura of normality. Slightly worn antimacassars draped the backs of both stuffed armchairs, and a matching cloth runner lay pristine straight on the top of the too large Edwardian dresser - obviously a family heirloom - which took up most of the space along one wall.

Family photographs in a variety of wood and silver plate frames occupied the space either side of a large silver candelabra, which seemed to be another remnant from a former, more genteel time.

Even the large ashtray stand and row of pipes on the mantle-shelf over the small fireplace gave notice that in this house at least, the strident protestations of the anti-smoking campaigners had yet to gain a foothold.

Deeply sunk into the cavernous depths of one armchair, apparently lost in contemplation of the plume of smoke curling gently from the bowl of the forgotten pipe resting between the forefinger and thumb of his right hand, Daniel Lynch matched exactly the nondescript appearance of the house.

Even seated it is clear that he is somewhat less than average height, somewhat overweight, somewhat thinning of hair and somewhat lacking in colour."Somewhat" described him perfectly, just your average, mid-fifties, somewhat passed his better days. To go by appearances you would without hesitation place him as a small town grocer, or maybe a gentleman's hairdresser

Of course you would be quite wrong!

Lynch was a killer, a cold-blooded, cold-hearted, matter of fact, no-fuss, no big deal - killer!

And of course you are not completely wrong. There is a small shop, not a Grocers or a Barbers, but a corner Newsagents which bears his name on the wooden painted sign over the door.

Not that he actually worked there himself. No, that would have been just a little unseemly for the chief of staff of the Provisional Irish Republican Army.

And of course, he never actually killed anyone himself, he just ordered it done. Never in those terms, naturally.

No. And of course he hated it! How often had he interspersed his swallows of Guinness with heartfelt denouncements of the need to kill? How many times had he shaken his head in regret and manfully accepted the onerous guilt upon his own shoulders. Didn't he allow his burden - manfully borne through necessity - to be glimpsed (if briefly) at many a council meeting where such deeds were planned and ordered?

Sorrowfully he would nod in acquiescing to a euphemistic 'hit'.

With a sigh he would authorise the kneecapping or punishment beating of those who transgressed his law and he managed to ignore the tingle in his loins when he dispatched the order to seize and shave the head of any pretty young colleen who had the temerity to take drink with the enemy.

There could be no-one in any doubt that if it weren't for the presence in his beloved land of the murdering Brits and their Proddy compatriots which demanded such huge sacrifices from men like him that indeed, life as a corner shop owner would be all that his heart would aspire to!

Naturally enough, no-one did doubt him. Especially Martin O'Shaunassy did not doubt him.

Hulking awkwardly in the other armchair - overhanging it everywhere - like a huge dog content to sit in the presence of his master - was a rough hewn lump of a man, whose size seemed designed to embarrass him next to the slight rotund smallness of his companion.

Sitting as still as he could so as not to disturb the other's concentration his body would every now and then betray him; his foot would slip off his knee with a jerk and wherever he placed his leg would become excruciating in a matter of moments, forcing yet another move.

Having settled his leg and resolved to bear the discomfort with stoic determination he would suddenly find his throat noisily clearing away a build up of saliva from a gland which for some unknown reason had gone into hyperactive overdrive, producing vast quantities of mucus.

Now with a mouthful of spit came the dawning realisation that the desperate search for the grubby handkerchief that he knew was secreted somewhere beneath layers of jacket and sweater would only create a further disturbance.

Sweating now from the embarrassment his own body was causing him, O'Shaunassy grimaced and swallowed loudly!

"Dammit Martin! Can't a man think in peace with you around!"

Ungratefully unaware of his underling's sacrifices, Lynch snapped irritably at the big man.

With a huge sigh, giving up the struggle Martin farted and let his body fall where it would. "Sorry"

The reason that Martin would not ever have doubted his leader's pronouncements of regret whenever an example had to be made was quite straightforward He was simply not the intellectual type; questions of morality, of right and wrong, were not matters of high principle with him, they were resolved not by questioning and soul-searching but by the simplistic code he had absorbed from childhood. He was not created with the capacity for brainwork, but for loyalty; unswerving, steadfast and most of all free from the need to analyse and conclude - these things he left to his betters

So when his betters announced that they had pondered deeply and concluded regretfully that the Proddy bastard Riley and his traitorous Catholic wife had to be made an example of, O'Shaunassy merely nodded.

"Ah, you were saying.." He thoughtfully lowered his booming voice to a more acceptably deferential hoarseness:

"You were saying about young Liam, Liam Kennedy....?" His voice petered out with the question hanging in the smoke-filled parlour air.

Lynch paused for a moment, his mind focussing again on the slight young man whose intensity and persistent eagerness to serve the cause had eventually been noticed.

"Hmm. Do you think he can do it?"

In the blank silence punctuated only by the big man's scalp scratching as he searched for a suitable reply, Lynch answered his rhetorical question.

"Well, he must be given the chance to prove himself."

At last he turned his attention to the other, jabbing his pipe stem at him for emphasis.

"You must go with him, but let him do it himself. If he does a good job, then fine.....if he doesn't....."

Big eyes stared at him willing him to finish the sentence and resolve the blank terror of an unfinished command.

The commander sighed: "If he screws it up Martin, then you must make bloody sure that he doesn't panic and get picked up. We can't chance him talking, so you know what to do!"

He pointed the stem of his pipe at Martin and jerked it sharply upwards as if it were a recoiling pistol.

The big man's face creased into a toothy grin as all mental conflict and irresolution vanished.

CHAPTER SEVEN

LONDON

There was no brass plate to advertise its presence, anyone who needed to know the whereabouts of The Gentleman's Club would already know the address. It was one of London's more select and private sanctuaries, where even women's liberation had come and gone without even rippling its tranquil surface.

Not that any of the members had anything against women, of course. Fond memories of matron's rule and nannie's fussing were practically sine qua non for the politicians, retired generals, judges and senior civil servants who formed the main body of the membership. In fact there had been the odd occasion when women had been admitted into the grand dining rooms - by special dispensation, naturally, but never into the inner recesses of reading room, lounge and bar.

The Gentlemen's Club was fractionally more lively than Boodles or Whites, but maintained the same Victorian atmosphere of civility and courtesy only possible for a ruling class with an empire at its feet.

A taxi pulled up in the soft, evening drizzle; that London speciality which frequently catches the unwary tourist at a disadvantage, as not at first appearing to warrant the wearing of a rain-coat, but which thoroughly soaked one to the skin if caught out in it for any length of time.

As the cab squealed to a stop, the uniformed doorman moved forward holding an umbrella high.

He opened the door of the cab, and touched the peak of his cap to the tall well-dressed athletic man in his early 50's who stepped out and walked briskly up the steps.

"Good evening Colonel Williams." In the cool marble interior of the foyer, the liveried club attendant smiled in welcome as Williams handed him his furled umbrella and signed in.

"Mr Grey is waiting for you in the library, sir."

Colonel Roger Augustus Williams DSO MM MC Retired, nodded and smiled back pleasantly. He slid the Mount Blanc back inside his blazer pocket and took the wide marble stairs two at a time.

The club library was very genteel. Lit by crystal-strewn chandeliers, the tall marble columns supported ceilings bedecked with clouds and cherubs. Worn brown leather armchairs and sofas formed little islands amongst the card and coffee tables, whilst white-coated waiters quietly ferried silver trays of drinks to the few members already ensconced, talking quietly, reading or simply dozing in the leather covered comfort.

Over in one corner Grey relaxed, nursing a drink, not untidily though. He didn't sprawl. Inelegance - even in repose - was the sign of a lack of self-control. It would also have been obtrusive in Grey's society. Public school had long since knocked off the edges of obvious nonconformity. Some of his contemporaries - like the Chief of the FCO - developed a charismatic public persona that they wore almost as a heraldic badge; in Grey's line of work however, it did not do attract attention, to appear in any way different from the others.

He looked up and smiled briefly as Williams approached.

"Evening Roger, do sit down." He waved him to a chair. "Drink?" Grey's finger lifted as Williams nodded and settled himself comfortably into an armchair.

"Oh Arthur." He beckoned to a passing waiter: "Two Brandy & Sodas, large ones?" He tilted his head enquiringly at Williams who nodded again. "Yes, large ones, if you would be so kind."

The white-coated Arthur gave a little bow and glided smoothly away.

After a brief moment of appraisal Grey decided not to keep his companion in suspense any longer.

"Well Roger, I expect you're rather keen to know if HMG will give its collective blessing to your little venture eh?"

Williams nodded slowly, then seemed about to speak. Grey held up his hand to forestall him as the waiter returned with the drinks.

"Thank you Sir." Arthur set the glasses down before them, then accepted Grey's signature on the proffered chit.

Williams sipped his brandy and waited.

Grey sat for a moment in silence. "There's a price!"

Once more the imperious hand cut Williams short. "You want the patronage of HMG, and in return for this we would require....." His lips formed a little moue in the brief silence as he searched for the *mot juste* ...

"Well, let's call it 'co-operation' in certain areas; occasionally certain very private, somewhat 'dampish' areas, if you follow me?

Williams grunted, in dawning comprehension: "Specifically........?"

Grey, leaned forward and stared straight into William's eyes continuing in a chilling and emotionless voice:

"'Thou wert not wont to be so dull.' To quote the Bard." His eyes grey colder as he continued emphasizing each word.

"What I mean, Roger, is that you get all the help that HMG can unofficially provide, with contracts and training and so on, and in return we get to place one or two of our people with you to keep an ear to the ground and when necessary to supervise certain - tragic but inevitable - accidents, which could just possibly befall - shall we say - enemies of the State."

He leaned back in the armchair and sipped his drink. "Specific enough?"

Williams looked reflectively into his glass, considering his reply, then glanced up at Grey:

"Enemies of the State...?"

The intensity of Grey's reply was curiously at odds with his relaxed posture: "Black September, Bader Meinhoff, Al Fatah, PLO, IRA, Mafia; think of a nice set of initials and there's bound to be a few crazed malcontents who have assumed them as a title for their pursuits of 'Freedom' and 'Democracy' - which are to be defined by them of course, even if it entails denying the vast majority the 'Freedom' to live free from fear in the 'Democracy' of their choice!"

Grey's casual veneer was momentarily discarded in the strength of his emotions. He put down his glass and leaned forward.

"We've used you and your chaps before, and we want to use them again, but this time without drawing attention to ourselves. Going through Embassy windows in the full glare of publicity might be exciting stuff for 'News at Ten', but it can be counter-productive in some parts of the world."

As if suddenly aware of his vehemence, Grey sat back, took a long breath and spoke normally again. "Same targets, same masters, only....... only now there must be no publicity, and no possible way for any of Total Security's actions to be laid on HMG's doorstep. Understand?!"

Williams took a large swallow and concentrated his gaze on the amber contents of his glass as if scrutinising them for imperfections. After a moment he looked up.

"I understand perfectly, Charles. I'm to do your dirty work for you, in return for which I will receive no thanks and no help if things go wrong! How can I refuse?"

"Not you , exactly, Roger." Grey continued, electing to ignore the irony in William's tone:

"You see, there's one little proviso. We've a chap we want you to use as head of operations. James Hunter. He's been very useful to us in the past, one of your old SAS chaps actually, as I'm sure you know, given his record."

William's mind was caught with a mixture of emotions. Naturally he was pleased - no, relieved even - that he would be receiving government patronage, but at what price.... He forced his concentration back to Grey.

"Hunter you say! Well. I can't deny I'm a little surprised, but yes, he made quite a name for himself with us, a good chap, but very much his own man!"

Grey nodded: "He is being a little difficult, at the moment, about 'Wet' work now that he's back in Civvy Street again."

"Couldn't that prove a little awkward then?"

Grey pulled a face, signalling to a waiter for a re-fill: "He's too good at it for us to just let him go, so, we want you to use his abilities, but - at least for now - keep him away from all knowledge of our...... 'special' contracts eh?"

There was barely a pause as Williams considered his options, then the replenished glasses clinked as the deal was struck. Knowing James Hunter somewhat better than he had let on, Williams was rather of the opinion that he could turn out to be a somewhat large fly in the ointment, but then, that wasn't his problem was it?

CHAPTER EIGHT

The Director of Operations office was more of a cubbyhole than a real office, thought Hunter; the biggest thing about it was the nameplate 'Total Security Inc. Director' on the door.

A good address was vitally important when dealing with foreign embassies and businessmen, Colonel Williams had explained when detailing Hunter's duties some three months ago now, and a West End location was expensive. So, at least to begin with, it was necessary to work from rather cramped premises until it was possible to expand.

James Hunter, ex-SAS captain, ex-married man, ex-MI6 operative had been more than glad to hear from his old C.O. He had been even happier to hear of the job offer that had accompanied the after-dinner cigars at the C.O.'s club. If he were honest with himself it couldn't have come at a better time.

The knee injury that had caused his medical discharge had been a bitter blow.

Of course the medical attention available in the Falklands was fast and workmanlike, but the delay in evacuation from field hospital to carrier sickbay and ultimately back to the Hereford clinic meant that the torn ligaments and muscles were more or less functioning again, but would always be liable to give way under a strain.

Mount Longdon, overlooking the capital, Port Stanley. Would he ever forget such an inhospitable place? God alone knew why anyone would want to live there anyway, never mind die defending it!

It had just been his section's luck to run into the last remnants of opposition before the Argies capitulated. Hunter's three-man team had been on a night-time intelligence gathering mission before the last push to capture Longdon when the helicopters ferrying in the main assault squads had come under ground-to-air missile attack from just beyond the knoll where the radio intercept equipment had been set up.

Unlike most regular units, (and a source of discontent to them) the SAS maintained their own direct satellite transmitting and receiving link with Command H.Q. back in England, which was capable of transmitting instantaneous updates in strategy and tactics dependant upon just such intelligence as Hunter was to relay.

Unfortunately, some of the few experienced Argentinean regular troops, had decided to pre-empt the attack that they were aware was coming, and had dug themselves into a strategic position behind great white rocks overlooking the DZ for incoming attack units and supplies.

Once the first Sea King helicopter went down, intelligence gathering became secondary to search and destroy. So, in the pre-dawn bitterly cold wind and damp of the exposed hillside, Hunter led his section over the difficult terrain to locate the enemy position.

It had been a long, slow job, made more difficult by the need for silence. The team was exposed and vulnerable in that featureless , rock strewn, wet scrub, and any sound travelled a long way.

Ironically the explosions from the burning Sea King helped to cover their progress, and it was sheer bad luck that an Argentinean head popped up from cover to search for another

42

target at the very instant that Hunter was about to drop a fragmentation grenade into the dug-out.

Hunter's number two cut him down instantly, but the damage was done, and as he fell the stricken Argentinean's lifeless fingers clutched spasmodically at his weapon, spinning a wheel of fire around him. In the same moment that Hunter's grenade tore apart the others in the slit trench, one of the stray bullets smashed into the rock by his right knee, sending a spray of shrapnel-like slivers agonisingly into his leg.

Hunter remembered the feeling of disbelief, not pain, at least not at first, but the sheer incredulity that overwhelmed him as he, as if from miles away, watched his leg collapse beneath him. Later, of course he felt the pain.

Still, that was long ago and far away, and to be honest, Hunter wasn't sure which was the worst pain, the wound in his leg and the subsequent agonies of rehabilitation, or the black cloud of despair that befogged his every thought when his marriage to Jean finally broke up.

Hunter's forehead creased as his mental shutters clamped down hard. He had gone that route, and tortured his every waking moment with self-recriminations, which were almost worse than the self-pity. He had tried the bottle, he had tried immersing himself in the new career offered to him by MI6, but neither had softened his sense of overwhelming loss. The Army had been his life, and the emptiness became enormous when even the private home-life that he had tried to maintain, also crumbled and vanished.

It had not been a good time.

As with all things, however, the intensity of his unhappiness had become a dull ache, always there, but at least he was now able to function, although he had drawn the line at some of the things his new masters had required of him.

It wasn't that he was squeamish, God no, but it had somehow seemed totally wrong to his sense of morality to be expected to simply kill someone just because some civil servant ordered it! O.K. Perhaps they were criminals or undesirables, whatever, but he had put his life on the line for the concepts of Justice, Honour and Freedom, and he was damned if he was going to tread all over his principles just like that!

Of course, they were very nice about it, but he knew that they had tested him and found him wanting. "Best to try something less demanding." They had put it, when regretfully terminating his contract, at the same time reminding him of his signature on the Official Secrets Act.

Colonel William's offer had been like Manna from Heaven!

He rocked backwards and forwards on the upholstered swivel chair behind the tiny desk littered with files, telephones, a computer terminal and empty coffee cups, trying to force his attention back to the file he had been reading. There had been quite a number of such files lately, as the reputation of the company spread.

Mostly straightforward close protection jobs, like this one seemed to be, but occasionally they contained details of more interesting contracts; the training of Royal Protection Squad members in defensive driving, lecturing the Improvised Explosive Devices disposal unit on booby-trap bomb recognition, and even supplying training personnel to a Middle Eastern Sheikh to help instruct his private bodyguard.

It seemed to Hunter that the Colonel's idea of making use of the knowledge and expertise of retired and invalided ex-SAS and SBS personnel was paying off handsomely. The more dangerous the world became, the more such services were necessary.

He looked down once again at the photograph of the Irish-American congressman attached to the file that contained details of his forthcoming visit to England. Leaning forward he clicked on the intercom to his secretary.

"Jenny, this visiting American. I don't recall getting any information on this. Anything I should know? Who's been assigned?"

The reply came instantly, as if she had been poised waiting for the question: "Three operatives, rotating, Sir, with Mr. Martin controlling and as standby."

"I see it's an FCO job?"

"Yes sir, I believe so."

"Thanks."

He looked thoughtful for a moment, then clicked open the intercom again. "Jenny, I want full details of the itinerary. Wasn't Mr Martin supposed to be lecturing to the new intake from the Royal Protection Squad on improvised explosive devices?"

"Yes sir, but Colonel Williams personally selected him for this job, something about not getting street rusty I think. Anyway, his lecture has been re-scheduled, and he's to head up this team instead."

Hunter closed the file. "O.K. Where is Mr Martin now?"

"I'll check with communications sir."

The background hiss cut off momentarily, then: "Sir, the American is on a shopping spree at the moment, with one cover. Mr Martin is back-up waiting at his hotel."

Hunter thought briefly then came to a decision. "Jenny, I'm going out. You can get me on the mobile if you need me." He didn't know why, but he felt uneasy. Something...God knows what...niggled at the edge of his brain.

CHAPTER NINE

BELFAST 25 YEARS EARLIER

If it hadn't been for the curious juxtaposition of the picture of the Pope on the wall next to the Wedgewood commemorative plate of the Coronation of Her Majesty Queen Elizabeth II, it could have been the interior of any house in Belfast. Most households, to be sure, might have one, or the other, depending upon their sympathies, but few would have both.

In the small but comfortably furnished lounge two young children, a boy and a girl, were sitting on the floor watching television. A big, curly-haired man in shirtsleeves and worn brown corduroys was seated in an armchair, the remains of his evening meal littered a tray beside the chair.

The first bullet missed entirely!

"In the name of God...!"

Aghast and terrified, Riley struggled out of the armchair, almost comically stretching his hands in front of him in an attempt to ward off the next shot which smashed into his left shoulder, spinning him back into the chair painting a wet crimson smear across the floral design..

"NO! Please NO!" The scream came from Riley's soul.

The butt of the heavy, so heavy gun, in Liam's right hand was slick with sweat and the recoil almost jerked it from his grip. He moved further into the room and aimed again.

It was difficult to decide who was the most terrified; the gunman, the target whose only crime was to be a Protestant and an easy victim, or the two young children sitting frozen into spastic immobility from the moment Liam kicked through the panelled glass lounge door and without a word began to jerk the trigger of what felt like the heaviest revolver in the world.

"Blam!" "Blam!"

The frightful disorientating blast of the shots was augmented by crescendoing wails of terror as the children, eyes huge in horror and disbelief - almost in slow motion it seemed - scrambled towards their dying father as more bullets - seemingly with nothing at all to do with Liam - slammed him further down into the chair, tearing gaping bloody holes in his chest and face!

The young killer grasped his right wrist to steady his aim, and fought against the overwhelming terror that tried to force him away from this place of slaughter. Teeth clenched he held the gun firm against the almost uncontrollable shaking, his heart clattering out of control in his heaving chest.

The tremendous sudden silence hurt his ears even more than the screams! The tableau was engraved into endless moments of immobility.

Liam realised that he had forgotten the advice to plug his ears with cotton wool, and the gunshots had momentarily deafened him. Suddenly the room came back to life.

The target - the corpse - for that was what it now was - slid slowly from the chair which scraped its way backwards across the floor, as if to gentle the fall, and the thing which used to be

Riley came to rest upon its back, with what was left of the head supported by the wet-smeared seat.

Liam stared entranced. He couldn't connect this scene with himself, it was like watching a Movie thriller; he almost expected the body to climb back onto the chair and carry on watching the T.V. as before!

Disgust twitched his nostrils.

The room filled with the stench of corruption as the empty sack, which only moments before had been the beloved father of three and husband to Aimee, relaxed control of its sphincter muscles and voided its bowels.

In the grip of terror Liam jerked into life and ran from the room and through the ruins of the front door. He only knew he had to escape from the children's enormous pain-filled, unbelieving eyes. He never saw the futile efforts of the two children trying to stop up the holes in their father's body with their little fingers, nor heard their half-crazed screams and sobs!

The car was waiting.

As he fell onto the back seat it moved smoothly away, heading from the Shankhill to the Falls Road and the safety of 'Home turf.' Not moving too fast, doing nothing out of the ordinary to attract the attention of the army patrols or the RUC.

"Christ Oh Christ, Jesus Christ!" Liam sobbed on the verge of panic and relief, unwittingly echoing the murdered man's supplication to the Almighty.

.

"All right lad" Soothingly the big man beside him in the back reached across and gently removed the forgotten revolver from Liam's fingers. He slid the gun into his overcoat pocket and patted the trembling killer's knee. "Hush now man, it's over. You did well, very well!"

He took his hand from Liam's knee and pulled the collars of his big coat closer across his chest. He was silent now. He knew that the next few minutes were vital, especially vital to the young man next to him.

There was nothing that he could now do, the die was cast. Liam was either going to be a welcome asset to the cause, or just another body to be found at the side of the road. The boy's reactions now would decide.

It started to rain.

"Typical" thought Liam, his whirling mind caught by the sheer ordinariness of things. He stared unseeingly out of the window as the car worked its way through the traffic of an early Saturday night. He sighed a long, deep shuddering breath and turned to O'Shaunassy.

"Jesus but I could do with a drink!"

The big man released his grasp on the butt of the pistol in his overcoat pocket and grasped instead the neck of a bottle of Bushmills. He proffered it to Kennedy, and leaned back in the seat, satisfied.

CHAPTER TEN

THE PRESENT

The smell of fresh French coffee drifted in from the little kitchen.

Dozing in that half-land between sleep and wakefulness, Liam stretched contentedly, he didn't often get many moments of such secure relaxation, and in the dark recesses of his drifting mind he was fully aware that such luxury was soon to be set aside once more for the higher demands of duty.

But, for the moment, he allowed himself a little indulgence. Lying in Nicole's bed, with his hands behind his neck, he was lost in thought.

Looking back over the years it all seemed inevitable. His first 'active service' mission! Could it ever have been different? he wondered.

Memories came welling up:

School playgrounds where Cowboys and Indians had given way to 'The Boys' and the 'Black and Tans.' Streets littered with the confused remains of petrol bomb, brick throwing protest marches and the burnt-out skeletons of barricades and cars. Parlour singsongs where the accents thickened with the smoke-ridden air, and every man woman and child drank in the heady atmosphere of alcohol and patriotism! The flushed faces and voices rough from keeping up with scraping violins, and the unsteady hands on his young shoulders as giants of men swayed unsteadily with tears coursing their cheeks as old ghosts walked again.

Liam knew that that first time had almost undone him. Never again would he come face to face with his enemy unless there were no choices.

Just sometimes, at first, he had felt dirty!

Oh yes, he knew that it was all for the cause, the greater good, but if it must be done, then by God it would have to be in another way, at a distance! Liam smiled almost ruefully at memories of this first mental shutter. He should have known. What then had seemed an answer had been just another lie! Just another way of hiding from the raw ugliness of murder.

Oh yes, the wary looks and careful attention of the others were balm to his ego:

"For fuck's sake, you don't want to mess with that one!" The whispered advice to those on the periphery who might be tempted to nudge his arm in Kerry's Bar, who couldn't see the deadly steel hidden beneath the surface of the slim, quiet figure with the unsettling eyes.

And women! Ah, they fluttered like moths around this handsome figure, whose air of quiet withdrawal in a sea of boisterous raucous effervescence marked him as different, interesting. They tried to mother him, entice him, use him, but they never even got close! Liam had retreated to a private place deep within, from which he watched with silent amusement as each attempt to breach his defences came to grief.

He could play them like the trout in a county Donegal stream; a gift - a sharp word; a smile - a cold and withering stare; an insult - a gentle caress, and - inevitably - his lovemaking.

Not for Liam the savage sweaty thrusting of alcohol-fired lust. No, for him it was a thing of power. Young or old, fat or thin, beautiful or downright plain it was all the same to him. Only with their complete abandon in a writhing, panting orgasm could he gain his satisfaction. Only then, with their spent bodies underneath him, could his rock-hard penis pump out release!

For all their ploys and wiles, they could never get to him!

He sighed, lying there on Nicole's bed, listening to the sounds of her clattering pots and preparing coffee, it all seemed so very long ago, Was that shy tongue-tied brat really him? How time had passed.

What was the score to date? Not counting mistakes of course, they were inevitable - just casualties of war.

Difficult to say really, with some lingering on for months! Anyway no-one could come close to him in either numbers or quality! Almost dozing, Liam's mind drifted back to that sunny Saturday; the date he would never forget; the 25th of August 1979.

The day that really set the feather in his cap!

From his vantage point in the car on the headland overlooking the little harbour of Mullaghmore, nestling lazily under a brilliantly clear blue County Sligo sky, he could see quite clearly the ant-like figures on the quay and the to-ing and fro-ing of the little dinghies as they bobbed around the larger boats like so many waterboatmen on a pond.

He leaned his elbow on the open car window to support the weight of the powerful Zeiss binoculars. The image wavered then solidified as Liam slowly turned the focusing ring.

Suddenly he saw it! Nosing smoothly through the water, the 28-foot motor launch *Shadow V* gave way and gently eased alongside a string of lobster pots.

Liam swept the length of the vessel with the glasses.

"Yes!" He exclaimed exultantly to himself! There he was.

Standing tall at the wheel, unmistakable in his white cords and worn black fisherman's sweater which had been a present from the crew of his old wartime command HMS Kelly, he saw the tall, imposing figure of 'Uncle Dickie', otherwise known as the last Viceroy of India, Lord Louis Mountbatten - Godson of Queen Victoria - Uncle to the Duke of Edinburgh - and arrogant enough to believe that he and his brood could come and go with impunity!

Liam looked down at his watch. It was precisely 11.44 am. He licked his tongue briefly over lips that had suddenly dried. He returned his gaze to the magnified image below him. *Shadow V* had almost stopped by the first of the pots.

Liam's left hand reached out to the device on the passenger's seat next to him. Not grasping it straight away, he glanced down and stabbed his finger at the small grey button seated on the top of the cigarette-packet sized electronic detonator.

The sound of the huge explosion washed over the car.

Liam clamped the binoculars back to his eyes and rapidly criss-crossed the area where the boat had lately been.

Smoke! Just smoke and ripples on the water. That was all! Tiny splashes marked the entry of minuscule pieces of debris, but otherwise, just smoke!

Forcing his satisfaction deep within his chest, Liam started the engine and gently eased the car back onto the road, and drove off past Classiebawn Castle where the standard of the Late Lord Louis still flapped from the flagpole in the desultory breeze.

He had other work to do that day, at Warrenpoint in County Down.

That too had been a major triumph, devised and masterminded by Liam. Several days before, in the derelict old Lodge house to Narrow Water Castle situated close to the dual carriageway which led from the village of Warrenpoint to Newry, he had supervised the burying of a massive 500lb landmine with its remote control detonator, directly underneath the crumbling stone archway entrance.

A second remote controlled device was concealed in a rickety old hay cart standing innocently at the side of the road. The plan was simple, and fiendishly deadly!

Shortly before 5pm., as a small convoy consisting of a Landrover and two four-tonners of the Second Parachute Regiment wound past the hay wagon, Liam, still flushed with the success of his destruction of *Shadow V*, flicked the switch of the model aeroplane control unit which he had modified to set off the explosive and the area around the hay-cart became a horrific killing ground.

The tremendous explosion smashed the rear truck into a crumpled steel coffin. Six of the platoon were killed outright, and two more were injured in the first blast, and, just as Liam had predicted, the others had raced to take cover in the apparent safety of the stone gatehouse.

Liam had waited. He licked his lips, experiencing once again the sharpness of his faculties as the excitement forced adrenaline into his system. He knew that the survivors would call up reinforcements, and he knew that the wounded would be hastily evacuated. All he had to do was wait.

Very shortly back-up troops, both paratroopers and men of the Queen's Own Highlanders reached the scene and joined the others in the gatehouse, taking up defensive positions both inside and outside.

Within minutes the air throbbed with the characteristic sounds of an approaching helicopter. Lulled into a false sense of security and under pressure to get the injured away, the C.O. had called in a Wessex helicopter to airlift the casualties to the alerted emergency medical unit, and just as it hovered behind the gatehouse, Liam pressed the second switch.

The results were devastating! The stone, which was to have been protection to the men, became in an instant a murderous maelstrom of jagged pieces of shrapnel, shattering bones and pulping flesh.

At the same moment, other members of Liam's team situated across the small nearby Loch opened up with automatic weapons, pouring a storm of lead into the smoking chaos.

Liam smiled in a quiet satisfaction at the memories.

In all, eighteen enemies lay dead at Warrenpoint, including the most senior officer so far, the C.O. of the Queens' Own Highlanders; and at Mullaghmore Harbour....Well, that really was the closest they'd got yet to those Royal bastards that ruled the roost! Oh yes, their day would come, in spite of the current 'Cease Fire' policy of his masters. "Adverse publicity, especially in America, and an end to all that lovely NORAID money for arms!" That had been the general council's main concern.

"Ah well" he mused mockingly: "We'll see."

At least killing that high and mighty bastard had brought it home to them! And all of the rest of the bloodsuckers preying on his poor divided nation! Again the warmth of almost sexual pleasure tingled in the pit of his stomach.

Not much left of him or his boat!

His masters issued a statement that fifty pounds of explosive had been planted on the boat, but Kennedy knew otherwise. The results of just five pounds of gelignite packed into a two and a half inch metal pipe, some seventeen inches long, had blown parts of the wreckage over seven miles away to the other side of Donegal bay!

The killing of the eighteen British soldiers by landmine later that same day in County Down had established Liam firmly as the number one bomb-maker for the Provisional IRA, especially following the death of his mentor Kevin O'Brady, who shortly afterwards accidentally blew himself up with his own bomb in Crossmaglen, Co. Armagh, thus ensuring Kennedy's value to his masters in the international terrorist market, as both assassin and instructor.

Not for money of course, 'though there was always a shortage of that; but in the clandestine world of international violence and death there was a constant need for arms and explosives, for which Liam's services could be bartered.

The deaths of innocents - the fifteen-year-old boy crewing the *Shadow V* and other family members young or old - were no problem to Liam. In his mind they were all guilty by lineage or association, and were thus justifiable targets!

Deep, so very deep, down within the deepest recesses of his mind, a little worm of doubt wriggled and turned. Without even realising he did it, he squashed it firmly. That was the way it had to be! Any other course led to madness! Best to keep the lid tight shut upon that dark and secret morass!

Liam knew doubt. Didn't any man? At least in the early days, but he was young then, and set apart from the roughneck crowd and their boisterous ways. Even at school he had turned a quiet nervousness into a pose of studied unemotional indifference. Never a troublemaker, he was seldom the victim of trouble.

He remembered with a cold satisfaction a warm Monday after school. How old could he have been then? No more than eight or nine surely. Malcolm. Yes, that was his name, Malcolm Doyle. Fat, wanting to be sure he got Liam's dinner ticket to sell for money to feed his gut! The playground confrontation with him and his two accomplices had been a one-sided episode of hot shame and a growing, burning anger.

Later, outside the school gate, Liam could still feel the coldness of his right shoe upon his bare foot, and the cutting of the stretched wool sock against his fingers as it swung in a savage arc towards the back of Malcolm Doyle's head.

The half-brick inside made such a satisfying sound as it impacted, with a devastating force. The crowd of children, watching in silence as the ambulance wailed off with its bleeding cargo, all knew. The pool of silence around him began to grow.

Playground bullies took careful note, hesitating to confront his coldeyed stare, preferring easier meat. Of course, there were no onlookers to see the other Liam Kennedy, beneath the protective veneer. Fighting the only way he could to be the man that now he had to be! For his mother's sake. Clamping down the soul-deep shout of grief that poised threatening to un-man him, to make him just a child again, as he was before the soldiers shot and killed his father in the Bogside on "Bloody Sunday"!

And with the passing of the years and the funeral of his mother - who betrayed him to follow her true love Sean so quickly to the grave - he assumed a mantle of quiet menace in much the same way as others developed pimples and grew into long trousers.

Figures making space for him at crowded bars, drinks "On the house Liam lad!" eased the way as his reputation spread, and the ill-concealed appraisal of certain 'known parties' smoothed his path into adolescence.

Inevitably he gravitated into the 'Na Fianna Eireanna', the youth section of the Provisionals, and in time he joined the periphery of these shadowy men, whose reputations were none the less for being largely built on hearsay and conjecture. Perhaps they too were intrigued or entertained by his unsettling air of edgy danger.

Amongst those figures in Belfast there were also the few who really mattered, the hard-line killers, staff officers of the three "Battalions" which covered the city and its surrounds.

Once in their company, and especially once he came to the notice of members of the third Battalion based in the Ardoyne and the Short Strand north and east areas of the city, the most violently anti-Loyalist, the rest was inevitable.....

Nicole walked up to the bed carrying two steaming mugs. She was naked.

Liam lay back feeling a stir in his loins as he watched her two large breasts jiggle and sway.

Her nipples fascinated him. Were they always erect? he wondered, or was the wantonness of her nudity arousing her? Her body was so white he could discern the blue veins surrounding those soft pink centres.

God but he wanted to bite them! Savagely! Tear them from her impossibly slim body! His penis jerked into life as a vision of her twitching in pain beneath his twisting, pulling fingers swam into his mind.

She smiled down at him, confident in her illusion of control. Her long black hair fell forward concealing her face momentarily as she leant over and placed the mugs on the bedside cabinet.

Liam reached up and cupped those pendulous breasts, slid his fingers down to grip her erect nipples between his fingers and thumbs and pulled her down on top of his naked body.

CHAPTER ELEVEN

LONDON

As Hunter entered the Hotel he paused and surveyed the coming and going of tourists and hotel employees, then his eyes fastened on a casually but smartly-dressed black man seated in the lobby, apparently engrossed in a copy of the Telegraph. It would perhaps be simply coincidence that his seat afforded him a full view of everyone entering or leaving.

Hunter strolled over and sat down casually in an adjacent easy chair. Dennis Martin looked up briefly at his approach but made no sign of recognition and carried on reading his newspaper. With a polite smile Hunter leaned over and gestured at the selection of newspapers on the table in front of Martin.

"Do you mind?"

Martin glanced up and nodded indifferently, as Hunter bending closer picked one up and continued in a whisper: "My car. 10 minutes!"

After unhurriedly scanning the headlines, Hunter put down the paper again, made a show of looking at his watch, got up and walked out into the street, crossed the road and climbed behind the wheel of his car. The passenger door opened and Martin slid in. From the look on his face Hunter could tell that he was somewhat annoyed.

"Jim." Hunter nodded as Martin continued abruptly: "What's up? You know I'm on assignment!...I should be..."

Hunter interrupted sharply: "What's going on Dennis? This assignment? Why you, and why don't I know anything about it?"

"Whoa Jim. I don't know, it's just a job...."

Martin seemed taken aback by Hunter's cold flat tone. Turning in the seat to look squarely at his colleague, Hunter cut off his protestations.

"It's not just a job, Dennis, this guy is a real big fish, a Senator for Christ's sake, with Irish connections and no doubt likely to be getting attention from all sorts of undesirables, and here he is, swanning around with just minimum protection! Something stinks!" Martin took a deep breath and continued in quieter tones in an attempt to placate him.

"Look Jim, I just do what I'm told. The Colonel himself assigned this one, obviously he's happy with the cover, who am I to argue?"

Hunter looked away, staring bleakly out of the windscreen, tapping his fingers irritably on the steering wheel: "It doesn't feel right Dennis...I don't know... Why wasn't I consulted?"

Martin replied with a shrug, more confident now: "Ours not to reason why..." He smiled. "Look Jim, I'd better get back. See you tonight in the Dojo?"

With an effort Hunter shook off his uneasiness and grinned across at Martin as he climbed out of the car: "Yeah. About 8.30 I should think. See you then."

He sat there, watching as Martin strode back into the Hotel. He still wasn't happy. So far he had been consulted on every contract, and as Director of Operations he should at least have been asked to O.K. the rescheduling made necessary by the Colonel's selection of operatives for this assignment. So what was different here? he mused, why should the Colonel have kept him in the dark on this contract? There was only one way to find out.

Hunter started the engine and eased the car out into the traffic. "After all," he mused, "he could only ask."

CHAPTER TWELVE

"Look Jim, there's nothing peculiar about it at all."

Colonel Williams cradled the handset between his shoulder and cheek as he motioned for his visitor to take a seat.

"Martin needs the experience, that's all. He's a first-class man to have in a combat situation, when facing a known enemy, or when it comes to dealing with explosive devices, but when it comes to day-to-day boring routine observation or low-risk protection work, well, he's got to learn the ropes, the same as everyone else!"

He listened for a moment:..."No! There's no question of it; this one is down to Martin. If he slips up. well, it shouldn't be too disastrous, after all, it's not as if the fellow is high profile, he's just a visiting Yank being shown the courtesies as far as I see it."

Hunter's voice is heard over the 'phone amplifier: "I appreciate all that sir, it's just that I should have been told! I've had a glance at the Yank's file, and I'm not so sure that he's all that 'low profile'. He's a senator, but he also seems to be heavily connected with NORAID, fund raising from Irish groups and donating the proceeds to the IRA, and....."

Williams cut in testily: "Yes, yes, Hunter; Mr. Grey is perfectly aware of all that, and he specifically requested that Martin be given his chance to run this one so...."

Hunter interrupted sharply: "Mr. Grey! What's he got to do with this?"

The Colonel could have bitten off his tongue, realising that he has said too much. After a moment's pause he continued briskly: "Hunter, it's simply another job passed on through the FCO and vetted by MI6, nothing unusual; so just let the man get on with his job, all right?"

Without waiting for a reply, Colonel Williams placed the receiver back on the rest and switched off the amplifier. With a sigh he leaned back in his seat and looked across the desk at his visitor as if seeking reassurance.

After a moment, Grey gave a slight nod.

CHAPTER THIRTEEN

A KARATE DOJO IN LONDON

The portrait of an elderly Japanese, Gichin Funakoshi, the 'Father' of modern Karate looked down from the place of honour on the otherwise blank walls at the Black-belt class in session.

Pairs of karate-ka engaged in Ju-Ippon-kumite called target areas to each other before launching fierce kicking or punching attacks. The screams of their Kiai shouts as they focused deadly techniques just short of the target echoed in the silence. The only other sounds being the cracking of the white suits as the limbs snapped out, and the occasional "Oss!" of acknowledgement at a good strike.

Over in one area, an obviously exhausted fighter, white Gi almost black with sweat; strong and muscular, but barely able to stand, faced the Japanese chief instructor: Isao Watanabe 8th Dan.

Each time the weary student attacked, Watanabe, with the ease and timing of a master, parried his techniques and swept his feet from under him, crashing him heavily to the tatami.

Watanabe - a former All Japan Champion - was big, very big compared with the normal Japanese. He stood practically six-foot, and was heavily built with huge gnarled fingers, knuckles enlarged from hours of punching the makiwara post, and feet like slabs of beef.

With narrowed slits of eyes he stood, firm but balanced. No wasted movements, no visible signs of breathing, the beating all the more terrifying for its total lack of emotion.

Once more with heaving shoulders, air was sucked into aching lungs. Once more courage was screwed up beyond breaking point, and once more the student's battered body thudded into the mat.

This was special training. Both Hunter and Martin had undergone this arduous forging of the spirit, and were quietly proud of it. This was no gratuitous bullying, but a master paying tribute to the tireless efforts of a senior student by forcing him time and again to confront pain, exhaustion, even death, and by so doing go beyond them to find the inner strength of the martial arts.

The student would know that he could end the beating anytime he wished. all he had to do was stay down. But he also knew that to hone his body and spirit into that of a that of a true martial artist he had to go beyond the merely physical, into the realm of sheer willpower, determination and commitment, even to death, and by so doing overcome his fear of dying. Once this stage was mastered he would be able to react to any danger spontaneously and intuitively, without even a heartbeat of possibly fatal hesitation.

In the far corner of the dojo Hunter and Martin sweated freely from their exertions. Hunter attacked Martin with a Front Punch. Martin slapped away the punch and countered with a fast roundhouse kick which smacked lightly into the side of Hunter's head.

They resumed their positions, and this time Martin attacked with Mae-Geri, a long powerful kick to the stomach with the ball of his right foot.

As his leg snapped forward, Hunter slid in to meet the kick and parried it, unbalancing Martin. He stepped to the side of the attacker's body and - spinning - slammed the bottom of his left fist under Martin's ear as he landed, then, spinning back again, with the calf of his right leg he chopped Martin's front leg from under him, dropping him in a heap. His sweeping leg drawn up, poised to stamp down on Martin's face.

"Yame!!!" The Japanese karate teacher stood between the two. "Ie! No Good!!" He thrust a stubby finger at Hunter as Martin clambered to his feet.

"You not thinking! Everytime you thinking Must Sweep. Must put man down! But not thinking also must protect head at same time!" Watanabe motioned to Martin to take up his stance, indicating that he should attack again with the same technique.

"Hai. chudan geri!"

As the kick snapped forwards towards his stomach, the teacher repeated the same defence as Hunter, but as Martin dropped to the floor from the sweep, Watanabe raised his right fore-arm beside his face:

"Reason - If he good fighter, then when falling must make mawashi - round kick - Neh? Kick your head! You not see, so then finished! Not to wait, Everytime making block so - Neh?"

Ruefully, Hunter made a slight bow to his teacher. "Oss! Hai! Wakarimasu. Thank you Sensei." With a perfunctory nod, Watanabe turned on his heel and walked away to the front of the class.

"Hai! Everybody line up. class finish!"

The sweating white-clad figures, with the familiarity of years of practice, quietly lined up and adjusted their wet dishevelled uniforms. Then, following the master's lead, they squatted with backs straight, knees wide apart, balancing on the balls of their feet. After a moment, moving as one, they placed first the left knee then the right down on the tatami, and closing their eyes and straightening their backs, began the meditation and recovery exercise known as Mokuso.

Later, in the lounge bar of the 'Bird in Hand', the Japanese master was almost sociable. In fact the regular after-training sessions had become almost a ritual for Watanabe and his senior students. During the actual sessions it was unusual to get more than a sardonic grunt or an exhortation to train harder from him, but here after a pint or two he would even unbend enough to explain the finer points of a technique.

Tonight, however, Hunter and Martin sat a little apart from the group around the sensei.

Martin took a long swallow of lager, and wiped his lips: "What can I tell you Jim? It's just a routine, boring waste of time; he goes shopping, he eats, goes to the Embassy. I believe he's got some business meetings set up, but - so far - just routine!"

Hunter leaned back wearily in his seat and massaged his aching knee: "Yeah! I know." He took a drink of the ice-cold beer and hiccupped as it hit his digestive tract: "But there's just something......." He sighed and downed the rest of his drink.

"Anyway, I've got to go. I promised Jean I'd look in and fix a shelf for her."

He pushed himself to his feet, picked up his training bag.

"How is she? Are you and she.....?"

Hunter pulled a face: "No. She's fine , but...well, it's just friendly now, you know how it is..." He nodded and walked over to the group as etiquette demanded, to say goodbye to the teacher.

Martin sat for a long time, staring thoughtfully after him.

CHAPTER FOURTEEN

Jean placed the coffee cups on the kitchen table, as Hunter dropped the screwdriver back into his toolbox. He hated DIY with a vengeance, he always had. In Hunter's experience each attempt was just one more opportunity for Sod's Law to operate.

He couldn't remember ever doing even the simplest of tasks around the house without something screwing up! Flat-pack furniture never came with the number of screws listed on the instruction sheet, dimmer switches didn't and he didn't even want to think about his attempts at plumbing!

It wasn't that he couldn't manage, it was more that because he judged these things so inconsequential, he never seemed to give them enough attention, and thus continually found himself the loser on these domestic battlefields.

And he felt strange, here in her apartment, in a place he once called 'Home' - so domestic, just like before, except now it was different, he wasn't staying. Now he wasn't sure that he wanted to.

At first, of course, he would have given anything to have had her back again. But it wouldn't work. Deep down he knew that he still couldn't settle into domesticity any better than before.

"Thanks Jim. That's saved me a lot of trouble, you know how useless I am with practical things like shelves." Jean smiled, her voice soft, the gentle brogue still so appealing.

"You do look a bit tired you know, too many late nights?"

Hunter pulled up a chair, sat at the table and gratefully took the proffered cup of coffee.

"No. You know how it is, I've a lot on at the moment."

He lapsed into a slightly uncomfortable silence and sipped his drink. She had remembered that he liked it really hot.

"Same as ever, Jim." She smiled again, but wistfully this time: "You always did spend more time away than you ever did at home with me, first the army, and now that security firm."

Embarrassed, Hunter cut her off with an apologetic grimace. He had the feeling that if he were to just take her in his arms, she would not object, he sensed that she still cared very much for him, but what would be the point, he hadn't really changed, and until he did....

He pulled a wry face and grinned at her: "I suppose I'll never get the hang of delegating." He drained his cup and put it down on the table.

"I must be going." He got up.

As always when in her company the sense of guilt for the disruptions he had caused to her life began to make him uneasy. He knew that it was his fault that she was now on her own again, and the knowledge somehow diminished him, making him less than the person he really was.

Jean rose and went around the table to Hunter, placing her hand lightly on his arm. Looking tenderly up at him, her eyes were sad. "You're never here more than five minutes before you say 'I must go'. Try and take things a bit easier Jim, you really look as though you could do with a holiday."

Hunter wanted to get away. He could feel the tension beginning to build up. If only she had been a bitch, he thought, then it would have been easier, but she wasn't; she was what she had always been, a really nice, warm person...He realised with a start that she was still speaking.

".....and your step-father called, he says you haven't 'phoned him lately and you know how he worries..."

Hunter gave her a quick hug and headed for the door: "I Know, I know. Time seems to go by and I don't even notice, but you're right, I should call him; I'll do it from the office tomorrow."

She went with him to the door: "Oh yes! Jim don't forget that Margaret is coming to stay with me for a few days, and you promised to take us shopping!"

Hunter metaphorically rolled his eyes at the memory of his promise to chauffeur Jean and his brother's wife around the West End and Knightsbridge.

"No" He lied, "I haven't forgotten. Just call me at the office and tell me when and where to meet you. If I'm not in. leave a message with my secretary, and she'll make sure I get it. Anyway, I really must go." Hunter almost bit his tongue as the words popped out. He shook his head, kissed Jean on the cheek and smiling ruefully, escaped.

CHAPTER FIFTEEN

Charles Grey's office, as usual, was a haven of quiet tranquillity, firmly rooted in a bygone age of solid affluent gentility. He sat at his desk, speaking to Dennis Martin, who is standing almost formally in front of it.

"It must be soon, Martin, he's been here two days now, and surveillance hasn't turned up anything interesting, so let's earn a few Brownie points with the CIA and get the job done!"

"No problem, sir;" Martin said confidently: "But Hunter is more than a little suspicious already, so I ....."

With a wave of his hand Grey cut him off:

"Don't worry about Hunter, he'll do what he's told, but since we're still repaying favours to our American cousins from the Falklands, and since the CIA are no longer authorised to carry out certain tasks, they've ...ah...suggested that we might be able to help them out."

He steepled his fingertips and continued in dry tones as though delivering a lecture on the water-colours of Charles Edward Wilson, a particular favourite artist of his:

"They know for certain from some of their own informants, that the man's a dyed-in-the-wool IRA sympathiser and activist, and that he's probably acting as a courier under Diplomatic Immunity to ferry either funds or equipment to the

IRA here in England. The feeling is that he's carrying something new from Silicon Valley which we really don't want to fall into the wrong hands. The CIA think that its some new type of transmitter, which is very small, and capable of outwitting radio frequency jammers.....which in a bomb detonator could be very nasty!"

He paused, as if considering the disturbing prospect.

Martin took the opportunity to speak: "Are we sure Sir? He doesn't seem to be bothered about anything much except his shopping and sight-seeing...."

His voice trailed off at the sight of Grey's exasperated expression:

"Really! So he's not waving a flag with IRA sympathiser plastered all over it! How surprising!" His voice dripped with sarcasm.

Martin apologised sheepishly: "Sorry Sir. I wasn't thinking."

"Hmm!" Snorted Grey, then continued briskly: "Anyway Martin, we want him dealt with right away, before he does get a chance to pass anything on.....if he hasn't already, that is!"

"I don't think he has," replied Martin: "we're watching him like a hawk, Sir, the trouble is we don't really know what we're looking for....if it's something very small...well.."

Grey's eyes seemed to grow darker and bore right through Martin: "I'm aware of the difficulties; all the more reason to get the job done quickly wouldn't you say?"

It wasn't that he was a big man, mused Martin to himself as he made his way out of the building, but he was so ...

intimidating. He seldom raised his voice, but Martin didn't doubt that if necessary Grey could be an implacable foe. "It was strange," he mused, "but on the surface Grey seemed so, so ordinary, but then, almost as if his guard was down, there were moments when something else seemed to be inside him, something cold. There was just something about his eyes, or rather the way they seemed to change on occasions, like a light switch being switched off, then they were just blank black holes, no spark, no warmth, just.......coldness....and death!"

Martin shook his head to clear the unsettling images and made his way hurriedly towards his car.

CHAPTER SIXTEEN

Selfridges on Oxford Street is spoken of internationally in the same breath as Harrods. These were the two stores that more than any other in London, attracted the visiting tourists, and the American was no exception.

Accompanied by one of Total Security's bodyguards, the Senator crossed from the perfumery department into the ground floor men's clothing section. They passed the suits, jackets and trousers and headed for the haberdashery department, stopping at the tie racks and stands.

The American gestured for his companion to put his collection of Harrods shopping bags down on the floor as he selected a particularly dazzling silk tie and held it up for comment.

A pale non-descript shopper brushed past, apologetically, intent upon the silk ties. He is also carrying a green Harrods plastic bag.

As the Senator held his selection up to his collar and asked the bodyguard for his opinion, on the other side of the rack, the browser smoothly bent down and switched his carrier bag with one of those at his feet, then strolled casually away.

Back in the American's hotel, the lift to his Penthouse Suite had an 'out of service' sign on it, and Martin, dressed in a brown overall, was working on the electronic door mechanism.

Kennedy's less salubrious hotel bedroom, in contrast, was fairly unremarkable, save that scattered across the bed are a number of packages of Semtex II explosive, empty lunch-boxes, detonators and other bomb-making equipment.

Seated at the dressing table, the Irishman was bent over a small box into which he carefully soldered a tiny circuit board dotted with transistors, resistors and silicon chips. On the floor nearby lay the empty discarded green Harrods bag.

CHAPTER SEVENTEEN

Later that afternoon, in the American's hotel lobby, Martin, now normally dressed, got up to greet the Senator and his bodyguard as they returned.

"Evening Sir." He smiled and shook hands with the Senator: "Enjoy your shopping?" He nodded approvingly at his colleague, weighed down by various bags, which are all carried in one hand, however, leaving his dominant hand free for emergencies. "Brian."

Martin relieved him of the bags as they walked towards the elevator. "I'll take over now Brian, make your report and get some rest."

He grinned at his colleagues discomfiture: "I do believe it's shopping again tomorrow, is that right Senator?"

The American laughed loudly at Brian's expression.

"I guess so! Wouldn't do to go home without a few things for the little lady huh?"

Martin pressed the button to summon the lift. When it arrived, he ushered the American in, and placed all but one of the bags quickly on the floor and leaning in, pressed the Penthouse suite button. "You go on up Sir, I'll be up in a few minutes when I've gone over a few points with Brian about tomorrow."

The doors closed before the American had time to reply, and Martin gestured to the shopping bag that he had deliberately kept back.

"Never mind. I'll see he gets it."

Chatting genially, Martin walked with Brian through the lobby to the hotel entrance and after a few moments wished him goodnight.

As soon as he had gone, Martin made his way over to the easy chairs in reception and sat down. He looked at his watch, then picked up a newspaper and began to read. After a few minutes, he put down the paper and went over to the house 'phone and dialled the American's room.

"Ah Yes sir, it's me. Sorry to trouble you, but you must have left one of your shopping bags in reception.....No, it's quite all right, I've got it here, but I'm afraid it looks as though I'll be stuck down here with Brian for some time yet sir; do you think you could possibly pop down and collect it?.....Great! I'll be in the lobby."

Martin replaced the handset and turned away with a smile of satisfaction on his face. As he turned he collided with Hunter who had come up silently behind him.

"Christ Jim! I almost had a heart attack! What're you trying to do to me?!!" Hunter laughed at his expression: "You're losing your touch Dennis. All this civilisation is making you soft!"

Martin pulled a face: "Yeah! You could be right, perhaps I could do with some IED work to liven things up eh? Anyway, what's up, checking up on me now?"

Hunter grinned: "You just thank your lucky stars you're out of that Improvised Explosive Device disposal unit! That sort of thing can be seriously detrimental to your health!"

"No, of course I'm not checking up on you, I just thought I'd pop in and...."

Martin clapped him on the shoulder: "I know, you were just passing.....anyway Jim, I'm just on my way up to check on our friend's plans for the evening, and deliver his shopping, so come up and meet him yourself." He steered Hunter across the lobby towards the lifts.

Up in the penthouse suite, the Senator placed his empty whisky glass on the sideboard and pressed the button to call the elevator. He waited patiently as the indicator lit and the doors slid open. He stepped in, and dropped like a stone into the empty lift shaft!

In the lobby Hunter and Martin stood waiting for the lift. Suddenly, an alarm bell shrilled startlingly and the lift lights all began to flash.

Surprised, Hunter shot a quizzical glance at Martin who shrugged his shoulders in bewilderment. He spun on his heel, shouting to Martin as he began to run across the lobby:

"The stairs! Come on!"

Both men ran to the emergency stairs and clattered up them two at a time. Fit as they both were, by half-way they were both panting for breath, but they forced themselves onward. Hunter, gasping and breathless reached the door first, hammering on it and ringing the bell.

Wet with sweat, Martin pushed him aside.

"I've got a key, Jim." He panted.

Shaking from his exertions, fumbling, Martin thrust a key into the lock and threw open the door. As it crashed open they heard a yell and ran to the open doors of the elevator.

Leaning over the edge, they could see down in the lift shaft the dishevelled figure of the American standing on the roof of the elevator car, stretching on tiptoe desperately trying to grasp the lip of the floor which was just out of reach.

The two men immediately knelt, reached down and hauled him up. The Senator was white and trembling with shock. Hunter helped him up and settled him in a chair, motioning to Martin to pour him a drink. The man was obviously badly shaken.

Martin passed him a glass. "Take it easy, you're all right." He spoke soothingly: "It's O.K. now, you're safe." The whisky vanished in huge gulps and the glass held out for more.

Hunter patted the trembling man comfortingly on the arm, Then, wiping the film of sweat from his face with the back of his hand, he walked over to examine the lift and the door mechanism leaving Martin to replenish the empty glass.

"What happened?" Hunter asked from the lift doors.

The white faced American exploded in anger and relief: "What happened?! I'll tell you what fucking happened! The motherfucking lift happened, that's what! The doors open, I get in, but there's no fucking floor is what happened!! I could'a been killed, that's what happened!"

Lapsing into silence, he took another deep swallow.

Martin pressed his shoulder encouragingly and walked over to Hunter. "Find anything?"

Hunter looked up from his examination of the door mechanism with a strange expression on his face.

"Didn't you check it?" He tapped the controls with his forefinger. "It's been tampered with. I'm willing to bet that the door will open a few moments after the button is pressed, whether or not the lift is actually there! It was sheer luck that it happened to be just one floor below, otherwise..." He gestured to the exposed control panel.

"Look, all the safeties have been bypassed. Surely it was checked?"

Martin replied defensively:

"It didn't seem necessary, Jim. I told you this was just...."

Hunter's fierce reaction cut his protestations short.

"I know Dennis, 'just routine.' Shit! you know better than that. Nothing is ever left to chance!" He walked away in exasperation, then turned on Martin: "Take care of him, and make sure that you double check everything from now on. I'm going to see Grey tomorrow and get to the bottom of this!"

With a nod to the still shaking Senator, Hunter walked out. Martin stroked his chin thoughtfully, staring after him long after he had gone.

CHAPTER EIGHTEEN

Next morning Grey's secretary conducted Hunter into the Bond Street office where Grey was seated at his desk.

"Thank you, Mrs Hemmings. Come in Hunter, Sit down. Coffee?"

Grey motioned Hunter to a seat and, getting up, poured two cups of coffee from the tray. "You don't take sugar do you?...no."

He handed the cup to Hunter and sat back down.

The older man gazed almost sadly at Hunter for a brief moment, then caught himself as if remembering his image as he leaned back in his chair.

"Now. I understand that you have a problem. Well, we must try to clear things up mustn't we?" He raised a hand to forestall Hunter's reply: "No! Don't interrupt. Hear me out, and then if you want to add anything or make any comments you can."

Nonplussed, Hunter sat back in his seat and waited.

Grey deliberately maintained an aloof silence as he leafed through a thick green folder of notes, open on the desk in front of him. Eventually he looked up and fixed Hunter with his hard gaze.

"This is you, Hunter; your life, your thoughts, your emotions; all the information that experts in psychology have gleaned from your service record, your security vetting, reports from various of your superiors and colleagues, even from your old school reports and past girl-friends, not to mention your ex-wife!"

The object of his scrutiny shifted uncomfortably in his seat and put down the un-tasted cup of coffee.

Grey continued icily: "We have taken you apart, Hunter, examined you like a fly on a pin, but we still don't understand...HOW YOU COULD CONTINUE TO BE SO BLOODY STUPID!"

Grey's sudden shout hit Hunter like a whiplash!

"You, of all people Hunter," Grey continued in his normal unemotional tone, as if nothing had happened. "Your father murdered by IRA thugs, your Special Forces activities, your active service in unspeakable conditions in the Falklands, and your tours of duty - three, if I'm correct - in Ireland. How then, can you not face your responsibilities?"

"Yes, Hunter," He leaned forward: "Your responsibilities to each and every innocent man woman and child in our society who look to us, you, for protection and Justice!"

Hunter felt like a schoolboy again, in front of his headmaster:

"That's not fair sir," He protested: "I.."

Grey cut him off angrily: "Fair! Fair! My God, Hunter."He continued almost sorrowfully: "Whoever talked of 'Fair'?"

He took a deep breath, then continued gently: "Yes, Jim."

Hunter's head came up at the unfamiliar and unexpected use of his first name:

"I know you've done your part - more than most - but just because you're not in a uniform any more doesn't mean that the war is over!" "You refused the opportunity to remain an official part of our team because of what? A sense of morality? What's moral, Jim, in allowing a known murderer to walk free because an extradition form was filled out incorrectly. Where's the justice in that? Come on!"

He got up from his desk and picked up another folder, this time a red one. He crossed to where Hunter was sitting and handed him the file.

"There's no way out, you know; like it or not, fate, has decided that you are to exercise your talents on behalf of the angels, even if we do appear to be most unlikely examples."

He returned to his seat. "You're worried, I know, about this American. And, yes, you're right, but Martin hasn't been lax in his duties - at least not in the way that you thought. Read the file."

Hunter opened the folder and noted the recent photo of the Irish-American pinned to the top, and the CIA 'Confidential/Need to Know Only' bright red stamp.

There followed a brief resume of his subversive activities and NORAID fund-raising, plus a note that the subject was suspected of being involved in obtaining highly sophisticated weaponry for IRA and other end-users. Next was attached a page of electronic blue-prints which made no sense to Hunter, except that he saw mention of VHF frequency shifting, which he related to some sort of broadcasting device.

Finally there were three sheets of photocopied text in German, with a typed translation. It was a Coroner's reports on the deaths of a British soldier and his wife blown apart in their booby-trapped car by a suspected active service IRA cell near an Army base in Dusseldorf.

Hunter looked up enquiringly at Grey, who moved back behind his desk and sat down.

"What's the connection? I take it there is one?"

Grey's eyes had turned cold again: "Our CIA friends know without a doubt that this man is no more than a terrorist. In fact, although he never personally pulls a trigger, he and the money that he raises are responsible for countless terrorist atrocities. But, naturally, as he never does pull the trigger himself, it is unlikely that he will ever be brought to account."

Hunter was shaken: "If the CIA are so sure of him, why don't they just pull him in then?"

"If only it were that simple, Hunter. They know for sure because of a 'Sting' operation which was set up by one of their moles on the inside of NORAID, concerned with obtaining and shipping certain anti-helicopter one-man ground-to-air missiles and launchers from Libya to Southern Ireland."

His lips twisted scornfully: "The trouble is, if they arrest him he will probably yell 'entrapment' and walk away, whilst the CIA cover will be well and truly blown! So,...they asked us to ....deal with the problem."

Hunter was in no mood for the niceties of language: "A Wet contract.....?"

Grey sat back in his seat: "Precisely!"

It was all becoming clear to Hunter now, but he had to be sure. "And Martin was to do the job"

Grey sighed. "Since we were aware of your 'reservations' yes. Martin, is a good man, but I'm afraid, he has been....not as successful as we would have hoped."

Hunter stared at him in silence.

Grey did not as a rule see fit to explain anything to anyone. Usually he issued an order, and that was it. But there was just something about this dark, solemn, intense character sitting opposite him that made Hunter like him. Powerful, deadly, yes; but essentially straightforward, and - to use a word that almost seemed inappropriate in view of what Grey was trying to get him to do - a good man, with a strong sense of justice.

He had taken note of Hunter's career, ever since he refused to accept the final MI6 desensitisation programming course, designed to adjust any inhibitions which might cause an operative to hesitate over certain 'required' solutions. Perhaps he could see in Hunter a reflection of his own early struggles with conscience and conventional morality, whatever it was, he decided to lay all the facts before him.

"You see, the CIA believe that the American is being used by the IRA to smuggle in a cargo of electronic circuit boards with a new type of chip which cycles radio frequencies extremely rapidly in short bursts. Now if these are used in conjunction with specialised receivers they could penetrate our security jamming devices and perform a number of functions - disrupt computers, jam our own sensitive frequencies, but - more significantly - they could detonate a radio frequency sensitive explosive device, in spite of defensive jamming, in micro-seconds."

Hunter leaned forward, his attention caught.

"Maybe I'm a bit slow, sir, but why would this be different from the video-recorder timing devices that they use now? And anyway, I thought we had reached an agreement with the IRA to end the violence......?"

"To take your first point, the difference is time. Hunter, time. You see there is a built-in limitation to the life of a video timer, plus it must have an electrical supply in order to operate; thus it can only be set a certain period before it is to be detonated, perhaps a few months at most."

Grey allowed his concern to show in his voice: "The devilish thing about this stuff is that it can be planted in sensitive areas years before it need be used, and with a hook-up to the latest long-life battery cells the device can remain undiscovered yet armed and lethal until it receives a micro-second signal which we cannot jam, then...!"

The room was silent for a few moments, then Grey leaned forward with his arms upon the desk.

"As to your second - well, we should I suppose simply take their words at face value, after all, it would save us all a considerable amount of time and effort - but..." He raised an eloquent eyebrow at Hunter.

He sighed: "Even if it were true, do you really believe that all those murdering thugs who have nothing in life except the twisted status purchased by their willingness to kill and maim innocent women and children indiscriminately will be content to simply fade back into obscurity?"

His tone hardened as he stared bleakly into the future.

"No. Mark me well, James, it is only a matter of time! The cease-fire is more or less over, and there will always be some supposed excuse which they can trot out to justify the continuance of their only claim to being a somebody!" He paused before continuing softly:

"And some have grown addicted to the thrill such power bestows. They will not remain silent for long!..The stirrings are already there, mainland bombs on motorways that – thank God – have so far claimed no lives but…….."

Grey pulled himself back from the horrors in his mind.

"Well, anyway - Martin was supposed to deal with this matter before the consignment could be delivered. Your zealousness may well have jeopardised that!"

Hunter looked uncomfortable, but he was not ready to capitulate yet. "One thing,...why the Dusseldorf report in the file?"

Grey looked grimly at him:

"A field test before delivery, to see if the device works to specification. The body of the husband, by the way, could not be identified. There was not even enough left in one piece to place on the mortuary slab. A black plastic bag, Hunter. A black plastic bag against a corner wall!..... At least the wife's relatives were spared that; the top half of her body was more or less intact! ....I suppose that's some comfort..."

The continuing catalogue of horror beat like waves on Hunter's resistance. He spoke hesitatingly, finding it difficult to verbalise his emotional responses.

"It's just that....I don't know; it's just that when I see someone pointing a gun at me, well, I feel justified...you know what I mean, but to ...terminate...kill..an unarmed person seems....I don't know..not right."

Grey just stared at him, forcing him to follow the logic of his thoughts. After a brief pause Hunter continued.

"If it were to stop all this slaughter.." He gestured towards the German Coroner's report: "I can see....." He lapsed into a thoughtful silence.

The intercom buzzer broke into the silence. Grey reached over and clicked up the switch. Hunter could plainly hear his secretary's apologetic voice.

"Sorry to disturb you, sir, but there's a message for Mr. Hunter, could he call his office before he leaves?"

"Thank you." He switched off the intercom. "Did you get that"

Hunter pulled a wry face: "Yes thank you, Sir...Look Sir, I realise that I've been...difficult, but it's not easy."

Grey got up slowly, and walked around the desk as Hunter also stood. He put a hand on Hunter's shoulder and spoke softly and emotionally.

"Jim, I do understand, you know. I have to sleep at night as well. But I made my commitment long, long ago. A murderer is a murderer as far as I'm concerned, and no argument or reason will ever persuade me that terrorism - the slaughter of innocent women and children - is ever justifiable, and, court of law or no, these inhuman bastards are a cancer in humanity which must be cut out before their evil sickness destroys us completely!"

He sighed, dropped his hand and walked back behind the desk, reverting instantly to the cold and calculating Grey that Hunter knew so well.

"So. You have to make your choice, you're either for the angels, or for the enemy. We need surgeons with sharp scalpels, not moralisers. There's no place here for fence-sitters!"

He nodded his head towards the door, signifying that the discussion was at an end. Hunter stared at him for a moment, then turned away, grateful to escape. Mind racing, he walked slowly out of the office.

Grey looked up as the door closed behind him, then pressed a button at the side of his desk. A few seconds later the door opened again to admit Dennis Martin, accompanied by Sir Hector Bainbridge.

"Did you hear?"

Both men nodded as he continued:

"I think, Martin, that you will find Hunter to be more co-operative from now on. Anyway, get back to the Hotel. You've a job to do! Get it done!"

"Yes sir." Martin turned and walked out briskly, as Bainbridge helped himself to a sherry.

Grey affably motioned him to a seat:

"Now Hector, what about your GCHQ intercepts. Have you turned up anything useful?"

CHAPTER NINETEEN

The Tea Room of The Ritz is one of best known meeting places in he world. Every afternoon it is filled to overflowing with people coming to see celebrities, and celebrities coming to be seen.

Chattering throngs of mostly middle-aged well-dressed women sat in little groups clustered around crisp dazzling white-clothed tables with elegant waiters moving briskly between them. In one corner a dress-suited trio of elderly musicians plays selections of chamber music.

Hunter's wife and his sister-in-law, Margaret, were seated at one of the little tables sipping tea and occasionally punctuating their conversation with tiny bites from delicate scones, baked fresh every day and served on the distinctive blue and white china.

Across the room, in one corner, a well-dressed man wearing a brightly coloured silk tie made his way through the throng. He noticed an empty chair at Jean and Margaret's table. Kennedy coughed politely to attract their attention, and with a friendly smile spoke in his soft Irish brogue.

"Good afternoon ladies, is this seat taken?"

Jean smiled and shook her head.

"No? Do you mind if sit here, it's so busy?"

Kennedy smiled warmly again in thanks as he eased himself into the empty seat and placed a number of shopping bags well under the table. "I'm sorry to disturb you, ladies, but oh dear! The crowds in London these days!"

He picked up the menu and studied it while the women went back to their animated conversation. After a moment, he beckoned over a waiter and ordered a pot of tea and some sandwiches. Leaning back, he made himself comfortable and gazed around happily while he waited to be served.

CHAPTER TWENTY

Still unsettled from his meeting with Grey, as soon as Hunter got back to his car after leaving the Bond Street office, he picked up the car 'phone and punched his secretary's number.

He pulled a wry face as she gave him Jean's reminder that he was to meet her and his sister-in-law at the Ritz were they are having tea and waiting for him. With a mental sigh of resignation he started the car and began to drive leisurely through the mid-afternoon traffic.

Back in the Ritz, Kennedy swallowed the last morsel of the delicious triangles of crust-less smoked salmon sandwiches, drained the last of his Earl Grey, and brushed a few recalcitrant crumbs from his lap. He dabbed fastidiously at his lips with the pure linen napkin, then laid it on the table and rose to leave.

"Afternoon ladies!"

He smiled a pleasant farewell then stooped to collect his shopping bags. As he did so he unobtrusively pushed one - a Harrods green plastic bag - further under the table. He straightened up, and with a final nod, strolled off through the throng towards the exit.

Outside in the afternoon sunshine, he casually strolled along, whistling and apparently without a care in the world. At the street corner he paused and reached into his pocket, withdrawing a small device, almost like a pocket calculator in size and shape.

He fingered it for a moment, then pressed a little red button.

With Radio One playing, Hunter drove easily on auto-pilot. He smiled to himself as he listened to another tirade by 'Mr Angry' on the Steve Wright Show. Suddenly he was aware of the intrusive wail of police car sirens, and then, almost immediately, the clamour of fire engines. He saw lights flashing in his rear-view mirror and pulled over to let an ambulance go racing past.

All at once there seemed to be a lot of activity in the streets, and yet another police car sped past, followed by another ambulance.

In the background the crescendoing wails of emergency service sirens increased, and, without knowing why, Hunter found himself starting to drive faster as a sense of unease settled over him. With a mounting sense of dread, he suddenly knew that something was wrong, terribly wrong! He accelerated along the inside of a slower car and fumbled for the dashboard, cutting off Mr Angry in mid tirade. He flicked on the Police Band.

The voice of the operator filled the car: "..all casualty flying squads. A mobile Incident Room vehicle is on the way, and DCI Mulready, I repeat, Chief Inspector Mulready will be co-ordinator. All units will report to him."

Slamming the accelerator to the floor, Hunter swung the car in and out of the traffic, faster and faster, at a reckless pace towards the Ritz, and the menacing pall of black smoke that he could now see rising above the buildings in front of him.

"....All mobiles to assist in crowd control and evacuation. We do not know if there is another device. The first priority is to ensure clear evacuation routes for casualties."

Knuckles white from his savage grip on the steering wheel, Hunter flung the car around the next corner and stamped fiercely on the brakes, slewing to a skidding halt almost colliding with the side of a patrol panda car blocking the road. As he wrenched open the door he could hear the announcement being repeated once again:

"All units, there has been a terrorist device exploded at the Ritz Hotel. No warning was given and the number of casualties is uncertain. The area is to be cordoned off with access only to authorised persons. Be prepared to facilitate access for the emergency hospital flying squads.."

Over the outstretched arm of the young police officer Hunter could see the vision of hell that had so recently been the Ritz Hotel. A vast black gaping maw yawned, smoking and rubble-strewn, where the entrance facade had been. The street was littered with debris and bodies. Secondary explosions had picked up parked cars and flung them chaotically like the discarded playthings of a petulant giant! The red of the fire-engines contrasted with the white of the ambulances and the blue of police vehicles. Splashes of colour so vivid against the blackness and the grey-blue roils of smoke.

"My God..Jean!" Hunter gasped, his brain refusing to function. Like an unstoppable automaton he knocked aside the restraining arm and ran, his head filled with a silent scream, towards the horror.

It was like a giant ant's nest. Blackened, bloody, dazed figures scrambled in and out of the ruined building, some emerged supporting stumbling, injured lucky ones, but, ominously, many worked in pairs, carrying still and unprotesting bundles. Fire hoses drenched the scene, and the shouted commands of the rescuers intermingled with the screams and sobs of the injured, as Dante's infernal dream became a nightmare reality!

Hunter picked his way frantically through the scrabbling groups of victims and helpers, making his way from one to another, his attention jumping this way and that as he sought desperately for his first glimpse of Jean.

Through all the blood, pain and dirt, all the faces were of strangers. Crying, grimacing, staring blankly or sobbing hysterically, but not Jean's face....maybe..Hunter clenched his fists in a spasmodic unbelieving anger, and clamped down savagely upon his sudden jump of hope.

Stumbling and almost falling over the wreckage, he forced his way past the swearing, sweating knots of struggling figures deeper into the shattered building.

As he made his way further in, the heat and the acrid smell of smoke and water stung his throat making him gag. With a crash, a blackened - something - fell heavily across his shoulder, thrusting it aside with a curse, Hunter rubbed the sweat out of his stinging eyes and peered frantically into the depths of the ruined tea rooms.

In the gloom he could dimly make out silhouettes of figures bending and straining, levering away broken tables and shattered fabric. In the yellow pools of light thrown by the emergency lamps it was impossible to distinguish features.

Helplessly, Hunter moved to the nearest group and began to lend a hand carefully easing a section of the bar off the shattered legs of a quietly moaning figure clutching the remnants of a violin.

CHAPTER TWENTY-ONE

It was quiet in the street outside the blackened remains of the Ritz, later that evening. Two fire tenders remained on standby to damp down and control any possible rekindling, and uniformed police manned the barriers to keep away the morbid onlookers always attracted to disaster and tragedy.

Forensic and Special Branch had collected and taken away for analysis the fragments discovered by the Bomb Squad, who had pronounced the scene clear of further devices. All the survivors had been ferried to casualty departments throughout London. Now the grim task of extricating the bodies was underway.

A small row of still, shrouded figures lay silently in the street awaiting collection. Hunter sat near them on the wet pavement, as if in a trance he stared blankly at the bundled figure next to him.

The row of bodies got steadily shorter as ambulance men rolled them gently onto stretchers and lifted them into the waiting vehicles. Then there was only one left to remove.

"Sorry mate, we've got to take her now." The gentle sympathetic voice fell on unheeding ears.

The ambulance man looked down understandingly at Hunter and rested a hand on his shoulder. "You can go with her, you know, if you want that is.."

There was still no reply. Hunter stared unseeingly into a different world.

"Sorry mate..." He gestured to his companion and they gently eased the broken body onto a stretcher and lifted it into the waiting ambulance. Before he climbed into the cab, he came back to Hunter. "Look chum, we've got to go now,...sure you don't want to...."

Still Hunter didn't answer.

He tried again: "You know, you shouldn't just sit..." He stopped abruptly as Hunter clambered suddenly to his feet.

Like a sleepwalker waking from a dream, Hunter stared at the ambulance man, then with an effort he spoke:

"It's... I'm O.K.... I..." He lapsed into silence again as he slowly surveyed the scene, as if committing it indelibly to memory.

He continued as if something had broken in him: "No, it's O.K......there's something I've got to do..."

Grim-faced, his mouth set in a white-lipped line, Hunter strode away from the pathetic removal vans of misery. Slamming the car door, he knuckled away the tears burning his eyes. His brain was like ice on fire. Savagely he jerked the motor into life and drove fiercely away, tyres skidding and squealing, narrowly missing one of the policemen manning the crowd barriers.

CHAPTER TWENTY-TWO

The Senator was a happy man.

Seated on a couch in front of a the largescreen TV set, he was watching the latest news of the bombing. Periodically he sipped from a large glass of Bourbon on the rocks. There is a curious expression on his face....almost of suppressed glee. Across the room Dennis Martin is also sitting, staring fixedly at the screen. On his face by contrast is a look of horror and anger.

The suite doorbell cut harshly through the commentary. Martin got up and crossed to the peephole. He grunted and slid open the safety bolt. The door crashed open and Hunter, dirty, dishevelled and grim-faced, pushed past him.

The sombre tones of the television reporter were accompanying the hand-held amateur video film of the early rescue attempts. ".....many casualties as no warning was given. As yet no responsibility has been claimed by any particular group, but it is believed to be the work of the IRA."

"You murdering bastard!" Hunter thrust the astonished Martin to one side and strode over to the Senator who had risen to his feet.

Martin stood as if paralysed as Hunter seized the blustering American by his lapels and spun him round, levering one arm savagely up into a hammer-lock behind his back. Hunter's other forearm choked off his cries of protest as he frogmarched the struggling man rapidly towards the balcony French windows.

"Open them!" he snarled, jerking his head at Martin, who, coming to life, reached around the heaving figures and slid open the heavy glass doors.

Without another word, Hunter forced the terrified struggling American out across the narrow balcony, over the guard rail and out into space. The horrifying despair of his diminishing scream was balm to his soul.

Abruptly there was silence, then, far below, a squeal of brakes, then silence again. Breathing heavily, Hunter turned on his heel and came back into the room. Without a glance at Martin, he picked up the telephone and dialled. After a moment he spoke:

"You were right Sir. I've made my choice." He tossed the handset to Martin and without a backward glance walked out of the room.

Martin stared after him, then remembered the 'phone in his hand, he lifted it to his ear.

It was Grey on the other end.

"Yes sir, It's me, Martin. No, that was Hunter....well, I don't know what happened, but...well, the contract's well and truly completed now.......yes.....from 30 floors up! No... that's no problem, I'll wait here and square it with the uniformed mob.....an accidental fall whilst under the influence I expect sir...Pity, but accidents do happen!"

CHAPTER TWENTY-THREE

Sir Hector Bainbridge looked grim. "For God's sake man!" his angry tones losing none of their vehemence because of the lack of volume!

"Surely you can't think that this is a decision that was taken lightly?" "We are talking about murder you know"

The normally imposing figure of Ambrose Wolsley seemed somehow smaller and more fragile slumped in the worn leather armchair in the corner of the Chief Whip's office. The pale light of the green capped brass desk lamp threw slanting shadows across his weary features.

He lifted his head: "This room" His hand traced an eloquent gesture, "Of all places, here, in the very heart of all that we hold dear.....that this room should hear such treason..."

"Phah!" Bainbridge snorted in frustration, leaning forward into the pool of light.

"Good God, man you must know that this isn't easy!" "Of course it's wrong, terribly wrong, perhaps the worst, most despicable thing ever contemplated, no-one in their right mind could think otherwise!"

His eyes burned into Wolsley's. "But think for a moment just how much good would stem from this one act, wouldn't it be worth it? In this one act we can stop the needless slaughter of countless others who will - mark my words - who will die if we do not have the courage to continue!"

He softened his tone and continued, inspecting his fingers as he spoke as if suddenly embarrassed by his earlier vehemence.

"There's many a soldier on a some nameless battlefield, an airman over some foreign city, even some poor mariner in the depths of an icy ocean who have been asked to give their lives for the greater good!" "Did they volunteer for such a fate? No! They did what they were told, told by us! They didn't want to die but we gave them no choice! Your country needs you and you must go!"

"No-one consulted them" he continued, quietly now. "They would each, no doubt, have preferred to have continued their little lives, seen their families grow and thrive and grow old in the company of their loved ones."

He sighed gently, "But we, the representatives of Democracy, the State, the elected Government, we never gave them the choice."

He looked up again, sadly, "Even as we speak, Ambrose, some Protestant or Catholic who has never so much voiced a political interest one way or another, other than to wish for an end to what seems like a never ending cycle of killing is being lined up in the sights of a gun in the hands of one of his own countryman who's sole and total ambition is to force an end to any talk of peace that the cease-fire might seem to have brought about."

"I'm afraid we're in a battle we just can't win! We never could!"

T he Home Secretary stiffened in his seat.

"Then what the hell have we been doing all these years?" All the men, the resources….the lives lost…."

"Wasted!" "Totally worthless sacrifices, I'm afraid Ambrose." A spasm of anger flashed briefly over Bainbridge's face as he continued bitterly: "Of course we wish it weren't so, the fact is however that many in HMG have always known this to be the case; the problem has always been the certain knowledge that to simply pull out of Ireland and wash our hands of it would be politically out of the question. Without good cause the public would see this as a defeat and the end of any party which brought it about."

"Year after year, decade after decade this senseless waste has continued because no-one has had the....the political balls...to do what needed to be done!"

He fixed Wolsley in the eye. "So now it has come to this.....this ...desperate act of treason, but there is no other way!" "We cannot be seen to be giving in to the Machiavellian posturing of those so-called 'Peace Talk' delegates, but we must end this wound which is leeching away the blood of our people and our economy."

His face tightened into grim lines.

"We have thought the unthinkable, and now we must turn thoughts into action!"

He turned away. "In order to force the withdrawal. we are co-operating with the Provisional IRA to bring about the assassination of the Prime Minister!"

In the deathly shocking hush, he continued:

"I have already arranged a meeting with certain... people... who are being helicoptered in to one of our West of England air bases. They have guarantees of immunity, and I have agreed to meet them tonight."

He turned back to face Wolsley: "I want you to come with me!"

CHAPTER TWENTY-FOUR

Jean's funeral was a horrendous experience for Hunter. Ironically it took place on a beautiful sunny day, the black of the mourners contrasting strongly with the brilliance of the flowers and wreathes, and the soft green of the grass.

Hunter's brother was distraught. The loss of his wife had completely unmanned him, and the double shock of first her funeral and now Jean's was just too much for him to bear.

Four years younger than Hunter, he still had nightmares resulting from witnessing the murder of his father. The family's move to England, his mother's eventual remarriage to the older retired army colonel Roderick Hunter, had all seemed to have a more unsettling effect on him than on Hunter or his sister. He had become a clinging child, and Hunter had many a time had to stand up for him at school.

Then their mother, never a robust person, had seemed to simply fade and die. Cancer, it was; but Hunter knew it was simply the result of too many blows and disappointments for her system to bear.

Finding Margaret, or rather Margaret finding his dependence so appealing to the mothering instinct in her, was the best thing that had ever happened to his brother, and now even that support had been taken away from him.

Hunter found it too painful to remain in the company of his relatives for long, even his sister's quiet strength only made him more acutely aware of how unjust and tragic life could be, to the most innocent and undeserving of people.

Jean's relatives were unsure exactly how to approach him, after all, there had been the divorce, so they tended to keep somewhat apart in their grief, so Hunter found himself standing in that sorrowful place, all alone, stony-faced with a tight clamp upon the vast ocean of sorrows which would drown him if he let it.

But how could he, on a day such as this, keep his mind off his old enemy death itself? He had never really been able to come to terms with it. He could remember how, as a youngster, he would lie in bed at night trying to imagine how it must be, to be dead!

And who was it that really shaped our ends? Was there a purpose to all this, or was it just fate? All he had been able to do was frighten himself with the terrifying inevitability of the enormous nothingness that made such a mockery of all human pretences and ambitions.

Even now, having faced death, and even as a man responsible for many deaths himself, he would have to catch his thoughts when they strayed in that direction, or he could feel himself tipping over the edge of panic and despair. So many deaths, such a... an unforgiving finality to so many hopes and loves and laughter...

On the periphery of the mourners he was aware of the presence of Dennis Martin, and of Charles Grey.

Martin had been physically supportive, staying with him in his apartment, sitting next to him in Church, accompanying him in the funeral car. Grey, on the other hand, had stood at the edge of the Churchyard, quiet, respecting the inadequacy of any words.

As the mourners drifted away from the flower strewn grave, Grey slowly approached Hunter, and without speaking pressed his arm firmly for a moment, as if giving him the strength of a shared experience.

There had been no tea and sandwiches after the funeral, Hunter knew that he would not have been able to cope with that. Instead he had walked aimlessly, deep in memories, along the green grassy banks of the Thames. The slight late afternoon breeze had ruffled his hair, but he didn't notice. On the river white swans glided past in majestic convoy, but Hunter saw only the warm summers of yesterday .In his memory he was back in his Irish childhood, basking in the warmth of his mother's laughter and the hazy, misty golden innocence when duty and responsibility were unknown.

Violent passions coursed his Celtic blood; overwhelming hatred of a younger brother suddenly became a shared delight in the blind-eyed antics of a little mongrel puppy.

Shouting matches with a flaxen-haired vixen, who, all at once, became a helpless sister in need of protection. All the sounds and tastes which cannot be defined, the jumble of shadowy memories, sudden heart-stopping smells, all wound about and bound forever untouchable in his mind, immutable as the never-never land of a magic fairy story, so far, so very far, from the grown-up bitter nowness of his present world!

With a mental sigh, Hunter folded the beautiful age back into its secret place deep within his memory. Such love, such ....such happiness! Where did it all go?

The murder of his father...

Hunter stamped upon the recollection, as he always did! Then of course, Jean... Poor Jean, what had she ever done to deserve......Was it his fault? If he had not made such a failure of the marriage then perhaps...

"Christ!" Hunter shook his head savagely as if to shake out such thoughts. "Fate, that's all, fate. No logic, just vile murdering bastards who cared nothing for the misery that their evil brought about. Grey was right! The angels need help!"

After a while, as the afternoon wore into evening, Hunter found himself driving through Kilburn. He realised with a start that his stomach had been talking to him for some time now, so he pulled onto the forecourt of a Pub.

A stodgy, but filling, steak and kidney pie, peas and chips later, Hunter lifted his drink from the wet bartop, pocketed his change and made his way through the throng around the small stage back to his quiet table in the corner. Imperceptibly, the tension began to seep out of his body and his mind, as the warmth of the atmosphere enveloped him.

Guiness-black, the laughter and shrieks punctuate the bass rumble of the comedian's thick brogue......"Had some bad luck with the first wife.....She died of poison!.....Second died of a broken neck!......She wouldn't drink the poison!"

Hunter grinned, in spite of himself, shaking his head at the female shrieks that rose in appreciation, paradoxically applauding the joke against themselves. Gently he drifted away, staring again with unfocussed gaze into yesterday.

Was there really no answer? Detached now, he knew such calm acceptance was not always possible. Sometimes he felt as though the tumult and intensity of his thoughts would split his skull wide open!

Such happiness..........such sorrow! Such loving

warmth..........such grieving cold! To and fro...to and fro....like a gigantic emotional pendulum. Was there some purpose? Any purpose?

He heard again his mother's soft voice, felt his father's strong back as on hands and knees he supported Jim and his brother both together in stumbling, bucking bronco rides across the living room carpet. The same living room carpet that soaked up his life's blood as...NO!!

Hunter caught his tumbling mind before it fell irrevocably into that slough of despair.

Jean's face swam up to the surface of his drink. Young and smiling. Seventeen. He should have known, expected the pendulum's downstroke. Marriage to a woman and marriage to the army, both at the same time was bigamy. Both were escapes of a kind, an attempt to regain what once was taken for granted, security, love, family...

But, as his ties with his squad grew, so those with his wife weakened; and with the increase of special work, there was even less to talk about with Jean when bodily appetites were sated and silences began.

So many barriers, growing, growing, until eventually he could hardly see his wife over them. SAS Intelligence gathering in the Bandit country of Armagh shifted his concerns from choosing curtains to watching backs. The Falklands from washing dishes to frantically clawing frozen mud from the writhing victim of an Argentinean anti-personnel mine. His dash carrying his bleeding burden with its missing leg to the waiting helicopter had been captured by the TV cameras and seen throughout the world, but his wife had never known that it was him. Not even that he was there!

The urgencies of day-to-day survival pushed Jean further and further into the background. "There'll be time to make it up later." Much later (much too late) he realised that this was just not true. The pendulum had swung again.

A sudden gale of laughter broke Hunter's introspection; the comedian took his final bow and left and the continent of faces broke up once again into little island groups as the serious task of drinking re-assumed its temporarily abandoned importance.

Across the public bar, on the periphery of his vision, two large figures were making their way from table to table, thrusting collecting jars into the midst of the little knots of drinkers. Hunter watched, but didn't comprehend, but he could feel the tangible coldness preceding them like an invisible wave.

He looked away, lost in memories once more. A hand nudged his arm.

Hunter looked up as a harsh Irish accent assailed his ears. "For the Boys." A coin-filled jar appeared under his nose. "You'll be wanting to make a contribution!"

The large figure bent over the table, leaning a meaty hand on Hunter's shoulder. He placed the jar with flourish in front of his nearly empty glass.

Cold ice drenched Hunter's brain, as his senses focused on the man. He could see quite clearly the large open pores in his fleshy nose, the small ginger tufts of nostril hair matching those sprouting from his ears.

His concentration centred on his enemy. This IRA thug, whose collections might have paid for the very bomb that tore apart his wife!

Time slowed as Hunter reflexively evaluated the task ahead. Large, broad-shoulders, big strong hands. Not someone to wrestle with. Weak points? Eyes? No! Throat? Testicles?

Smiling disarmingly up at the looming figure, he reached into his pocket for loose change. He paused momentarily, his right hand poised over the jar, then released a cascade of coins.

As the big man's eyes followed the falling money, Hunter reached up and driving his body from his chair he seized the ginger hair with both hands. Using all of his body-weight, he smashed the collector's face down onto the jar, driving the rim completely through the flesh above the top lip and breaking every one of his top front teeth, and probably the bridge of his nose!

Hauling the bloody head upright again, Hunter stiffened the ridge of his right hand between the thumb and forefinger edge, and drove it with all of his power into the exposed throat.

The big man dropped, as if pole-axed, his initial scream stuck in his mangled trachea. He rolled between the chairs, eyes bulging, clawing desperately at his throat, bubbles of pink froth welling from his toothless ruin of a mouth.

His companion, momentarily frozen in shock, galvanised into motion, hurling himself towards Hunter, knocking aside tables and glasses as he came. Invincible in the icy fury of a terrible anger, Hunter stepped to meet him, driving the ball of his right foot deep into his stomach, doubling him over. As his head came down, Hunter's left knee came up to meet it, with a sickening crack, driving it back up again.

As his opponent arched backwards from the force of the

blow, Hunter swept both legs from under him, dropping him to floor like a felled tree in thunderous crashing of splintered table and broken glass.

The coldness in his head receded, and time ticked again. With a deep shuddering breath Hunter walked between the wrecked tables and the shocked, silent onlookers, through the door and into the comforting normality of the sounds of early evening.

CHAPTER TWENTY-FIVE

In the Cabinet room at number 10 Downing Street, The Prime Minister sat at a fine long mahogany refectory table together with the Home Secretary Ambrose Wolseley and various Privy Councillors.

On the other side facing them sat Charles Grey and Sir Hector Bainbridge together with others of the Special Security Liaison group. The Home Secretary was speaking. On a large video monitor in the corner of the room a video loop was playing and replaying scenes of the carnage caused by the Ritz bombing. The sound was turned down.

"...from information gained from our GCHQ 'Dictionary' telephone monitoring, it is quite apparent that this latest outrage is merely the forerunner of what is to come! Factions of the Armagh Brigade and INLA are out of the Official's control. Calling themselves "The Real IRA" They are determined to bring the Cease Fire to an end in a manner in which even those opposed to them would be powerless to forestall"

Wolseley let the import of his revelation sink in to those opposite him.

"We also have confirmatory intelligence from SAS agents in the field. These unofficials blame the soft element of the IRA general council with failure as they see it of Gerry Adams and Sinn Fein to make any significant progress after many months of a Cease Fire - so, they are committed to forcing the Irish issue back onto the breakfast tables in every home in Great Britain."

"Their view is that the only way they can do this now, having had their olive branch rejected, is to perform some outrage so...so diabolical that it will so sicken the British public that they will throw up their hands and insist upon a complete withdrawal of our troops from Ireland.."

The Prime Minister leaned forward, interrupting Wolseley: "We cannot allow that! A political defeat...and that's what it would be, make no bones about it..!"

The Home Secretary nodded sagely in agreement as the P.M. continued passionately: "It would mean the downfall of the government. Not to mention the total abrogation of all our responsibilities to those in Northern Ireland who do not want reunification at any price!"

His finger stabbed the air to emphasise his words: "The resumption of armed insurrection and terrorism cannot be allowed! This bomber must be caught! Caught and brought to justice, and before any more damage can be done. And...if necessary....as a last resort.... if detention is impossible, then he must be nullified as a threat!"

The smooth urbane tones of Sir Hector Bainbridge broke quietly and respectfully into the ensuing silence that greeted these remarks.

"Ah. Prime Minister, I'm sure you realise just how difficult...ah....provocative... it might prove to apprehend such a man, even where we to be able to track him down!"

He paused but the P.M. just stared at him. After a moment he continued:

"..In which case it may well prove expedient to..."   His

voice tailed off.

The Prime Minister leaned across the polished wood table top and cut short the prevaricating:

"Just do it Sir Hector!"

Later, when the others had departed, in the small private lounge, the inner sanctum of No.10, the one place of refuge free even from the constant interruptions of his PPS, the Prime Minister pinched the bridge of his nose between finger and thumb and wearily massaged the ache from his tired eyes. With a sigh, he replaced his glasses, and leaned back in his comfortable worn leather armchair, somewhat out of place amongst the fastidious elegance of the period furniture, crystal chandeliers and regency wallpaper; but for him a necessary indulgence, perhaps a memory of the simplicity of his past, an echo from a time when the highest burdens of office had not figured even in his wildest of dreams.

This was his chair, brought with him in the face of muttered opposition from interior designers given the task of smoothing away the evidence of the building's former occupant, 're-masculising' was the dreadful term he had caught from one of their interminable little conferences.

In his private room, where he was to remain undisturbed except for the direst of state emergencies, in this little sanctuary he could relax his calm, almost bland, mask of office.

He was used to ministerial responsibility, of course, but he had never imagined the pressure of ultimate office to be like this. He sometimes felt that his body itself were bowing under the constant buffeting of total responsibility....and now this!

These terrorist outrages, especially after the months of peace had built up so much expectation in the minds of the public, both at home and over there, it was just ....it was unthinkable!

It was bad enough before, with the sheer bloody nerve of that attempt to destroy No.10 itself (not to mention himself and the Cabinet with it) by firing mortar shells from a van parked in a nearby street. Sheer lunacy, and incompetent, but no more so than the security forces who allowed it to happen in the first place. Surely it wasn't all going to start again!

He knew now why one of the first official tasks carried out by Maggie Thatcher when she took office was to order the delivery of two armoured Daimlers as her official cars. She never trusted a word of what came out of the mouths of the so-called spokesmen for the IRA, had he been wrong to try?

The pressures of state were bad enough, but now....now it seemed that MI6 intelligence was positive that the major target...he smiled ruefully at the unconscious pun...the main target was to be no less than him personally!

The Home Secretary, Ambrose Wolseley, a large bluff but elegantly dressed figure with a shock of unruly white hair, eased the creases from the trouser leg of his deep blue pinstripe as he crossed one knee over the other and leaned back in the lacquered chinoiserie bergere sofa.

He looked across at the weary figure, almost enveloped in the huge battered chair. "If you don't mind me saying, P.M." Wolseley's deep resonant tones exuded waves of imperturbability, "I think we'd better tread a little carefully on this one, nonetheless, at least in public!"

The Prime Minster shook himself from his reverie and turned to Wolseley.

"I know you feel that we're at a disadvantage" the Home Secretary continued, "but are we really sure that this is the way forward? After all, elimination of politically awkward opponents has been seen to be counter productive in the past, and indeed, went by the name of assassination!"

"Yes, Ambrose." The often imitated dry incisive voice cut off the mellifluous flow. "Look, I do understand the objections, both politically and morally. Yes morally," he repeated emphatically denying the Home Secretary's raised eyebrow. "But in the end what choice do we ...I...have?"

He shook his head and continued: "God knows, if it were possible, but it isn't. We just can't beat them if we are playing a different game to a different set of rules; so, there is no choice. They've got to learn that there will be no more posturing from the White House, no luxury of a well-furnished prison cell, no more railing and ranting to the press over how our actions or inaction forced the breaking the cease-fire, no more....."

His voice died away. "And no more attempts on my life without fear of retaliation!" He concluded savagely!

He glanced up, looking Wolseley directly in the eyes: "I know that our policy must officially remain as it has always seemed to be, due legal process, and so on, but you and I are both fully aware of the realities of the situation. Still, we can in no way be seen overtly to be condoning a policy of 'shoot on sight' or 'take no prisoners.'"

His gaze through the thick lenses of his horn-rimmed glasses was almost mesmeric, thought Wolseley, who could feel the steel behind the veneer of boyish affability which normally characterised the persona of the Prime Minister. The lines around his mouth tightened as he continued: "We're losing a war that we're not even officially fighting, Ambrose, and I don't just mean against the IRA but against all those in society who simply don't care a damn about rules and regulations, about any morality at all that gets in their way. Well, I do give a damn!"

The Prime Minister hauled himself abruptly from the depths of his seat. "What's more, Ambrose, I'm going to bloody well do something about it!"

The big man pushed an unruly lock of hair from his forehead and watched in silence for a moment as the figure perched on the edge of his seat in front of him subsided once again in an angry silence, deep into the enveloping armchair.

He cleared his throat and spoke almost soothingly to the troubled man.

"It's not for me to be giving you a history lesson, Prime Minister, or to test you, but I had to ask if you were convinced that there is no other way; you see, there are some of us who do realise the enormity of the problem that you've inherited."

His interest caught, the Prime Minister turned his head as Wolseley continued:

"We, we who have been involved in the problem over the years, know full well that we will never beat the terrorists in the long run!"

The Prime Minister's blood ran cold as he listened to his most senior cabinet colleague voice the unspoken fears born of a long line of failures, setbacks and abortive attempts to solve the Irish question:

"We realise that those at the heart of our enemy consider themselves to be the legitimate governors chosen by the ballot-box and forced into exile by us, the British. Therefore any excess must be endured for the greater good of all Ireland!"

The Prime Minister snorted.

"I know, I know." Continued Wolseley wearily, "But there we are, that is how they see it." "And look at the quality of the active service units that they are able to field now; often men - and women - of many years training and experience, and no shortage of new recruits to fill any gaps that we might occasionally create in their ranks; even during the Cease-Fire they were still training."

His voice became harder as the bitter truths poured out.

"Years ago all we faced were either romantic dreamers or ruffians ready to disguise any form of mischief and disorder with the cloak of Republicanism, that's no longer true. Nowadays although there are indeed still plenty of out and out no-goods who find in the IRA a ready home for their psychopathic personalities, there is a steady increase in both the number and quality of members who actually do belong through conviction, and ...."

He raised his hands, almost helplessly:

"...Well, I'm afraid that I... we..." He shrugged. "There really is no answer if we are to discount withdrawal.....?" He left the question hanging in the air.

The Prime Minister rose angrily from his seat.

"So what do I do Wolsely, tell me that? Do I become famous

in the history books as the first leader of the great British nation to give in to the threat of the Armalite rifle and the bomb?"

He paced to and fro as he considered the eventuality:

"Good God man! The Government wouldn't last two minutes! And how long would it be before the voters ever trusted in a Tory leadership again? It would destroy the Party utterly. No! It's unthinkable!"

The Home Secretary's quite tones slid like a steel blade into his wrath:

"Well then, you must grasp the thorns of the only alternative that you possess. You must on the surface make all the right reconciliatory noises for public consumption, and in reality you must pursue the only damage limitation course open to you, as it has been to others in your position, you must as far as possible use every available means to weed out the active service units and destroy them!"

A tangible silence filled the room as the PM stood, stock-still, gazing unseeingly out of the window.

Ambrose Wolsley joined him in silent reflection, but in his brain another worm wriggled uncomfortably.....could he go ahead with what he must do? Yes! The logic of the argument was irrefutable, but could he, the Home Secretary of Her Majesty's Government really carry out what must be done...the further betrayal... and of this honourable man in front of him?

What he had to do was unthinkable! Treason even! But – the pulse in his forehead began to throb as once again he fought the turmoil in his anguished mind. The PM's own words had determined the course of action he was now committed to, and the knowledge that he had no way out except the coward's way sickened his stomach!

CHAPTER TWENTY-SIX

Dark Mahogany and hand-tooled leather chairs give a room respectability. Add high ceilings and works of art on the walls, and you have an ambience completely at odds with the subject of violent death.

Nevertheless, if it were true that inanimate objects can somehow retain a record in their molecules of all that transpires in their vicinity, then Grey's MI6 office in the Art Auction Gallery would be a storehouse of untold incongruity for anyone able to unlock its secrets.

Grey leaned across the handsome leather inlaid desk and passed Hunter a folio of enlarged photos of the carnage at the Bologna station and Madrid Airport.

Hunter took the file and began leafing through the sickening catalogue of horror and misery, as Grey spoke in flat emotionless tones: "We have now accurately identified the bomber who is responsible for your wife's...sorry, ex-wife's death!" He paused and stared fixedly at Hunter as if seeking any weakening of resolve.

Apparently satisfied, he continued: "There's now no possible doubt! The Ritz bomb was set by the same man who is implicated in both the Bologna station and the Spanish Airport incident, and our Spanish friends are also convinced that the ETA bombing at the barracks near Barcelona was by the same hand."

He gestured angrily at the photos: "There were more than twenty dead at the Ritz - I'm afraid!...including...Yes well."

He hesitated, slightly uncomfortable to be reminding Hunter of his loss, then resumed: "Not a military or political target amongst them! Just ordinary people going about their ordinary business!" He sighed wearily: "All expendable in the cause of the new Democracy I suppose..."

Grey cleared his throat in the silence and picked up a red folder from his desk and tossed it over to Hunter, who caught it and placed it on his lap on top of the photos.

"You remember, I'm sure the unfortunate death of Policewoman Fletcher, following which Britain cut off Diplomatic relations with the Libyan Government?"

Hunter nodded, he clearly recalled watching the incident on the T.V. and being moved by the poignancy of the fallen officer's hat lying in mute condemnation on the bare pavement outside the Libyan embassy.

"Well," Grey continued: "There is now a change in the political climate in the Middle East, and thanks to the Libyan government siding with the West and its allies against Saddam Hussain in the Gulf War, and now seeking to re-establish Diplomatic contact with us, we have had a minor breakthrough."

"As a sign of their 'good faith'..." His mouth twisted in distaste at the thought of such an inappropriate term: ..."They have quietly passed on some information regarding their terrorist and in particular their IRA connections, so now we have a name, and a photo, albeit a little blurred."

Hunter opened the cover of the folder, and there, slightly out of focus but recognisable, the face of Liam Kennedy stared up at him.

"We've very little hard evidence to go on." Grey continued: "But our sources indicate that he is probably the number one IRA explosives specialist, trained courtesy of Libya in Palestinian camps, loaned out by his masters in return for supplies of weapons and ammunition. He is suspected of countless killings...."

Grey paused until Hunter looked up from the file. "This man is not an ordinary terrorist....he is very, very special. He must be taken out, Hunter!"

Hunter looked down at the smiling face in the photograph again. Fighting to keep his emotions tightly under control, he could not hide the anger that threatened to overwhelm him.

"It would have saved a lot of trouble if our people in Ireland could have taken him out long ago!"

"Look Hunter!" Grey allowed some of his frustration to show through: "Our masters have decreed that even covert activity of this nature is just too sensitive. If it ever got out that we officially condoned a shoot-on-sight policy, especially after the fuss over the SAS and the Gibralter incident, well, just think of the capital our enemies would make of that! You see Hunter, you don't understand..."

Hunter cut in savagely, his voice trembling with repressed fury: "No! You don't understand! You've no idea how it feels. You get these bastards in your sights, and hear them planning murder, and then simply let them walk away because Whitehall wants to fight a war where the rules only apply to one side - us!"

Grey replied defensively: "Not exactly walk away Hunter, the undercover squads are supposed to place all information discovered in the hands of the appropriate body, and if your intelligence gatherers make direct contact with the IRA in the field they're supposed to call in the nearest official army unit to deal with them."

Hunter jerked himself out of his chair and rounded bitterly in exasperation on Grey:

"Oh yes! Then some bunch of squaddies with no local knowledge, on rotation from West Germany come helicoptering in and run rings around themselves while the IRA simply melt into the landscape! Very effective!"

He tossed the folder back onto the desk, then with hands in pockets he began to pace the office. After a visible effort he regained control of his anger. It hadn't gone away, but instead of boiling over in all directions now it was sitting there in his centre, waiting.

"So when do I go, and what help do I get from the Spanish with this?" His voice was calm and resolute.

Grey got up, crossed to the sideboard and poured two generous measures of Glen Fiddich into crystal glasses before he replied. He handed one to Hunter, and sat back down.

"To answer your question, Hunter, none at all! At least officially! It seems that our friend is a guest of ETA terrorists over the border in France, acting as bombmaker and instructor, so you can bet that any operation instigated by the Guardia Civil or Policia National would be passed on by sympathisers within hours, and the French would certainly be non too pleased!"

Hunter stopped his slow pacing and stared intently at Grey: "Can't the French do something then?"

"The French!?" The older man looked sourly amused: "Ah yes." Long experience of the vagaries of French diplomatic practice had left its mark on Grey:

"It seems that our French cousins are pragmatists at heart. The Basques have let it be known that they will not act against any targets on French soil as long as they are left well alone. In spite of more than 200 known ETA guerrillas actually living in France the fact is that not one move has ever been made against them."

Hunter said nothing. He sipped his whiskey as Grey continued.

"Colonel Rodriguez of Spanish Intelligence has had his people bug and watch the target's apartment, and his girlfriend's, and tap their 'phones. Apparently they've come up with details of the next major arms shipment to be delivered to the IRA, and it seems that our man is to return with the consignment. It would appear that he is needed for something very special, the 'biggest yet' to quote directly. The trouble is we've no idea yet what this is, nor do we know when or where he'll meet the shipment."

"So it's up to me then?" Hunter's eyes bored into Grey's.

It was as if a cold wind had chilled the warmth of the afternoon sunshine.

"Yes Hunter, It's up to you!" The reply was matter of fact, leaving no room for doubt.

For long moments the two stared at each other in silence, weighing, assessing, probing for the least sign of weakness.

This was a turning point in Hunter's life, and he knew it.

From this moment on his personal conscience would be secondary to the demands of this man sitting calmly across the desk in front of him. Did he trust him? Could he trust him? Was there no other way?

Grey reached down and picked a single sheet of paper off his desk and, hesitating briefly, passed it across to Hunter. He spoke in a flat, emotionless monotone:

"The Irishman's file also includes a run-down on the number of his victims, we believe it to be fairly accurate to date...."

Hunter took the proffered sheet and dropped it on top of the open file. He began to read.

Grey's voice suddenly seemed far away, as if coming from a long distant tunnel. Hunter could make no sense of what he was saying.

His head swam and he stopped breathing. He could feel - as if from somewhere deep within himself - the blood drain from his face as he read the one paragraph over and over again. It kept splintering and fragmenting before his frozen gaze, but each time the sentences re-constructed themselves to form the heart-stoppingly clinical statement:

"....Intelligence sources indicate that Kennedy is also implicated in the deaths of...." and then followed a list of some ten or twelve names of mainly Protestant murder victims, but Hunters eyes were locked rigidly on the last phrase:

"...including the probable initiation shooting of....HIS FATHER'S NAME....!"

Across the desk, Grey had fallen silent. He sat, like some colourless bird of prey, following intently the play of expressions on Hunter's face as he sat in shocked silence before him. If anything would confirm Hunter as his, then this would be it. This was the critical moment upon which so many future possibilities would hang. This was the moment the waiting angler would know, as the fishhook slid home. This was the matador lining up his sword for the ultimate thrust, the last possible time-stretching opportunity to escape. Would Hunter escape?

Grey sat still, just the slightest tightening of his jaw gave any indication of his inner tension.

Not that Hunter was aware of anything at that moment, his whole being was concentrated on his father's name, spinning, fragmenting, reforming blackly on the whiteness of the paper.

The horror was upon him, all the squashed and forbidden memories coursed through his brain as once again he was running, terrified, shouting for his mother, his screaming mother, momentarily transfixed by the nightmare in the tiny living room. Suddenly he was there again, bare feet on broken glass from the shattered door, his nostrils filled with the acrid gagging smell of cordite, blood and excreta. Eyes wide with shock as the tableau burned itself onto his retina and into his memory.

To the inane laughter of the television set, his father - Christ,

"God Almighty - HIS DA - OH God! DAD, DAD, DA!"
The loop played again and again in Hunter's shocked mind as he relived the moment of his father's bloody end.

Long minutes passed in silence as the two men sat there. Now was the time to strike!

Grey quietly got to his feet, walked around the desk and

poured another generous measure of Malt into Hunter's glass. Gently he touched the seated man on the shoulder and pressed the glass into the automatically raised hand.

Hunter lifted his head, slowly focusing on the stooping figure. He took a breath and tried to speak, coughed and worked some spittle into his dry mouth.

"Y..you knew!"

Grey didn't answer. He turned away and went back behind his desk and sat down.

Leaning back in his seat he closed his eyes for a moment, then sighed gently and leaned forward, staring straight into Hunter's accusing gaze.

"Yes and no, Jim, yes and no." His eyes bored mercilessly into Hunter's: "I didn't know before I received the file, but yes, I knew it when I gave you the file to read."

"Hear me out!" He raised his voice slightly as Hunter's expression showed his hostility.

"I had to do it. You had to be faced with the realities of just what sort of people we are dealing with. I suppose I could have done it more diplomatically, but I don't have the time for such luxuries." He continued firmly:

"Whilst you exercise your sensitivities more people, innocent people just like your father, are being murdered by slime like Kennedy!" The nerve in his cheek twitched: "Who seems to care anymore that yet another family mourns a father, or a daughter or a son'?"

"Well, I DAMN WELL CARE!" His sudden shout shocked

132

Hunter.

"How many funerals must there be Jim, before you help us stop those murdering vermin?"

Hunter dropped his eyes once more to the paper on his knee. The turmoil in his head was subsiding. He took a long swallow of the fiery liquid; as it burned its way down his throat it seemed as though it also burned away his doubts. The lines around his mouth tightened briefly and his eyes seemed dark and empty.

"I don't like it Sir, I'll never like it..." He spoke slowly and deliberately: "But I've no option really have I?"

In what could only have been seconds an eternity of doubts and consequences burned through Hunter's mind. It had to be, of course, there was no other way. All of his life, everything, his grief, his anger, his training, all had been roads bringing him to this room on this day, for this decision, for his total commitment. It was fate.

Without speaking, Hunter levered himself slowly upright, walked across to the desk and put down his empty glass. He gestured inquiringly at the folder.

"Keep it.""You'll liaise directly with MI6 and Colonel Rodriguez but all arrangements are to be deniable of course, we don't want any diplomatic feathers to be ruffled on this one."

He got up and walked Hunter to the door. "But what we do want is our bomber friend out of the picture....permanently!"

Closing the door gently behind Hunter, Grey walked slowly back to his desk and lowered himself into his seat. He sighed.

"Illusion, delusion, disillusion…!" He leaned back wearily into the chair and closed his eyes.

"What was life but a paring away, a pruning….It begins in blissful ignorance and continues through a perpetual cutting away of possibilities until all there was left was a grim certitude that after hacking away all the dross and glitter of love, religion, and friendship, all that remained was the cold and lonely certainty of loss, bereavement and the cold earth."

He clenched his eyes shut but the memories insinuated their way into his mind.

White – that's what he could remember; the antiseptic soulnessness – the sheer bloody whiteness of it all! Cold, the coldness – and the quiet – the stillness and the silence. The only movement the inexorable "drip….drop…..drip" of the painkilling medication in the transparent tubing which hardly impinged upon the overall featurelessness of the room and the small insignificant figure lying motionlessly tidy in the tightly made bed.

It shouldn't have been his impression, of course, as the room in the tiny hospice was clinical but not overly so. No. On the walls were colourful flowery prints, and the carpet on the floor was a warm and functional mixture of russets and dark golds.

However none of this could uplift the very essence of the little room. Nothing could turn his thoughts from what it really was – simply a waiting room. Not a boisterous holiday-airport type waiting room, but a quiet, austere and calm comma of a room, no, maybe a semi-colon of a room. Paused upon the moment of dying; an interlude in time before loss and anguish could be addressed.

There had been flowers, of course, initially, but now the flowers and the artificial gaiety of the cards from friends (there were no family) had quietly been removed. All was waiting on the moment. The Full Stop.

No matter how he churned it over in his brain there was no way that Grey could convince himself otherwise.

Not for him would be the salve of religion, the prospect of meeting her again "in a better world" was antithetical to both his intelligence and his experience.

He reached out from where he sat, had been sitting for hours unobtrusively at the side of the bed, and tenderly stroked the pale, colourless skin and bone hand which lay delicately unmoving as she slept.

The picture was one of calmness, of inevitability, of almost dignity. Inside his heart, however, stormed a volcanic disruption of anger and fear, of recrimination and helplessness which – were he to let go for but one moment – would transform this modest façade into a maelstrom of rage and tears!

She groaned slightly, and with a jerk Grey forced open his clutching fingers.

"There, there, my sweet; I'm here, it's all right." He lied, quietly soothing her back to sleep.

The eldest son of an old Lincolnshire Vicar, Charles had not always been so empty of hope. The earliest years of his life had revolved inexorably around the calendar of the Church of England – and high Church at that.

His earliest memories were of Sundays at the old Church

adjoining the Vicarage, where together with his mother, his two sisters and a miscellany of his father's current guests, his tiny voice swelled the volume of the equally tiny congregation.

Even in this changing age, parts of the Lincolnshire fens seemed caught in an earlier century. Here the local workman still wore flat caps and touched their peaks to the portly clergyman and looking kindly down at the boy and called him "Master" Grey.

His father truly was of another age. Older than his wife, he had never learned to drive, so he had to be chauffeured everywhere by his longsuffering but loving spouse. He even kept a carefully annotated cellar book in which he recorded every bottle of wine ever consumed at the Vicarage, together with comments as to its flavour and subtlety, as well as *bon-mots* from the after-dinner conversation.

Every Sunday was the same, a careful admixture of Christianity and slightly impoverished fine living.

An education at a good public school (aided by friends of the Church and by the local Freemasons for whom his father performed various offices) confirmed the growing Charles in the accepted religion of the State and of all right-thinking Englishmen.

Not that he ever really questioned anything. The very institutionalism of religion, permeating his daily regime at home, and at school punctuated his life in a consistent and never varying substructure.

University was unsettling, but not overly so, as a first in the Classics, with forays into mediaeval art and modern languages kept him busy with little time for the free-thinking which seemed to affect his two sisters.

Grey's first real inkling that all might not be so cut and dried as the Authorised Version would have it, came one unsettling evening when during vacation he was at home again.

Naturally, as a boy there had been the questions – but as they were invariably answered with a religious certainty he was never really troubled by concerns of the world to come. The passing of little-known aunts and uncles, indeed a constant stream of interments presided over by his father, only served to provide him with an easy acquaintanceship with "passing".

That is, easy until that evening when tired and slightly flushed from a fine claret, his father, looking morosely into the dying drawing room fire, confessed his own uncertainty.

"I don't know, boy, I just don't know." His father stared fixedly into the red embers. "Sometimes I just don't know." He heaved a sigh: "But if we are just deluding ourselves....."

He lapsed into gloomy silence, and a quiet Charles was shaken by this glimpse of fallibility – and inwardly afraid to question further. He wanted everything to remain as it was.

The comfort of certainty.

The fire in Grey's head erupted in a shout of silent anguish: "God?" His lips tightened into a thin line as he ground his teeth in futile anger. "What a sick joke!"

"Where are you now, God?" "Where are you now when my wife is dying, where were you when we lost our unborn daughter?" "Where....."

He screwed his eyes tightly shut and forced his churning

brain to stop. He smiled slightly at his own weakness and gently stroked her forearm so gently with the tip of his index finger as though afraid to wake her.

Leaning forwards over the bed he fixed the sight of her into his mind, as his soft slow tears dripped quietly unheeded onto the pristine bedcover.

Now, in his chair, he was all cried out.

CHAPTER TWENTY-SEVEN

Kennedy's "Rest and Recuperation" after the success of the Ritz bombing did not last long, but he had made the most of it, spending his time making love to Nicole in her apartment in the tiny French town nestling in the foothills of the mountains. He was full of sexual energy; successful missions always did that to him.

The afternoon had been swelteringly hot, and the evening breeze of cooling air from the snow-capped Pyranees was blowing the wrong way towards Spain, so the air in the little town close to the border, between the mountains and the flat plain, was hot and humid. Any physical activity brought a sheen of sweat to the skin, especially if there were no convenient air-conditioning unit to bring the temperature down.

The bedroom in the dilapidated apartment contained no such unit.

It was not surprising, then, that the passion of their love-making had made them hot and sticky with sweat. The bed top sheets lay crumpled in a heap upon the floor; under their squirming bodies the bottom ones were covered with damp patches.

Balanced on straight arms, keeping only his groin in contact with her thrusting hips, Kennedy drove his rigid penis deep into Nicole's liquid heat, grinding his pubic bone rhythmically against her jutting clitoris. The girl's eyes were screwed tight shut in her private erotic fantasy as her climax welled up through her body like an unstoppable wave.

Reaching her hands between them, she pulled open her cunt lips with her fingers, allowing the top of the root of his penis to rub directly on her swollen bud of pleasure with each rhythmic stroke.

Suddenly the animal grunts from deep within her throat became fiercer, as she transferred her grip to his buttocks. He could sense the subtle change in the cadence of her thrusting hips and the responsive clutching of her fingers began to reflect the rising moment of her own desires.

Her head went back exposing her throat as she arched against his belly, he dropped his lips to her dark berry-brown nipples and teased them with his tongue. As her passion increased, he began to bite them and squeeze them hard between his fingers.

The violence of his thrusts brought loud involuntary gasps from her open mouth, her eyes screwed shut with concentration.

Like the trainer of a wild animal enjoying his domination, he revelled in his sexual mastery of this twisting, sobbing woman. He pulled himself from her pulsating vagina to delay her climax for a moment, then, drinking in the vulnerability of her passion, he began to stroke her engorged clitoris firmly with his fingers, in seconds her thighs clamped tightly over his hand as she moaned and spasmed with pleasure.

Moments later, when her climax had subsided, he turned her and pushed her onto her face.

Pulling the plump cheeks of her buttocks open with his thumbs, he forced his swollen penis deep into her rectum. The rubbery tightness after the wetness of her cunt closed around his erection in exquisite sensations. Helpless under his body, the feeling of power he felt from both her climax and her position drew the semen from him in thick pulsating jets. He collapsed for a moment, breathing heavily, tasting the sweat on her shoulder. Then he rolled off her and reached for a pack of cigarettes.

"Gouloises! Shit! For all their civilised pretensions the French can't make a cigarette that tastes of anything but merde!"

Nicole turned on her side, her voice still thick with sex she laughed and grabbed at Liam: "Then do not smoke it, Idiot!" They wrestled playfully over the cigarette.

"Oh Leeam, I will miss you so much, why do you not take me with you?" She pouted her lips in mock dismay, her French accent very attractive:

"I do not believe you are going on business at all! I think you must have another woman!" She turned her back on Kennedy, who laughed, pulled her back and kissed her firmly.

"Another woman is it? Sure and where would I be getting all the energy from to be having another woman?" He flicked the unlit cigarette onto the floor and pulled her body under his.

"You know that you're my only woman." He kissed her again lingeringly: "As soon as I've delivered this order to my bosses in Ireland I'll be back like a shot!"

Kennedy caressed her face and slowly slid his lips down the line of her throat and to her breasts; her eyes closed and her face began to express her pleasure as her body reacted to his touch. He could feel his penis begin to twitch and harden once again between her thighs as he exulted in his power.

Outside in the street, in the back of a battered old Citröen van, nondescript amongst the lines of vehicles parked all along one side of the road, a dark haired man and a very attractive woman, two French speaking Spanish undercover agents, listened to and recorded every sound the rutting couple made.

CHAPTER TWENTY-EIGHT

Hunter didn't mind flying, at least not short-haul, and the flight to Madrid airport from Heathrow was relatively quick.

As he walked from the customs area into the arrivals lounge he fell into step with the big man in a long overcoat who, upon seeing Hunter, had turned on his heel and begun to walk out through the automatic doors into the refreshing cool of the evening. Hunter followed a few paces behind him. They walked casually out passed the taxi and bus ranks, and around the corner.

The man climbed into the back seat of the parked car with darkened windows waiting at the kerb. Without a word, Hunter got in the other side. As soon as the door closed the car pulled away. In the back seat the two men appraised each other in silence for a moment, then the man in the coat reached down and picked up a briefcase which he passed over to Hunter who placed it on his lap and opened it.

The big man looked at Hunter.

"The Passport is genuine, British, the former property of a very careless Mr Robert Miller." "The weapon is a 9mm Walther PPK, with three spare clips of ammunition. It is not known on our files, it was collected from a suspect and unfortunately "lost", as was the quantity of Semtex and detonators which you will also find."

He continued as Hunter picked through the contents: "The three radio handsets are available over the counter in many electrical stores throughout the country and were paid for in cash, so no receipts and names were necessary."

Hunter picked up the weapon and tried the mechanism: "So if anything goes wrong your people can pass it off as a falling out between thieves!"

Colonel Rodriguez of the Spanish special anti-terrorist secret police smiled grimly. "Si! Señor Hunter. And of course should we be lucky enough to apprehend any of these criminals I would not be at all surprised if none made it to the court room!"

Rodriguez placed his hand over Hunter's as he slid the gun back into the case and closed it. Staring meaningfully he continued quietly: "It would be most embarrassing if my department's involvement with this ...situation....became known. It would at the least create a very bad diplomatic situation with the French government who would not wish any incursions to be made into their territory, and here at home we would stand accused of trying to revive Franco-ism and bring back a Police state!"

They both looked at each other for a moment, then the Colonel slumped back in his seat and looked out of the window. With a deep sigh he continued sadly:

"It is the same all over the world now, my friend: Italy, Ireland, Lebanon, Israel....everywhere. Small, violent, petty people ....they find some cause to uphold to justify their small, petty acts of violence. Any cause will do, it doesn't matter, at heart they thrive on the machismo of terror!"

The big man's gaze was far away. With another sigh he continued, still staring out of the window:

"They cannot make, but they can break! And for a little while they become something in the world! What do they care for the countless innocents that they maim and kill? ....All in the name of Freedom, or even God!" Abruptly he turned back to Hunter, businesslike again, taking back the briefcase.

"Our people have learned that the Irishman is leaving on Friday to travel to Marseilles to meet the shipment which is arriving from the Middle East in a container. Apparently the container is to travel to Brest to be loaded as cargo on a boat which is then scheduled to dock in Southern Ireland."

"Agricultural Machinery?" Hunter knew that more often than not arms shipments from Libya were hidden in crates disguised as tractor and machinery parts, and described on cargo manifests as 'Agricultural Equipment.'"

The Colonel nodded: "Si. To be delivered to a company in Cork. Naturally, it will never reach harbour; a little fishing boat will meet the ship off the Irish coast, and FFtttttt!" He waved his hands expressively.

"Can't your people simply stop the cargo before it reaches Marseilles?"

Rodriguez shrugged: "Alas it is not that simple; we have discovered what is going to happen when the container arrives at the port, but no-one knows from where it is coming, nor from whom the arms were purchased. Probably an agent of Gaddafi, or the PLO, but which...."

He pulled a face: "Now if we could somehow have a little talk with your target's friends who will be travelling with the cargo, well, it might be possible that they could be persuaded to reveal one or two little clues...?"

He raised an eyebrow and looked meaningfully at Hunter.

Hunter grunted: "In return for which I suppose I will receive help from an unknown source which might just be able to assist in disposing of any 'embarrassing' remainders!"

"Exactly Señor!" He laughed suddenly and clapped Hunter on the knee: "Ha! Yes! We will be in the 'scratching of backs' situation Señor Hunter and we will be most happy to remove any - as you say - remainders!"

The car pulled up outside the entrance of a nondescript back street hotel. Hunter picked up his overnight bag and followed the Colonel up the steps to the entrance. Gripping the briefcase firmly, the Colonel continued talking as they went.

"Of course you will also be provided with a travelling companion who will help you with your terrible Spanish and French! We have reserved a room for you both in the Marseilles Hilton, and we can, at least, use Diplomatic channels to get this.." He gestured to the briefcase: "Into the country for you. Meanwhile you can get to know your colleague in these not so luxurious surroundings."

Hunter followed Rodriguez as he passed briskly through the sparsely appointed foyer and down a long adjoining corridor, finally stopping outside the door of the last room. The Colonel knocked briefly, opened the door and ushered Hunter in.

A broad smile split his face as the younger man stopped dead in his tracks, taken aback by the breathtaking beauty of the young woman who got up from a chair and walked across the room to meet them.

Hunter could almost feel his jaw dropping. He couldn't remember seeing anyone this gorgeous except on a Pirelli Calendar. Tall, slim-hipped with long raven-black hair that draped her shoulders.

At a loss, he didn't know where to look; her dark lashed brown eyes laughed at him as his gaze jumped from her face to her narrow waist, then up to her breasts which seemed to sway in opposition to her hips as she walked. He had to crush down an almost overwhelming urge to sink his teeth into them.

The Colonel's voice retrieved the situation for him, as the vision of his dreams held out a hand:

"Señorita Mercedes. She and her colleague Juan have been tailing the Irishman for some weeks now in France, and she has become familiar with his habits. She also looks far too beautiful to be dangerous, don't you think?" He laughed: "Quite an asset in our business!"

The Colonel nudged Hunter as he held out his hand for her cool firm grip.

"Mr Robert Miller, meet Mrs Miller!"

The Colonel's booming laughter filled the room!

CHAPTER TWENTY-NINE

The empty container lorry, with two men in the cab, approached the Marseilles Dockyard trailer park. It bore Swiss plates and the logo of a Zurich freight-handling company. The driver was a skinny tousled-haired man in a flat cap, wearing the ubiquitous boiler suit and battered Donkey-jacket, typical of long-distance truck drivers everywhere.

His companion in the cab dwarfed him. He was a gargantuan Arab, with enormous hands and head, with a full black beard that covered most of his face and his dark weather-beaten leather-like skin. His outcropping black eyebrows were almost lost under the wild tangle of greasy locks that cascaded over his forehead. He looked for all the world like a wild man peering through an entangled hedge, but no-one would ever have said as much to his face!

When Donahue, the driver, had first met him he had immediately been scared of him, and closer acquaintance had not altered his initial reaction. Normally garrulous, The menacing monosyllabic grunts that had greeted his attempts to shorten the journey by conversation had intimidated the driver into a nervous silence.

Donahue was not the regular driver, and by God, he was never going to do this again. All he wanted to do was load the shipment when it arrived at the docks, meet the passenger that he had been told to expect at the pre-arranged rendezvous, and get the container and its frightening protector to Brest as quickly as possible!

CHAPTER THIRTY

Marseilles railway station, like that of any major city is always busy, but at rush hour it is packed to overflowing with seething bustling crowds of shop assistants and office workers fighting to escape to the sanity of their own homes.

Marseilles is also a major shipping centre, with a busy port and dockyard, even if many of its most profitable transactions in drugs and guns take place under the cover of darkness.

Extremely cosmopolitan, the city teems with life both high and low, and attracts all levels of humanity eager to take advantage of its opportunities, from the entrepreneur businessman to the small-time villain, ready to hustle and cheat where he can. With a thriving nightlife, the city also boasts a complete range of whores, from the 5,000 francs a night hostess to the half-caste hooker offering hand-jobs for 50 francs in the dark doorways of the back streets around the docks.

For those not of that persuasion, there is also the theatre, the opera and an abundance of art galleries.

Curiously, some of the most successful drug smugglers and gun runners were in the latter category.

Tucked away in Liam Kennedy's wallet was a prepurchased ticket for that night's performance of Don Giovanni. Not that he was an opera buff, he actually much preferred Tina Turner and Elton John, but as, bag in hand, he alighted from the train and threaded his way through the frantic rush-hour throngs towards the taxi ranks, he was quite looking forward to dressing in good clothes again, even if it were only for a short time, for it would soon be back to jeans and a sweater in the confines of the container truck's cab.

With his mind dwelling upon the coming evening's events, and the covert meeting set up for him by his IRA masters with a confidant of one of the senior Basque Separatists who had need of his services, he never gave a thought to the dark-featured figure that climbed down behind him from the next carriage and followed him out of the station exit towards the line of waiting taxis.

If he had noticed him, he would have paid him no attention, for Kennedy had never looked inside the van parked outside Nicole's apartment, and had never seen Juan, who had taped every incriminating word and every passionate groan that they made.

The Irishman leaned in through the open cab window to issue directions to the driver, and then, sliding his case in first, he climbed into the back. As the taxi drew away from the kerb, a second pulled away and remained behind them.

Some 20 minutes of stops and starts later, Kennedy was leaning casually over the guest book in a clean but unremarkable hotel of the kind so beloved of travelling salesmen the world over.

He signed the register and smiled his refusal to the porter waiting to take his bag and conduct him to his room. "No thanks, I'll manage, just tell me the way."

As soon as the Irishman entered the lift, Juan, who had been watching from the entrance, crossed over to the desk carrying his own suitcase and beckoned to the receptionist. As she came to the desk he leaned across:

"Ça va. Ou est le monsieur?" She stared at him uncomprehendingly. "Le M'sieu, Il-y-a un autre valise dans le taxi!"

Taking him for Kennedy's taxi driver, the receptionist rolled her eyes expressively at the forgetfulness of foreigners:

"Il est au-dessus, deuxième étage dans numeraux deuxcent cinq, nous avons un porteur.."

Juan cut her off with a shocked expression on his face: "Porteur? Non, merci..." He rubbed the tip of his forefinger on that of his thumb, in the world-wide sign for money, as he made his way towards the lift. He waved and winked as the doors slid shut and he punched the button for the first floor, not the second where the Irishman would be.

As soon as the doors opened he walked briskly down the corridor to the stairs and went back down to the lobby. He waited for a moment until he was sure that the receptionist was busy elsewhere and quickly made his way out of the hotel and into a nearby telephone kiosk.

CHAPTER THIRTY-ONE

The suite booked by Colonel Rodriguez for 'Mr and Mrs Miller' in the Marseilles Hilton was functionally elegant, and except for perhaps a certain Gallic quality to the furnishings and the selection of French Impressionist prints on the walls it could have been anywhere in the world. As in Hiltons everywhere the emphasis was on a classless luxury for the nouveau-riche and the up-market business executive.

Hunter stretched out on the large king-size bed, wearing just a towel around his waist. He had to admit that the meal had been good, and the company excellent. From the bathroom he could hear the sound of water running into the bath as Mercedes busied herself with her toilet.

The leisurely journey by car from Madrid had given them chance to get to know each other, and every minute had been a pleasure!

Hunter couldn't remember a time in the last few years when he had been happier. Of course as soon as he realised that, he immediately felt waves of guilt threatening to destroy his mood and bring him back to his normal level of everyday stress and dissatisfaction with himself and with life.

Actually it wasn't that Hunter was an unhappy man, on the whole he rather enjoyed life, but it was always as if every happiness was only the precursor of some minor crisis, every stroke of good fortune the harbinger of a brown envelope. Still, he imagined that such was the lot of most men, so he couldn't complain.

He realised that by far the greater part of his discontent stemmed from his own feelings of falling short of his own standards, and that what he really needed to do was to forgive himself for his own humanity!

Of course, he had felt guilty when he first looked at Mercedes and with something of a shock realised that she was appraising him with the same look of interest that he knew was on his own face. It hadn't been that long since he was standing over his ex-wife's grave, and here he was seriously considering his chances of taking this gorgeous sexy woman to bed with him.

He recalled with embarrassment the colonel's elbow digging into his ribs and his loud guffaws of laughter echoing around the spartan office. It must have been written all over his face.

Hunter had been totally disconcerted by this tall, leggy woman, who was quite self-sufficient and coolly capable of taking care of herself in most situations, in fact according to her record which the colonel had shown him, she was an expert shot with a pistol and had gained her brown belt in Uyeshiba aikido.

The leisurely drive from Madrid, on the winding roads over the snow-capped Pyranees and down through the little French villages and eventually into the hustle and bustle of the great port city of Marseilles itself had been like a waking dream for Hunter.

With Mercedes beside him it was as if somehow he had been transported onto a gigantic film set to play the part of the romantic hero. There was no initial hesitancy between them, no coy shyness, not even any jockeying for emotional supremacy. Just for once Hunter was faced by a supremely self-assured and beautiful woman who did not seem to want to flaunt her independence, but who was as interested in him as he was in her.

This attraction between equals was completely novel to him, and, although in his heart he was convinced that it was just a transient thing, with a hidden emotional price-tag that would reveal itself at the worst possible moment, he was more than content to go with the flow of events and feelings.

The driving itself was often done in silence; not the awkward silence between people who have little in common and who don't know what to say, but that special kind, where words would be unnecessary intrusions into shared experience and where silence gave room for the more intimate communication between eyes and hands, and simple togetherness was conveyed by the warmth of a leg or the breeze blown hint of perfume.

When, in the quiet and warm twilight of a country hotel bedroom he had reached for her, he was pleased, but not surprised, to find her reaching out for him.

The first tentative touch of his lips to hers had been met by her wriggling tongue worming its way between his teeth. In all things she matched him, not in a contest, but as an equal. When he slid his lips along the nakedness of her torso to the tips of her jutting nipples, it was Mercedes who had arched her back and grasping her breasts in both hands, had forced the puckered erect morsels deep into his mouth.

There was no rush, each needed to give joy to the other. When Hunter felt her hands cupping his scrotum he leaned back praying silently for the wetness of her mouth around the crest of his penis; when it had happened he was unprepared but driven into uncharted ecstasy by the gentle probing of her long slim index finger deep into his anus.

The first boiling climax had not softened his aching erection, but there was no hurry. Time had ceased to be, only the discovery of each other's body was important.

Mercedes had been greedy for sex, both selfish and selfless in turn. As the throbbing of her orgasms died away she turned again to Hunter's naked body and began to play it like a living instrument driving him into new pitches of writhing excitement, sometimes tender and caressing, then, just as his body became attuned to her touch she would seize him almost roughly and pull and jerk at his tumescent erection until he would cry for relief.

The liquid heat of her vagina pulsating around his cock drew the orgasm from him, he lost himself in her hot centre. Then he would retaliate. He twisted her onto her belly and forcing her legs wide apart he began to lick her gently. Starting with the back of one ankle he worked his way up over her calf, across the ticklish hollow behind her knee, and slowly upwards across the fleshiness of the back of her thighs until he reached the fold of her plump but muscular buttocks.

Ignoring her grunts and the squirming of her body to entrap his busy tongue in her dark moist centre, he began again from the ankle of her other leg, moving slowly upwards until she almost screamed at him to drive his tongue deep into her fleshy lipped warmth. The catch of her breath and the opening surrender of her widened cheeks as she pushed her backside up at him when he hesitantly tickled the tight rosebud of her anus almost drove him mad.

It wasn't just the sex, though. Somehow, for once with a woman, Hunter felt completely at ease. Perhaps it was because there was no pretence between them, he didn't know. He didn't want to analyse it, in case the bubble burst. No, he was content to just savour the moments.

His reverie was broken by the sudden ringing of the telephone at the side of the bed.

He reached out and picked it up:

"Miller."

He said nothing as he listened to Juan's voice on the other end of the line.

Picking up the pen and pad which were lying on the bedside cabinet by the telephone Hunter scribbled down the name of the Irishman's hotel and room number.

"Good. Stay in touch with him and contact me again in two hours unless anything happens, and I'll arrange for you to be relieved. As an afterthought he added: "Oh Juan, now that we're in range use the radio to contact me, O.K?" Satisfied, he replaced the handset and rolled onto his back, staring thoughtfully at the ceiling.

"So far so good." Now it was all up to the Irishman to make his move to rendezvous with the shipment, and when he did one of them would be watching.

With a sigh, Hunter allowed himself the luxury of feeling pleased that it was Juan out on surveillance duty and not him. He must be growing old he thought, looking down past the well-defined pectoral muscles of his chest at just the slightest hint of thickening around his waist.

His gaze wandered further down, past the end of the towel and on to the cluster of hairless scars around his knee.

Memories.

All at once Hunter was lost in visions of his past. The warmth of the room and the sound of Mercedes in the bath re-awoke recollections of a childhood, oh so impossibly long ago, when all the summers seemed composed of entirely sunshine days, and school holidays went on for ever; of misty Irish mornings and a loving family, of a big rough bristly father towering gently over a striking redhead, smelling of warm bread and mother love, her French ancestry so noticeable in her delicate features and auburn hair.

How she, with her Catholic family background, had ever fetched up with a big 'Proddy' like his dad still made him shake his head! He shivered involuntarily as if to shake off a sudden chill as the light died out of his reverie and the lately unfamiliar, stabbing, overwhelming pain of hate and loss-filled anguish threatened to wash over him again like an overpowering wave.

He could still see through smarting, soap-filled eyes his mother's jerk of shock and the flannel falling from her nerveless fingers as the sound of breaking glass and gunshots from downstairs joined with his father's dying screams to form the symphony that marked his childhood's end!

Jerking himself back to the present, he blanked the vision from his mind and carefully unclenched his knotted fists. He knew that he should not spend so long in the past; but how to stop....

The bathroom door opened and Mercedes, little-girl like, wrapped in a huge pink towel, walked across to the bed, the glowing skin of her bare shoulders glistened with droplets from her wet hair, as she began to rub it dry with a small hand-towel.

Hunter looked up at her. He knew he could never love a woman like her, not really love. He would probably be afraid to; really beautiful women had always somewhat daunted him, as if he was never really sure of his own attractiveness. Mind you, it had been so different with Mercedes....

Could there be a chance?

His body made up its own mind, however. He could plainly see the projected outlines of her erect nipples, even through the thick pile of the towel. He felt his penis twitch involuntarily as she just stood there smiling down at him. He caught his breath as, slowly, very slowly, with her dark eyes burning into his, she leaned over and gently grasped the evidence of his arousal.

With a look of amused appreciation she eased the towel out of the way and wrapped her fingers around the thickness of his cock.

For moments that seemed an eternity, she milked the first beads of stickiness from him. Never taking her eyes off him for an instant, she lifted her wet fingers to her lips, and licked them clean. He reached up and pulled her slowly to him, her towel dropping to the floor as she lowered her body onto his.

Much later, Hunter belatedly remembered the phone call: "God, I'm losing it." He thought to himself, realising he hadn't even told Mercedes of the call from Juan.

Disentangling his arm from around the dozing girl's bare shoulders he looked at his watch. Good, just time enough for a shower before he had go and take over from Juan, to allow the Spaniard time to get some rest.

Awoken by his movement, Mercedes reached languidly for a cigarette and lit it. "What now, James?"

With an exaggerated gesture of distaste, Hunter waved the smoke away and sat up. "I have to go and relieve Juan before he gets mad enough to come and get me!" He smiled ruefully at the thought.

With a laugh of pure devilment Mercedes blew a cloud of smoke at his naked backside as he swung his legs over the side of the bed.

Mustering what dignity he could, in the face of her chuckles, he stood up and walked, naked, into the bathroom.

CHAPTER THIRTY-TWO

In the Gallery Bond Street office, Grey was placing some documents in a filing cabinet drawer in his desk, sliding it shut he reached across and clicked on the intercom.

"Send them in Mrs Hemmings."

Moments later, the door opened and Grey's secretary ushered in Sir Hector Bainbridge who was accompanied by a tall thin man in a grey suit.

Bainbridge, immaculate as ever, made his entrance. That was actually the only way Grey could describe it. He had been friends with Hector ever since Eton, but he still found a quiet amusement over his flamboyance. Mind you, he had to admit that it had gone down well with many of the foreign diplomats that Bainbridge had to deal with, and who were somehow put at their ease by the very 'Englishness' of the man.

Nodding to Grey, Bainbridge affably waved a hand towards his companion: "Morning Charles, I think you know Chief Inspector Douglas of Special Branch."

Grey stood and crossed to meet them. He shook hands briefly and seated them both in comfortable chairs.

"Yes, of course." He smiled at the Chief Inspector: "But I'm a little surprised to find you keeping such dubious company."

Douglas looked at Bainbridge and grinned.

"Sherry?"

Grey poured three small dry sherries from a crystal decanter on a small silver tray set out on a little table at the side of the easy chairs.

The two nodded their thanks as Grey handed them each a glass and, taking one for himself, crossed back to his desk and sat down.

Allowing himself an appreciative sip, Bainbridge pursed his lips: "Well Charles, I'm afraid we've rather a ticklish problem, and it seems that we might be needing some assistance from your chaps."

Grey looked a little mystified: "Yes, but, you'll forgive me for being blunt." He gestured at Douglas. "Why or how is the Special Branch involved? You know that our concern is strictly limited to foreign matters, or with visitors from abroad, unless it is simply a matter of surveillance; all internal affairs are Special Branch or MI5 matters, and as such not within our operating parameters. Unless...."

Bainbridge's lifted finger forestalled him:

"This is a little different, I'm afraid, Charles; it seems that in these particular circumstances we might be forced to utilise some of your peoples'...He hesitated as if a little loath to be too explicit, then continued: "'Special skills' as it were."

He looked meaningfully at the Chief Inspector, who leaned forward in his chair and took up the thread:

"This is a bit difficult really, but I daresay that you're aware of the decision by the Home Office to authorise some of our Police vehicles to carry out constant armed patrols?"

Grey sat back in his chair and focused his complete attention upon Douglas. This somewhat unnerved the Chief Inspector who felt himself almost mesmerised by the cold gaze. He faltered for an instant as he tried to pin down the reason for the sudden sense of discomfort that Grey imbued in him. Suddenly he realised what it was; Grey never blinked! He sat still behind his desk, almost like some great bird of prey.

The eyes bored into his, dark and emotionless.

With an effort Douglas brought his mind back to the subject and continued:

"Well. this is something that we never wanted to do, but there's really no choice. So many villains these days - especially where drugs are involved - have taken to using firearms and we need to be able to respond rapidly to any situation that may arise. The usual practice of signing weapons out from the station officer was just taking far too long, and placing our unarmed PCs in danger.....and now there is another dimension!"

He fell silent, looking across at Bainbridge for support.

"Not to put too fine a point on it Charles, the situation in some of our larger cities is out of control, and we - you - are going to do something about it!"

Bainbridge leaned forward, the urgency of his feelings apparent in his voice: "In Manchester, for example, certain Mosside estates are almost principalities in their own right. Thugs and drug pushers run them as if they were their personal territories, and they also maintain their own private armies of enforcers who rule by sheer terror."

Grey moved at last, leaning forward about to speak, but

Bainbridge, warming to his task, held up his hand to cut him off.

"Let me finish Charles. In the last few weeks alone there have been numerous beatings, some severe, two victims of attacks by machetes, and two shootings, one by shotgun, one by a 9mm. automatic."

"Yes but....I still don't see...."

The Chief inspector cut in, outrage clearly apparent in his voice: "Two of those were our own men, sir! One found almost in pieces in an alleyway, one shot to death outside a night-club! Both plainclothes undercover constables - both dead!"

Grey stared at him in horrified silence, then Sir Hector added, diffidently:

"There is a rather interesting factor..."

The Chief Inspector reacted explosively to Bainbridge's tone:

"Interesting!!!" Bainbridge cut him off with a sharp wave of the hand. "Yes, it rather seems that ballistics have come up with a remarkable connection. It would appear that the weapon used to murder our DC...."

He paused and looked across at Douglas, who supplied the name: "Elliott, Detective Constable Charles Elliott."

Nodding his thanks, Sir Hector continued: "Yes, DC Elliott."

"Well it seems that he was shot with bullets from a Browning No2. Mk1 semi-automatic pistol. The same weapon that was issued last year to one of our undercover SAS captains in

South Armagh. An officer subsequently murdered by the IRA!

Almost as an afterthought, he added quietly:

"His body - by the way - has never been recovered. Intelligence tells us that he was chopped up - dismembered - and then fed to the dogs!"

In the numbing silence that followed, Grey looked first at one then the other, then he leaned forward. Resting his right elbow on the desk, he stroked his chin thoughtfully with his thumb and forefinger, He directed his gaze to the Chief Inspector:

"Any doubt?"

Douglas sighed and shook his head.

Bainbridge's face wore a grim expression as he continued. He knew Grey of old, and could see by the stony look in his eyes that inside he was shocked and angry.

"What we've got here is subtle, Charles, subtle. It's bad enough that vicious criminals are attempting to impose a rule of terror in our streets, but we've now got positive proof that they are being encouraged and even armed by the IRA, in a further bid to cause murder, mayhem and the downfall of Law and Order! - so much for the cease-fire!"

He took a breath and sat forward:

"There seems little doubt that this peace initiative isn't sitting well with some of the more 'free-thinking' elements, and they appear to be working in devious fashion to outwardly comply with the no-violence agreement, whilst in fact they are merely disguising their activities by promoting unrest and supplying arms and explosives to various native and ethnic elements on the UK mainland."

"The IRA general council has a major problem here. On the one hand they need to maintain control of their own brigades and others – like those so-called Irish National Liberation Army dissidents – who are not so keen to comply with this new scenario. On the other hand, they realise that they will still need enormous amounts of ready cash to enable them to continue to function at all, and this cash must be obtained somehow - without obviously compromising their public stance in the peace initiative."

He sat back.

"I've just come from another special cabinet meeting with the PM, and it has been agreed that we are left with no alternative: we must either give up the streets to these killers, or we must 'eliminate' them!"

His eyes held Grey's:

"That's where you come in. Your chaps have the necessary expertise in these affairs, and it goes without saying that not one word of authorisation will ever be given outside these four walls!"

"Trace this IRA connection, Charles, and eliminate it! We cannot send in unarmed Bobbies, even in plain clothes on this one; this is a war, a dirty, bloody war, and it will be up to you to use whatever means you think fit. Just get the job done!"

With a nod from Grey, Bainbridge and Douglas got up to leave. As Grey moved to escort them from the room, Bainbridge held up a hand.

"If you don't mind, Charles, can you spare me a moment more? I have a few private thoughts to discuss with you?"

Grey raised an eyebrow as Sir Hector crossed to the door and pushed it firmly shut behind the retreating Inspector Douglas.

"Sit down please Charles." "Before I begin I need your word that what we are about to discuss will never be revealed to anyone – no matter who and whatever the circumstances!"

"Is it that important?"

"So important Charles, that you will literally hold my life in your hands!" His quiet intensity shook Grey.

He paused, then slowly put out a hand and flicked off the switch that controlled the surreptitious recording of every word that was spoken in his office.

He sat back and waited.

Thirty minutes later Sir Hector quietly clicked shut the door behind him, leaving Grey to his whirling thoughts.

CHAPTER THIRTY-THREE

Naturally, if live explosives were to be used in the introductory lecture for the new intake on Total Security's Close Protection trainees, then it would have been held in one of the old Nissen huts that dotted the perimeter of the disused (officially, that is) airfield in Kent, not here in the old East End factory.

They would all be billeted in Kent eventually, for the small-arms practice, the anti-kidnap evasive driving and skid-pan experience, and, when they had passed this first theoretical course, for their hands-on taste of Improvised Explosive Device recognition and containment.

However, all close-quarter armed and unarmed combat skills; in particular a specially devised Third Party Protection system drawn from a mixture of Karate, Aikido, Judo and Wrestling techniques which concentrated on manhandling the protected person into cover with one hand whilst dealing with an attacker with the other, were taught and practised in the old Rag-trade factory off Brick Lane in London's East End.

Here members of close protection squads from a variety of Commonwealth and Middle Eastern countries had learned their trade, with its particular concentration of awareness and protection in the killing zone, that space of a few feet around a potential target which presented the greatest danger from cutting weapons and bullets.

Lectures in 'Pest Extermination', as it was euphemistically called, the detection and removal of unauthorised electronic information receiving devices, that is to say 'Bugs,' were also held here, as also were the introductory lectures in bomb, car-bomb and boobytrap awareness, at this stage utilising only dummy explosives.

The tiny improvised lecture room was full of electronic equipment and circuit diagrams of bombs and booby traps.

The latest intake of Special Branch, and Royal Protection Squad trainees, a small group of six people including one woman all dressed in combat fatigues, were seated in front of a table upon which were scattered video-recorder timers and other bomb-making material.

Dennis Martin, ex-Special Boat Section sniper and demolition expert, similarly dressed, was seated casually on the corner of the table, talking to them:

"So, what does it look like then?" He was toying with a glass jar in one hand. Suddenly, without warning, he tossed it to the girl.

Startled, nevertheless she caught it and lifted it up to examine its contents. After a moment, an expression of distaste crossed her face: "Err. Well... it actually looks like..."

Her eyes widened as she realised what the jar contained: "Ugh.. It looks like a finger, someone's finger!"

Martin laughed loudly in pure delight.

"Yes! Yes! You've just made the acquaintance of Mr Paddy Jameson. IRA bombmaker and Irishman of some repute - unfortunately not for making bombs!" "It seems that our friend here was attempting to add to the world's stocks of improvised explosive by mixing a certain nitrogen based fertiliser with diesel oil in his bath tub."

He grinned broadly, warming to his story:

"Well it would appear that after stirring the mixture thoroughly with a wooden paddle and being fully satisfied with the explosive qualities of the end product, Mr Jameson then set about to prove the truth of every Irish joke by banging the paddle on the side of the bath to dislodge the residue sticking to it!" He paused momentarily for effect:

"How successful he was we shall never know. What we do know is that he managed to take out the gable ends and two complete walls of his house, and vanish totally into thin air, leaving only one finger to remember him by!"

Still smiling hugely, Martin reached over and took back the jar. he stood up and walked back behind the table placing the jar in front of him. Just as he was about to speak the telephone rang shrilly. He picked up the handset:

"Yes. Martin speaking." He listened intently: "Yes....No, they are just about through here for the moment, going on to...." He looked quizzically at the group.

The girl, her face still slightly pink spoke up; "Driving sir."

Martin turned back to the 'phone: "Defensive Driving skills Sir.......Yes, I'll come over straight away.....about an hour I should think....Yes Sir. He replaced the handset and looked up thoughtfully.

CHAPTER THIRTY-FOUR

MARSEILLES.

Kennedy was in a good mood. Last night's Opera performance had not been as painful an experience as he had expected. Still not for him, although he could readily own up to being moved on occasion by the power of the drama and the voices. Something of an acquired taste, however. Nevertheless, it had felt good to be wearing decent clothes again, and the meal afterwards in the tiny Bistro near the Opera house, had been excellent.

Of course, his companion had been a little hard going at first, but a couple of bottles of red wine and a few exchanged confidences about mutual acquaintances had eased the atmosphere somewhat.

Nothing was ever said straight out, naturally. Both men had been aware that even casual conversation could be dangerous if overheard by the wrong people.

It would be necessary for Liam to take a little trip to a place where plain speaking would be possible. Even the go-between had no idea of what lay behind the request that Kennedy accept an invitation to a meeting with a Señor Ricardo Nuñez, on the island of Mallorca.

Kennedy had received his instructions from the General Council's chief of staff to go along with any arrangements, as long as they didn't jeopardise the delivery of the shipment. It was obvious to him that whatever it was had already been agreed between his masters and this Señor Nuñez, so he had

170

no option but to agree. The thick roll of 1,000 franc notes pushed surreptitiously across the table to him 'For expenses' had cheered him considerably, however.

After memorising details of the rendezvous, Kennedy had taken his leave and made inroads into his expenses first in a very intimate revue club, and then in the embrace of a long black-haired half-caste with big eyes and long legs who swore that Liam was the love of her life, and that only a sick mother's hospital bills forced her to accept any 'little present' that he might care to leave on his way out.

He couldn't complain; he had made her work for her money!

This evening, after another call to Ireland to confirm his instructions, Kennedy left the hotel carrying a small overnight bag. Walking briskly through the lobby, he climbed into one of the waiting taxis. As it drew away, Juan, his shadow, followed him in another cab.

Working eight-hour stints, Hunter and Mercedes had each taken their turn watching Kennedy's Hotel, allowing the others to get some rest, and making it less likely that Kennedy would become aware that he was being tailed.

Inside the taxi Juan reached into his coat pocket and pulled out one of the three walkie-talkie sets which Rodriguez had provided in Hunter's briefcase. He checked the battery strength. Satisfied, he slid it back in his pocket for the time being.

CHAPTER THIRTY-FIVE

2300HRS an old Nissen Hut on a disused airfield.

The security cordon around the airfield was provided by 22 SAS regiment ostensibly out in force on a night penetration exercise.

In the gloom, other than the visible pairs of sentries, all around the perimeter, invisible in their camouflage and dug into ditches and hedges, sniper units lay, as they had been trained, silent and unmoving.

The inside of the Nissen hut which years before had housed the standby Spitfire and Hurricane fighter pilots who stood against the might of Goering's Luftwaffe, was lit by only a single bulb hanging from the ceiling which struggled to penetrate the shadows.

The cold, decrepit building was absolutely bare except for a group of hard-backed wooden chairs. Not a cabinet, not a telephone, not even a table to support the plastic coffee cups which stood unused on the floor, next to a Thermos flask. Nothing which could conceivably hide a microphone or any transmitter bug – not even a carpet on the floor - disturbed the emptiness.

Each of the five figures seated in the little group had submitted to a painstaking search of their clothing; Bainbridge had performed the task on each of the Irish contingent and both he and Sir Ambrose had submitted stoically to similar treatment. Neither side would wish their discussions ever to be revealed!

The task of bringing the three IRA leaders in from Southern Ireland was a simple matter, it was not an infrequent event that a low flying helicopter dropped out of the night sky to embark and disembark shadowy figures, units on special covert operations and the like.

Daniel Lynch, cold and in a bad temper from the long journey from Belfast down to the pickup point near Cork pulled his coat more loosely around him, staring at the two representatives of British Imperialism that he was avowed to bring down.

He didn't care that neither had proffered a hand as the three entered, stiff and cold from the confined space of helicopter. He would have refused it anyway, "Let's get on then." His flat Belfast accent sounded harshly in emptiness.

Bainbridge grimaced:-"We are here because we all wish to bring an end to hundreds of years of unrest." "We don't have to like each other…" His eyes noted grimly the accuracy of that statement, as he stared hard at the three representatives of all that he had been born to despise.

He tried and failed to shrug off the almost overwhelming feeling of dirtiness at what he was about to do.

"We will all be adjudged traitors if even the slightest hint of either this meeting or its agenda become known! We just have to agree to a course of action – and then.." He paused, the muscles along his jaw contracting as he gazed bleakly at the silent figures and continued: "Then God help us all!"

CHAPTER THIRTY-SIX

Back at the Hilton, Hunter and Mercedes were finishing a meal in weary silence. The strain of the around-the-clock surveillance was beginning to tell on all of them, and they picked desultorily at the plates of food balanced on the small coffee table. A high-pitched bleeping noise suddenly broke the silence. Hunter leaned over in his chair and quickly picked up one of the walkie-talkie sets from the sideboard and pressed the receive button.

"Yes!"

Juan's voice crackled into the room as he responded, speaking good but strongly accented English. "I think we maybe are in trouble! I'm still with Kennedy, We're at the airport, and he's just bought a ticket on the next plane to Mallorca!"

Hunter sprang to his feet, spilling his coffee onto the table as he did so. Urgently he motioned to Mercedes to pass him his jacket. Nodding a thank you, he struggling into it whilst talking rapidly to Juan:

"Mallorca, shit!" He bit his bottom lip: "When's the flight? O.K. Stay with him. Mercedes will try and book us two tickets on the same flight. God knows what's happened! But stay with him at all costs. I'll meet you at the airport. I'm on my way!"

He thrust the radio set into his jacket pocket and turned to Mercedes:

"He's booked a flight to Mallorca of all places!" "Well he can't be going on his holidays, so go down and use the reception 'phone, call the airport and book two seats on the next flight for Juan and me; I'll call the Colonel and see if he's had any news of a change of plan!"

Wasting no time, Mercedes hurried from the room while Hunter strode over to the bedside cabinet and snatched up the room 'phone. The switchboard operator patched the call straight through to colonel Rodriguez' office, in Madrid. Luckily he was still there.

He listened to Hunter's urgent query:

"I've no idea! As far as we know the meet is still to be in Marseilles." He listened again: "No, there must be another reason, a shipment of that size could only be handled at a port like Marseilles."

He thought briefly: "There's one possibility, and it's only a chance, but if there's no connection we have a very big co-incidence." "We have had information that a Ricardo Nuñez, one of the top ETA bosses is visiting Mallorca on his yacht, we thought on holiday, but.....but it would now seem not!"..... "One moment."

The colonel opened a drawer in his desk and pulled out a file. He placed it down in front of him and opened it.

"As a matter of fact we have a current file on Nuñez as suspected of being behind the Carero Blanco assassination... Not as a trigger man, you understand, but as the brains behind it and many others of late, but.."

Hunter could hear the heavy sigh clearly over the phone: There's no proof, naturally."

The colonel spoke again: "To be honest with you, we also heard a little story that an Accion Nacional Espanola anti-ETA hit-squad was preparing a little surprise for him, and.." He broke off as Hunter exclaimed in surprise:

"Yes! Anti-ETA. A right wing group who oppose the Basque separatists, and fight fire with fire as you say!"

Hunter's silence was eloquent.

The colonel continued: "Well, we were about to look the other way, as removing Nuñez may have worked to our advantage . But - and it seems likely - if the Irishman is going to meet him, well then, it would ruin everything if he were to come to any harm. Go after him and make sure he is well protected."

"Use any means...the strongest if necessary. We'll clean up any mess of course. I will give you a contact number on the Island. This man will provide you with all necessary equipment. Good luck!.....The name of the boat?... Ah yes. a moment..."

The colonel leafed through the open file.

"Yes, here, it is. Not very Spanish, it's called the *'Geisha Girl'*, moored at Puerto Portals, in the Punta Portals harbour."

CHAPTER THIRTY-SEVEN

Nunez

Grey waved a hand in the direction of the tall cadaverous looking man wearing a suit that looked as if it had been cut for a slightly smaller body.

"This is Chief Inspector Douglas, Martin, Special Branch. He'll brief you on the background, and fill you in on local colour and things that don't appear in the official records."

Martin shook hands with Douglas and they both sat in the seats indicated by Grey. Douglas cleared his throat.

"Well. We've got rather a bad situation in Manchester, Mr. Martin. And I'm afraid there's a lot of reading, for you, and after I give you the general background we'll go down to West End Central where I've set up a meeting with some of the other officers who've been working on this for some time, but whom we've had to pull out...for obvious reasons....naturally we couldn't take the chance of doing this in Manchester itself, just in case any of the locals happened to see you."

Martin looked curiously over at Grey: "Manchester Sir?" "I gathered that I was here for a particular reason, sir, but surely this is just a police matter?"

Grey stared at him. "Not any more, Martin."

He pursed his lips and looked judiciously up at the ceiling for a moment, before continuing:

"It seems that the clampdown of the Drug Enforcement Agency in the USA is forcing the Drug barons, and especially the Jamaican Yardies, to look elsewhere for their marketplace, and there's no doubt that they've selected us as their soft option!"

"And that's not all! They are not only importing their drug problem but also their predilection for the use of firearms!"

"Putting it bluntly, Martin, it seems that the black gangs in Manchester are flooding the streets with Ecstasy tablets and Crack Cocaine and they're using guns almost as a status symbol, and – God help us - there is now an added dimension. We have hard evidence to show that they are receiving the weapons from the IRA, so it now becomes a matter for us! God knows where this could lead if it isn't stopped."

His expression grew hard as he spoke:

"If things go on as they are at present, England could end up like Chicago or New York, with every minor thug carrying a gun and prepared to use it!" He lapsed into silence, contemplating the enormity of the prospect.

After a moment Martin bitterly broke the spell:

"So, in spite of all this fuss over Peace Talks the IRA were never serious? They were simply buying time to infiltrate themselves deeper over here?" The sour note in his voice was evident.

There was a silence as Grey simply stared at him with an expression in his eyes borne of long experience and one eyebrow lifted slightly, subtly rebuking him for his naivety

Martin pushed away the slight feeling of resentment:

"So, I'm to go in undercover and ...well, then what? Who do

I take out?"

Douglas cleared his throat and with a glance at Grey began to answer: "It's not quite that simple, Mr. Martin. For a start we know the leader well, he's very high profile, and he's sharp. He won't be easily taken in, but.."

Grey cut in sharply:

"But, Martin, there is another complication! We don't want you to go in and just 'take out' as you put it, anybody this time. We desperately need to trace the IRA connection."

There was no mistaking the steel in the voice now.

"GCHQ Intelligence confirms now the peace initiative is seen to be a failure the dissident section in the general command, the INLA, are seeking to overthrow the General Command whom they despise as 'soft'." "To counter this situation and regain respect it is considered likely that the IRA will initiate another bombing campaign here in England.... that last bomb at the Ritz was simply the first of a whole series of atrocities, a sort of reminder."

Martin began to feel a peculiar prickling along the back of his neck. This was not going to be as straightforward as he had first thought.

Grey's voice pulled back his concentration.

"We know – don't ask how – that there is now a death list of political figures drawn up as well as a detailed analysis of 'soft' targets like railway stations, airports and motorway junctions, the compilation of this list has been one of the major activities of IRA units in this country during the time that their compatriots were making highly publicised overtures of peace back home.

"If we can infiltrate an active service cell, then perhaps we can get a lead on the bombmaker himself. We believe him to be out of the country at the moment, but due to return after letting the dust settle from the Ritz operation."

There was no sign in Grey's cold discourse that he even recognised the pun. His flat unemotional tones continued:

"We need a line to him, Martin, a connection, anything. "The only way, as far as we can see, is for you to somehow make contact with this cell through the Moss-side gangs, and then we may - if we're lucky - use them to get to him!"

Martin spread his hands: "But why me? After all I don't even know Manchester! And if you don't want me to actually remove anyone.....?"

Grey looked at the Inspector.

He swallowed and took up the challenge:

"Well, to be frank Mr Martin, you're black! We don't have that many black officers that we could put in. For another thing, the last one that we did use was shot dead! So your special skills might well prove necessary. As for not knowing Manchester, then with luck Manchester won't know you!"

Martin sat deep in thought - this wasn't going to be easy; no long-range marking of an unsuspecting target and a quick unemotional pulling of a trigger, and how on earth was he going to get close enough...Grey's voice cut across his introspection:

"We have prepared a rather unsavoury background for you,

keeping your name as Dennis Martin. Learn it well. Lots of minor transgressions plus there are some fake Metropolitan Police discharge papers which have you leaving as 'temperamentally unsuitable' after probationary service, but which you ascribe to monumental police racism."

"This should help you to establish yourself as someone with no love for the authorities!" "You are to pose as someone looking to buy drugs and a firearm, and you will be supplied with a sum of money to do this with."

"Your cover story is that you want to move in on an operation here in London, but you need to establish a secure pipeline to a major supplier of drugs." "In short. You need the right connections." "This, together with your obvious distaste for your ex 'Met' colleagues, should prove your bona-fides to the gangs."

His voice rolled relentlessly on:

"You will be entirely on your own until such time as you contact this office directly to arrange cover when a meeting with the Irish cell has been set up. Any problems and I'm afraid it will be up to you!"

CHAPTER THIRTY-EIGHT

MALLORCA

It had been warm in Marseilles, but muggy. Here in Mallorca it was glorious! Hunter had been on an assignment once to act as instructor to the personal guard of a minor Sheikhdom in the Far East; he had seen blue skies before, so it wasn't just the sunshine that affected him so. It was more the ambience of the island.

It was almost as if it had been fashioned - with its high mountains to the north and its convoluted coastline of tiny bays and golden beaches - for the sole purpose of providing a small glimpse of perfection.

Hot, but not too hot and arid, enough rainfall to allow greenery to flourish. Even the spectacular electrical storms that occasionally ripped the night sky apart seemed unthreatening; more like a splendid theatrical performance of The Twilight of the Gods, rather than the mean and spiteful English thunderstorms that frightened children into cupboards under the stairs.

Of course, thought Hunter, as he entered the cool gloom of the tiny bar, sweating slightly from the weight of the attaché case that swung from his left hand, it was only to be expected that eighteen-to-thirties lager louts and topless provincial secretaries would take this perfection and alter it into a beer-swilling, fighting, fucking, music-blaring pandemonium!

He glanced across the little table at Juan, who was indistinguishable from the native Mallorquins.

"Another San Miguel?"

The prospect of another bottle of ice-cold beer brought a wide smile to Juan's lips."Si, Señor. It looks as though our friend is happy to sit in the sun for the moment."

Through the little cafe door Juan had a good view of Kennedy, sitting under a parasol at another of the little bars that seem to dot every few yards of the Paseo Maritemo, the long stretch of Palma's yacht harbour that began with the enormous gothic Cathedral at one end and ended with the distinctive windmill at the other.

As he ordered the two beers, Hunter's dark eyes twinkled and he smiled ruefully to himself.

If he were younger, different.. whatever, no doubt he too would be a part of that group of young tourists that he so despised!

Probably working 50 weeks a year - or perhaps not even working - he reminded himself. So why not escape, just for a week or two from the grey drabness of their everyday existence?

Drink, fight, fuck.....tomorrow back to the dole and the realities of a way of life where disco temptresses would slap away a groping hand that only a few days before had been given licence to explore naked breasts and buttocks in hot, squirming, sandy ecstasy!

Teenage girls who here, in the careless abandon induced by too many San Miguels and the Mediterranean sun, would queue up in wet t-shirted droves to pout and posture in a frenzy of erotic breast-bouncing competition to the delight and

183

raucous encouragement of drunken, shouting, Romeos, would in an instant revert to being haughty, insulted virgins once they were back in Leeds or Rochdale...

"So," thought Hunter..."Why not?"

Through the open door he could see the white acres of expensive boats, swaying gently at their moorings. The late afternoon sun reflected dazzlingly from the myriad windows, portholes and burnished, gleaming fittings.

His attention lingered on one in particular. "That's not a yacht" he thought. "It's more like a cruise liner!" Momentarily the huge opulence of this privately owned vessel, towering even above the largest of its companions, seemed like a slap in the face. Just the thought of the amount of wealth required simply to pay the crewing costs of such a fantastic craft was almost obscene!

"Give me not poverty lest I steal." Schoolboy memories of a literary criticism seminar on Defoe's 'Moll Flanders' suddenly swam up in Hunter's mind. For a moment he realised that it was obscene, that such wealth could be for the sole use of just one man, whilst others in the world were starving!

Juan's urgent summons cut through his reverie. Hunter threw down a 1,000 peseta note on the counter and, picking up the little case, quickly joined Juan outside as Kennedy began to walk away, obviously unaware of the attention of his two shadows.

They strolled casually along behind the Irishman as he made his unhurried way up from the marina until, almost in the shadow of the towering cathedral, he turned into a little side-street to the left of the imposing Admiralty building.

Through the late afternoon throngs of tourists, Hunter and Juan had little difficulty in remaining un-noticed in the narrow street, occasionally stopping as if to consult the menu del diaz of the various Tapas bars that seemed to infest every available corner and crevice of the ancient buildings.

At the top of the street, Kennedy paused briefly in front of a small door set into another pair of enormous wooden ones. With a glance, he checked his watch, then entered. As the little door clicked shut, Hunter and Juan were nonplussed. They ran to the entrance and stopped. Was it a trap? Had they been made?

There was nothing on the facade of the building to indicate its function. A private house? A Church or Museum? As they considered their options, a small group of German tourists shouldered their way past and pushed open the door.

With a sigh of relief, Hunter motioned Juan to follow them into the Aladdin's cave that opened up before them. Great grey stone vaulted arches towered over a stone-flagged floor strewn with piles of apples and oranges; everywhere wicker baskets of limes, lemons and bananas were heaped in casual abandon.

Hundreds of long thick, white candles provided a flickering illumination that reflected in the rows of spirit and liqueur bottles that lined the rear of this imposing bar cum-restaurant, and the voices of the thronging tourists seated in sprawling easy couches and chairs around little tables were augmented by the chatter and squawks of dozens of multi-coloured cage-birds.

Juan gripped Hunter's arm and grinned as they sat at a tiny round table near the wall:

"'Abaco!' I remember, I have heard of this place señor Hunter, it is quite famous on the island, but I have never been here before. Look. Over there." Juan nodded to one dimly lit corner by the huge open fireplace. At a small table Kennedy was deep in conversation with another man. From Colonel Rodriguez' description Hunter guessed that it was Nuñez, the ETA contact.

The Irishman was sitting with his back to the room, in animated discussion with a large, thickset figure in a crumpled off-white linen suit, whose eyes, as he drank, were everywhere, in complete contrast to the Irishman's apparent unconcern.

Hunter was scornful. "Not very professional, this one." He thought, "sitting with his back to the door like that, not able to see what was going on around..."

Then: "Shit!" The expletive burst quietly but savagely from Hunter's tight lips.

As he raised his eyes from the Irishman's back Hunter found himself looking directly into his coldly calculating mirrored gaze. Kennedy was using the large ornate wall-mirror to check every movement behind him!

At that moment, the door crashed open and a small group of swaying, sweating and obviously very drunk Scandinavians fell in. Kennedy's attention snapped immediately towards the intruding clatter, as two waiters attempted to shepherd the noisy youths firmly out into the street again.

With a prayer of thanks, Hunter shifted his chair so that he too had his back to the room, and to the Irishman, leaving Juan to keep a check on him.

The interruption had seemingly wiped any concern from Kennedy's mind, as he resumed his earnest conversation with the Spaniard.

All at once both Kennedy and the Spaniard got up. The Irishman dropped a couple of 1,000 peseta notes onto the tabletop as they made their way through the crowded bar and out of the door.

Hunter didn't want Kennedy to see him following, so he urged Juan after them: "You go. I'll give it a moment and then I'll follow. I'll keep you in sight, but I don't want him to see me again!"

Juan nodded, and casually sauntered after the two, not looking back. Hunter waited for a few seconds, and began to rise from his seat, thrusting a handful of coins onto the table in front of him. As he did, he noticed another figure across the room, who was also making his way to the door. There was something about him that jarred. Something that ...didn't seem quite right.

Cautiously, so as not to attract his attention, Hunter fell in behind him. In the distance he could see Juan, but not the Irishman. But that was as he wanted it. As long as Juan kept contact, and he kept Juan in sight, then it was O.K.

The scruffily dressed lank-haired figure was also going in the same direction.

"That's it!" Suddenly Hunter knew. There was no way that such a down-at-heel Mallorquin would ever be able to afford the inflated prices in that gothic, jet setter's paradise!

The hairs on the back of his neck prickled, as if a cold breeze had wafted in from the darkening sea.

Without a doubt, Hunter knew that he and Juan were not the only ones following Kennedy and the ETA boss!

Tightening his grip on the little case that still swung from his left hand - no weariness would ever compromise the immediate readiness of his right hand - Hunter strode briskly past the third follower, and caught up with Juan just as Kennedy and Nuñez reached the taxi rank by the Admiralty building.

"Stop! Wait a moment!" Hunter whispered urgently to Juan; flinging an arm around his shoulders as if greeting a long lost friend. "Let them go!"

Not understanding, but obeying, Juan fell in with the charade, and, seemingly deep in friendly conversation, they watched as Kennedy and the Spaniard climbed into a taxi and drove off. "Dios! We've lost them!" Juan turned angrily on Hunter, who raised a finger to his lips.

Following Hunter's gaze, Juan saw a second taxi pulling away, after Kennedy's.

"Now! Quick!"

Diving into a third cab, Hunter thrust a handful of large denomination notes into Juan's hand. "Tell him not to lose that taxi! Not too close, but don't lose it!"

Quickly Juan translated the instructions for the taxi driver who seemed mesmerised by the amount of pesetas waving under his nose.

With a lurch that threw Hunter and Juan back into their seats, the cab pulled out into the Paseo Maritimo traffic, no more than 50 metres behind the second taxi.

The tension eased from Juan's face as Hunter explained that as long as they kept the anti-Basque shadower in sight then they would be able to retain contact with the Irishman without getting too close. With a sigh, Juan relaxed, watching the rear lights of the taxi in front.

The convoy drove in that noisy, nerve-wracking way that had long since ceased to trouble hardened natives, but which was guaranteed to break the nerve of any unfamiliar tourist. Red lights were seemingly placed in just such positions that they could not be seen until it was too late. Pedestrian crossings were apparently constructed to make it easier to knock down anyone foolish enough to obey the crossing signal.

Soon the traffic thinned as the cars made their way out of Palma on the western coastal road.

Through the side window Hunter could see on his left the huge walls and gates of the Marivent Palace, the summer home of King Juan Carlos and the Spanish Royal Family. Also a popular summer holiday home for their regular visitors, Charles and Princess Di.

"But a terrible place for security," mused Hunter's professional mind, but better since his last visit as they'd removed the enormous Campsa storage cylinders which had formerly overlooked the grounds and which would have given a tremendous vantage point to any sniper!

CHAPTER THIRTY-NINE

MANCHESTER

It was two A.M.

Dennis Martin brushed past the cursory glances of the two huge dinner-suited doormen and pushed his way through the crowded lobby of Isaac's, a dingy but notorious Moss-side discotheque. The lights are very low, and the music very loud with that heavy Reggae bass beat that Martin could feel as a physical thudding in his chest. The thick haze of Ganja prickled at his eyes as he elbowed his way through to the bar. With the exception of a few pale skinned blonde girls, the place was full of black men.

Sweating from the heat of the crowded gyrating bodies he squeezed his way to the front and caught the barman's eye. "Gimme a Red Stripe."

When the cold can arrived he placed his hand on the barman's arm and held up a £20 note. "Who's the man?"

The barman stared at Martin and said nothing, then he pulled his arm away and snatched the note, surreptitiously nodding his head towards a group seated at a table in the corner, watching the dancers strutting and posturing on the dancefloor.

Martin followed his glance. Under the flashing disco lights he could see four dreadlocked Rastas sitting talking to two young white padded-bra-clad wannabee's laughing and shaking their bare shoulders in pathetic imitations of Madonna in heat.

Taking his beer, Martin wove a path through the dancers. As he neared the table, the conversation suddenly ceased. One of the men got up and barred his way. Big and massive fisted he reminded Martin vividly of old newsreels of Sonny Liston, a giant bear of a heavyweight champion.

Martin gave him a cold stare, and then ignored him, speaking over his shoulder to the obvious leader. Dressed in black leather, eyes invisible behind round shades, the man was an inky shadow, enlivened only by the dull gleam of gold jewellery.

Impassively he sat tapping his fingers in time to the heavy bass beat on the silver top of an ebony cane. Curling around him like the coiling plumes of the Ganja smoke rising from the table was a tangible sense of menace. The others sat grouped together, but there was a distinct space around the black clad figure, as if even his own men were afraid to come too close.

Martin projected his voice above the thudding rhythmic beat: "I hear you're the man!" His flat tones showed no sign of fear.

Stick nodded his head briefly to the man standing between Martin and the group. With a heavy-lidded menacing stare he moved to one side. The black impenetrable lenses looked him up and down, glinting in the strobe lights. "Who wants to know?" The strong Jamaican tones were light and unconcerned.

"Somebody that wants to buy, who's lookin' f'somebody that wants to sell!"

"You got the bread?"

"Yeah! I got the bread!"

Almost disdainfully, the shades turned away from Martin as if in dismissal. Seemingly the dancers had once again claimed the man's full attention. He leaned back in his chair, his head swaying in time to the music.

"I'm busy right now. I'll check you later." His unconcerned arrogance tightened the nerves along Martin's spine, but he had to force the issue.

"When?"

The head turned back, contemplating, weighing. "Outside... in a couple'a hours." The tone was no longer light, but cold and flat!

Martin glanced slowly around the table. All the eyes were fixed on him, assessing, calculating. He nodded, then turned and made his way through the dancers back to the bar.

CHAPTER FORTY

PALMA - MALLORCA

From the slight rise behind the Punta Portals quayside cafes and restaurants, Hunter and Juan could plainly see Kennedy and the Spaniard as they made their way through the lines of parked Porsches, Mercedes and Shoguns onto one of the jetties that projected from the sides of the yacht marina.

In the late of the evening, groups of figures criss-crossed the tiny road and flagged patios, moving from bar to bar, punctuating the cool air with sudden bursts of laughter. As they watched they could also see the slim dark figure that slipped unnoticed in the shadows behind them.

Reaching into the little case, Hunter took out a tiny pair of Zeiss binoculars. Easing the gnarled focusing ring, he followed the two figures as they walked along the rows of moored craft. He grunted in satisfaction as the Spaniard abruptly turned and clambered over a gangplank, motioning Kennedy to join him. Focusing on the stern plate the name: '*Geisha Girl*, Bennetti Suntripper' swam into view.

Watching as Nuñez and Kennedy climbed on board and vanished through the rear glass doors into the cabin, Hunter then swept the quayside, back to where the following figure, apparently settling down for a long wait, could be clearly seen seated at a table by a quayside bar from where he could maintain a good view of the boat.

"Right" Hunter handed the glasses to Juan and reached into the case again and this time he drew out a small package, wrapped in a black plastic bag.

Quite openly in the gloom, Hunter unwrapped the package, revealing two Heckler and Koch VP70M 9mm 18 shot burst-fire pistols, each wrapped again in a pair of large-size flesh-coloured rubber gloves. Rummaging in the case once more, he found the two separately packaged spare ammunition clips.

"Don't touch anything until you've got the gloves on." He muttered, pulling on his own pair as he spoke. "They're clean and untraceable according to Rodriguez's contact."

In silence they checked the actions of the pistols, and slid home a full clip. Juan pushed the weapon into the waistband at the front of his trousers, Hunter favoured the rear. In a grappling match an unlooked-for shot would do less damage to his rear than to his front, or so he theorised.

Pushing the attaché case out of sight behind a collection of rubbish bins, quietly, without drawing attention to themselves, Hunter and Juan strolled towards the bar, exchanging friendly banter.

The ANE man gave them no more than a cursory glance as they stepped up from the road onto the raised bar patio. Over his beer he was concentrating on the Spaniard's boat.

Without breaking stride, suddenly it was done! Hunter went to one side of the seated figure, Juan to the other. Two hands dropped heavily onto his arms, pinning them to the table whilst in the same instant two guns pressed into his stomach beneath the table as Hunter and Juan slid into vacant chairs on either side of him, to a casual onlooker no more than two friends joining a third.

"Tranquillo por favor, Señor, y silencio!" Juan whispered fiercely!

It seemed an eternity before the startled man remembered to breathe again.

"Como se llama?" Juan leaned closer, pushing his face right into his. Petrified with fear, his eyes bulged in terror, it was as though he had lost the power of speech.

With an audible 'Click', Hunter snicked off the safety catch of the automatic and nuzzled it closer, boring its snub nose into the terrified man's ribcage.

"C - Carlos, Señor" the terrified man forced the words out.

"O.K. Juan, Tell him to walk slowly towards the end of the Quay," Hunter said: "Two paces in front of us, and remind him of what happens to the back of someone's head when hit by a 9mm bullet!"

The rigid fearful stiffness of their captive's back attracted no attention as the little group moved away from the lights and towards the quiet concealing darkness at the end of the jetty. Stepping carefully over the mooring lines of the little dinghies that bobbed gently in the slight swell, Hunter motioned to Juan to get the man into one of the them, out of sight of any casual observer.

Keeping his gun pressed firmly and painfully in the terrorist's kidneys, Juan preceded him down the short ladder and into one of the rocking boats.

Sitting carefully on the bow seat, he forced the trembling man to sit cross-legged in the swilling bilge water of the keel with his back to him, facing Hunter who clambered down after them and took his place in the mid-section seat leaning over so that his face was inches from his prisoner's.

Hunter's eyes were dark and deadly, his voice quiet and charged with menace. He motioned to Juan, not for the first time mentally cursing his lack of fluency in languages:

"Tell him that we know who he is and why he is here. We know what they plan to do, but we don't know when, nor how....He is going to tell us!"

Carlos's cracking voice whined in nasal protestations, understandable in any language. His spluttering denials cut off in mid sentence as Juan reached around him from behind. Jamming the top of his automatic hard up against his upper lip, holding the butt with his right hand and the barrel with his left, he savagely jerked the man's head backwards against his chest, grinding the cold metal forcefully into the sensitive spot between top lip and nose.

The pain was excruciating! So bad, in fact, that it took away his power to scream!

Hunter didn't like this part. It was the necessity of doing these things, even to such miserable worms like Carlos that created such conflict in his mind. The memory of the still, lifeless figure, lying on the damp pavement outside the Ritz cut across his doubts, however, and gave him the steel to continue.

Eventually, of course, Carlos talked. Between sobs, the spitting of blood and pleas for mercy, names and details came tumbling out.

Yes, there were five of them all together. He gave the address of the apartment. Yes, they were to assassinate the ETA boss, Nuñez. No, they had no idea who his guest was, but that was not important; it would simply be 'unfortunate.'

He - Carlos - was to watch until it was obvious that their target had settled down for the night, then he would telephone his accomplices who were waiting with explosive which they would then attach to the boat under the cover of darkness and .....

"But why not booby-trap the boat anyway?" Demanded Hunter.

The shivering man explained that they could not be sure whether or not the Spaniard would be staying on board the boat, or in a hotel, so they had to make certain. Also if he were to sleep on the boat it would allow them to set a time delay to the explosive, which would give them a better chance to be a long way away when it happened.

In the awkward silence that followed, Carlos knew, Juan knew, and Hunter knew.

In an instant Juan seized Carlos by the back of the neck and twisted him over the stern of the violently rocking boat so that his head was forced down under the water. Hunter threw himself upon his kicking legs, lying on top of them, ignoring the ineffectual flailing of his arms.

It didn't take long. A few moments of muscle-tearing struggle, a last rush of bubbles, one or two final convulsive jerks, and then an eternity of stillness.

They let the body slip quietly into the water. With luck it would look as though it were an accident. An unfortunate carouser who slipped, perhaps knocking himself unconscious on the edge of a dinghy before falling in and drowning.

Chatting casually, they made their way back along the jetty, past the 62ft twin diesel craft that now would still be in one piece tomorrow.

Retrieving the briefcase, and slipping the weapons back inside, Hunter and Juan walked casually over to the taxi rank.

As they took their place in the small noisy queue of people, waiting to be ferried into the night-spots of Palma, Hunter couldn't help but wonder about Kennedy and Nuñez. Why had the Irishman come all this way? What was it that was so important as to bring these two together?

Had he been a fly on the *Geisha Girl*'s cabin wall, he would have found the conversation more than interesting.

Because of the extremely high profile being maintained by the security services and the constraints forced upon them by the remnants of their own Cease-Fire, Kennedy's IRA bosses had secretly arranged a contract for his special accomplishments to be made available to their comrades in the Basque separatist movement, in return for the use of ETA safe houses in France for the IRA active service units who had formerly been operating on the Continent against British NATO servicemen and their families.

Like the IRA, ETA - translated as "Basque Homeland and Freedom" - was a paramilitary group, predominately of young men, which had murdered more than 800 people in an ongoing campaign for an independent state in northern Spain and south-western France.

After Kennedy had 'taken care' of a 'most urgent' task awaiting him on his return to Ireland, he would be placed at the disposal of Señor Nuñez and his compatriots. His job then would be to ensure the elimination of one of the senior Spanish Security men, who had been causing them more than a few problems of late, a certain Colonel Rodriguez!

Perhaps the Colonel would have appreciated the irony; by helping Hunter to keep Nuñez alive he had as good as signed his own death warrant!

CHAPTER FORTY-ONE

MANCHESTER

The back alley behind 'Isaac's' was dark, very dark. Very dark and deserted. Martin held up his arm to check his watch, twisting it to catch any stray beam of light. It was well past the time.

With a mental shrug Martin began to walk back up the alley. As he neared the street, a dark doorway of shadows moved and solidified.

Out of the blackness came a glint of gold and suddenly the boss-man in the round shades was in front of him. With him was Sonny Liston.

"O.K., I'm here, so what do you want?"

Martin stood still, senses straining to penetrate the darkness, where were the others? "I want to buy some Crack!"

"How much?"

"One Key!"

Stick pursed his lips and audibly sucked in air between his teeth. "You' talking some serious money!.... You got it?"

Martin's reply was flat and monosyllabic:

"I got it!"

The man's voice came out of the darkness, suddenly thick with menace: "Well,...I t'ink you'd better give it to me now!"

Martin felt rather than saw the other two in the darkness behind him. He relaxed his shoulders and breathed quietly and deeply. "First I wanna see the stuff?"

Stick snarled his reply: "Fuck you man! We'll just take the money!"

Martin heard the sharp metallic click as Stick loosened the blade in his cane. The steel glinted wickedly as he started to withdraw it.

Instantly, Martin dropped his weight slightly, and smashed the heel of his left foot backwards and upwards into the belly of one of the shadowy figures to his rear, catching him in mid-stride and lifting him off his feet. The air exploded from his paralysed lungs, and before he had even hit the ground Martin spun to his right, the edge of his stamping foot driving sickeningly into the kneecap of the second attacker. As he fell forward, Martin rammed the point of his elbow hard into his throat.

The big bruiser at Stick's side rushed forward with the wickedly keen blade of a machete in his upraised hand. Martin ducked the fierce swing that would have taken his head from his shoulders had it connected, and side-stepping, slammed both hands into the man's back and shoulder, forcing the lumbering attacker off-balance and head first into the wall.

As the big man's face impacted, he dropped to his knees. He shook his head and tried to regain his feet, but before he could rise he felt strong fingers seize his hair and the pinsharp point of Martin's own blade against the back of his neck. He froze like a statue.

Less than 5 seconds had elapsed between the first move and the last!

Adrenaline pumped through his system. With eyes wide and teeth clenched in a snarl, Martin glared at Stick, who had only just had time to fully draw his blade from its sheath. Even in the half-light of the Alley, Martin could tell that Stick was scared. This just hadn't gone according to plan.

He opened his free hand expressively, and lowered the swordstick.

He tried to placate the angry and very dangerous man facing him. "Hey! It's cool man!....cool!"

Martin shouted in his face:

"Cool! Call this fucking cool! This is shit man! I come to you 'cos they said you were the man, and instead you fucking try to rip me off!"

Stick tried another approach: "Listen brother, we had a bit of a misunderstandin'....."

Martin jerked the knife away from the big man's neck and thrust it sharply into Stick's face. "I'm not your fucking brother! I came to do business. If you can't do it, then I'll go somewhere else!"

Stick backed away trying to regain control: "That's cool, man. Look, let's have a drink and talk it over."

Martin released his grip on the big man's dreadlocks and glanced down at the other two on the ground, clutching themselves and groaning in pain:

"Just you and me this time?"

The relief in Stick's voice was evident as he replied: "Yeah man, just you and me!"

He turned and walked away.

As Martin followed him out of the alley he heard with satisfaction the second attacker sobbing in disbelief to his two companions: "Bastard! He broke muh leg! He broke muh fuckin' leg!"

Once back inside the almost deserted club, Stick led Martin back to the same table and motioned him to sit down. He pulled up a seat and sat opposite, leaning his sheathed swordstick against an empty chair.

Martin leaned back, stretching out his legs. He stared at the man opposite: "So, what do I call you?"

The dreadlocks swung, as with a wry smile the man in black gestured towards his swordstick: "They call me 'Stick'......for obvious reasons. Anyhow, who are you man, and what you want with a Key of Crack? You don' look like a user, and I know all the dealers 'roun' here!"

Martin's eyes narrowed, he knew that he had to convince the man opposite that he was no threat to his organisation, or - martial skills or not - he would end up back in the alley with holes in him.

"The name's Martin; and I need the Key to trade for something."

He got the reaction he had hoped for. If there were to be any trading in this part of town, then 'Stick' was going to make very sure that it was by his rules:

"Hey, I make all the deals 'round here..Mr..er..Martin...Me an' my posse run everyt'ing here, so maybe you'd better tell me what you really want!"

Martin knew he was almost hooked; he spoke quietly: "It's heavy!"

"What you mean, man, heavy. How heavy?"

Stick was irritated by the implication that maybe whatever it concerned it was out of his league.

Martin leaned forward across the table: "Is a 9mm Uzi heavy enough?"

Stick flipped up the dark hinged lenses of his glasses and stared at Martin with narrow thoughtful eyes. Eventually he spoke: "That is fuckin' heavy!!"

"Well?" Martin's challenge fell like a stone into the silence which continued for a dozen heartbeats.

At last the beginnings of a tiny smile tugged at the corner of Stick's mouth. He had taken this newcomer's best shot. He obviously didn't know who he was dealing with. Why, with his connections he could supply him with a whole trunk-full of Uzi's! Confident now Stick leaned back expansively:

"No sweat. I can get it man, but maybe it' take a few days."

Martin tried to pin him down: "What do you call 'a few days'?"

"Ah, you know – maybe two, maybe t'ree" He leaned forward again conspiratorially:

"Anyway, as I've seen the way you work......Jus' maybe you can do a little somet'ing for me.....to sort of prove yourself, if you know what I mean?" He left the question hanging in the air.

Martin knew what he meant all right, being handy with his fists would not be enough, he would have to show that his hands were as dirty as Stick's, that way there was no chance that he could be an undercover cop!

"Maybe!"

Stick's teeth gleamed in the half-light:

"Good! Come back tomorrow night; then we'll talk again."

Martin nodded and got up to leave. As he reached the door, Stick motioned to another figure who had been watching invisible from the shadows by the bar. Nodding to Stick, he moved quietly out after Martin.

The black-clad figure sat in thoughtful silence for a few moments, then glanced towards the bar and raised a finger.

The barman hurried over.

"Bring me the phone." He held up a hand as the man started to turn away. "And I think I'll just have a bottle of Sol."

Within a matter of moments he was pushing the slice of lime into the neck of the bottle and sipping the cold beer through it as he dialled.

When the 'phone rang three times at the other end, he hung up and dialled again; after two rings he pressed down the receiver and then dialled for the third time. This time he let it ring.

When the click came as the receiver was lifted he spoke:

"It's me, Stick. I want a meet, it could be int'resting to you."

He sat quietly as the lilting Irish voice on the other end gave him instructions. Satisfied, he hung up and relaxed back in his seat, savouring the sweetly sour taste of the imported Mexican beer.

CHAPTER FORTY-TWO

MALLORCA

Hunter and Juan were sitting quietly, out of sight in the thick shrubbery surrounding the pool area outside the terrorists' apartment in Illetas. The building was a typical holiday apartment block, which would make it easier for Hunter and Juan to move about un-noticed, but they would have to be careful even here not to attract too much attention.

As they waited in the warmth of the Mallorca evening, Hunter glanced at Juan; slim, handsome, eager for the work ahead. A visual memory of Saturday morning matinee's bubbled up into his consciousness.

"Just like a Spanish Errol Flynn" he thought, "in some swashbuckling adventure movie. He can't wait to leap in and kill the bad guys."

It was strange, he mused, how his brain seemed to work on so many levels at the same time.

He was intensely aware of every detail of his surroundings. His eyes constantly checking and rechecking every shadow; his ears tuning into, evaluating and dismissing the sound of breeze-borne revelry, the movement of every passing car, a door slamming shut, a barking dog - it was as if all the sounds for miles around were suddenly within range of his hearing.

In the stillness of another part of his brain Hunter was watching the frenetic activity of his adrenaline suffused nervous system. His breathing was slow and regular, heart rate slightly increased. Palms of his hands a little damp, but then, it was a warm night. Stomach? Hunter checked, fine, no nausea, no urge to urinate; so, everything tuned up and ready for whatever might come.

Nervous? Of course! He remembered Cus D'Amato's advice to the mighty Mike Tyson: "There is no difference between how scared a brave man feels and how scared a coward feels; the only difference is that a brave man acts, whilst a coward runs."

"Mike Tyson where are you when I need you?" The facetious thought wafted up, almost making Hunter laugh aloud. Simultaneously his memory provided the reason for his earlier thoughts about Errol Flynn, for it was right here in Illetas, he realised, that the filmstar adventurer spent so much time in pursuing his conquests!

Straightening up, easing the stiffness from his right knee and with a brief nod to Juan, Hunter pulled a bunch of keys from his pocket and ruffling his hair a little, walked into the building and up the stairway to the third floor.

Effecting a slight stagger for the benefit of anyone who may be watching, he moved down the corridor. Outside, he paused unsteadily, as if drunkenly deciding which key to attempt. Listening carefully he could hear the sound of a TV set. He could just make out through the thin walls that Real Madrid were playing.

"Good!" he thought, that should help, knowing the Spanish love of soccer it would be a fair bet that the match would hold some at least of their attention.

Hunter studied the door. For once, it was quite thick and sturdy, not the usual apartment standard fixing. There would be no way that he could smash it in and get into the apartment before at least four guns would be pointing at him. The door, then, must be the second element.

Rejoining Juan outside the building, Hunter pinpointed the apartment. Like many such edifices, the apartment block had been constructed on a plot of land that had been cut out of a rocky outcrop, thus the garden at the sides actually came level with the second floor. There were large balconies overlooking the garden. Being apartment D, however, it meant that it was impossible to gain direct access to that particular balcony, which was next but one to the end of the building.

"It's got to be the balcony." whispered Hunter.

"Look, you can get to the end one, 3E I suppose, by climbing up from the side of the one beneath, which you can reach from the garden. It's a bit of a jump, but not impossible."

The gleam of Juan's grinning teeth indicated his agreement.

In the darkness of the shrubbery Hunter once again opened the little attaché case and passed over to Juan a short silencer, and one of the shoulder stocks which attached to the butt of the Heckler and Koch. Fitting this automatically switched the gun into 3-burst fire mode, which gave the user 6 three-round bursts with a full clip; with the silencer very quiet and very effective at close range.

Clipping the second stock and silencer to his own weapon, Hunter outlined his plan to Juan, then watched as the tall figure melted into the darkness.

From his vantage point, Hunter saw nothing of Juan's progress until, gaining access to the end balcony on floor two, Juan was forced to balance momentarily on the balcony railing before leaping upwards to grab the floor of the one above.

Hunter's breath caught as the dark figure, silhouetted briefly against the white stucco of the building, scrabbling for a grip. He eased a sigh of relief as the long shadow swung upward and out of sight.

By moving along the balcony, Juan could now see directly into the open sliding glass balcony doors of the next apartment where the four terrorists were waiting for a call that would never now be made.

In position, he raised a hand and gave a quick wave.

Hunter slid the gun inside his open shirt and feeling its comforting cold hardness against his sweating body, he walked boldly into the building and up the stairs. Once again, luck was on his side, he met nobody.

As planned, he rapped sharply on the apartment door.

From the next balcony, Juan watched three heads snap round! Two men had been seated on a couch, watching the football match, and one had been sitting at a table, eating. The forth was out of his line of vision. All three figures were concentrating on the door, fumbling for weapons. Then the fourth man, came into view, also carrying a gun. He moved towards the door, obviously asking who was there. The three behind him made a tight little group.

The moment that the fourth man's hand went out to grip the door knob, Juan leapt onto the balcony and through the open patio windows, spraying the room with rapid-fire bursts. The effect of the special fragmentation bullets was murderous at such sort range. Little rippling pops from the silenced gun went almost un-noticed amongst the roars of the football fans on the television.

The group of figures scattered, hurled apart by the lethal force of the bullets as they tore into flesh and bone.

At the same moment, Hunter who had been listening at the door, fired a burst into the lock and kicked it in, firing into the room, confident that Juan, as planned, would have dropped to the floor to change magazines after his initial onslaught.

It was almost too easy - too quick. All four of the targets had been hit in the first few bursts of fire from Juan. Hunter's bullets changed the direction in which one or two were falling, but that was all. Two were dead, both head-shot. and two were choking on their own blood, jerking and writhing in agony on the blood-spattered marble floor.

As Hunter watched, not shifting his aim for an instant, one gave a convulsive heave and lay still. He walked over to the other who was rolling frantically to and fro, attempting in knees-up spasms to hold in his protruding intestines. Leaning over Hunter shot him through the head. The three bullet burst tore it apart in an explosion of pink-misted ferocity!

"Gooooaaalll! Real Madrid's fans roared their approval from the TV in the corner of the still and otherwise silent room.

It was a good thing, thought Hunter, that these Israeli loads had been specially prepared for close-range work, or there might have been a few surprises in the adjoining apartments. Small but dense, these special rounds were designed to disintegrate on impact, and though still capable of creating a deadly wound, they posed less of a threat of ricocheting and injuring bystanders.

As it was, no outcry or alarm was apparent. They moved

quickly, stepping carefully around the leaking bodies and the spreading pools of blood. The room looked like an abattoir.

Hunter and Juan carefully wiped both weapons - just in case - and placed them in the dead hands of two of the terrorists. Pulling off the rubber gloves, they checked each other front and back for any evidence of the slaughter, and tossing the gloves into the clutter of plates and pots in the kitchen sink, they walked briskly and un-noticed from the apartment.

The cool of the evening breeze felt refreshing on Hunter's hands, still hot and sweating from the rubber. He retrieved the case from its hiding place in the bushes and transferred the little Zeiss binoculars to his trouser pocket.

Walking down the one-way system towards the local bars and restaurants and the local taxi-rank, Hunter paused for a moment and deposited the empty case in one of the overflowing rubbish skips that seemed such a part of the island's scenery.

"Back to Puerta Portals, senor?" Juan's question cut into Hunter's reverie, as they approached a waiting cab. The slim Spaniard looked cool and unruffled by the evening's events.

"Yes, that's it." Hunter eased the tension from his neck muscles:

"Now all we can do is wait for Kennedy to do whatever it is that he's here to do, and then follow him back to try and locate the shipment."

CHAPTER FORTY-THREE

The door of Martin's cheap hotel room slowly opened. With a grunt of satisfaction the dreadlocked figure quietly clicked it shut behind him and moved directly over to the wardrobe. Momentarily fingering the quality of the few garments hanging there, he quickly ran his fingers over the pockets, and finding nothing, turned to the chest of drawers.

Rummaging carefully through socks and underwear, his fingers closed on a black leather wallet. Pulling it out of the drawer, he sat down on the bed and began to go through the contents, forcing himself to ignore the thick wad of twenty pound notes in one section. He peeled open a central flap and withdrew the little collection of newspaper cuttings and documents revealed.

Laying them down beside him, he read with interest of Martin's dismissal from the Metropolitan Police, and the cuttings detailing his complaints of racism against his former colleagues.

Moments later he refolded the papers and slipped them carefully back into the wallet.

Across the street in the run-down 'Bernie's All-Nite Diner' Martin toyed unenthusiastically with the remains of the 'All Day Breakfast' that had seemed the least offensive item on the blackboard menu. His heartburn reminded him that he should have known better.

Finally, he wiped the grease from his lips and took another sip of the dregs of the disgusting brew euphemistically advertised as cafe latte as he waited for his shadow to finish turning his room over and leave to report back to Stick.

He sighed as he realised that this might take some time, and it could well mean that he would be forced to buy another drink. Tea this time, he resolved firmly.

The next evening, in the snug bar of a rundown pub on the fringes of Stick's territory, but not exclusively patronised by blacks, the gang boss sat nursing a scotch, across a low table from a young white couple.

There was nothing extraordinary about them at all, nothing to indicate that they were anything but what they seemed, young, working class, and out for a quiet drink. The girl was reasonably pretty, Stick thought, in an unpolished scruffy way, not at all like the tarted-up white bitches that hung around the posse-members like flies around shit. Slim with long un-styled brown hair, in her worn blue jeans and brown woollen sweater she could disappear in any crowd.

He sipped his drink as he turned his attention to her companion, also casually dressed in jeans and an open-necked shirt. It wasn't necessary to hear his voice to place him as Irish. He was a walking stereotype from his mass of brown curly hair, to his large thick-necked frame and his bright-eyed cheerful freckled pink complexion and plump cheeks. All that was missing sniggered Stick to himself, was a tattoo on his forehead saying "Paddy!"

Naturally, Stick never considered that anyone with one functioning brain cell would take one look at him in his immaculate black leather and festoons of jewellery and see the stereotype of a black pimp.

This early in the evening the bar was never busy, which is why it had been selected for the meet, even so not a word was spoken until the hotel porter stopping in for a homeward wet had finished his drink and left.

The girl leaned forward. "So?"

Stick leaned towards her over the table, conspiratorially. "Wee-ell it's like this you know..."

"Cut the Jamaican crap!" The flat Belfast accented voice cut across him like a whiplash! "I know you can speak English as well as you want to, so don't give us any of the poor immigrant shit, just say why you wanted to see us."

Stick took a deep breath. If anyone in his posse had spoken to him like that, with such...disrespect, he would have their tongue cut out and forced up their arsehole.

This girl was different. He was uneasy in her company; she seemed so sure of herself, not at all overawed by his black masculinity, nor intimidated by his ability to command violence. Not in the least; if anything she always appeared to be somewhat amused by Stick, like an adult over the behaviour of a recalcitrant child.

The problem for Stick was that he knew that she would - and could - kill him at any time without compunction! What was more, she was representing a whole fucking army, a REAL army, with explosives, M60 heavy machine guns, rocket launchers and everything!

Stick took another deep breath. "Right."

She waited, staring coldly in his eyes.

"Look, I know who and what you are."

He held up his hands expressively: "Hey, I'm with you, fuck the authorities I say, and if you want to run your own country, then great, I'm for that." He took another sip of the amber liquid as the girl just stared.

"Well, it's like this, you've done me a lot o' good, what with the guns an' all; but I know you don't give a shit about me or my brethren, what you want is just to fuck up the system, right?"

"I figure that you only backing me 'cos I'se the man to feed whitey with the dope to screw him, and 'cos I got the manpower to shit all over the police and the courts right?"

He waited for her reply, all he got was a cold unblinking stare. He gave up and sat back:

"Ah fuck it!"

He won a minor victory. Intrigued she prompted him:"Go on."

He sat forward again: "There's a guy, a black guy, not from round here, from London, but he wants to buy a piece, not just any piece, but an Uzi!"

Before she could speak he continued:

"Yeah, I know what you thinking, but I've had him checked out, he's some serious bad news, and he's goin' to do some stuff for me, not pretty stuff you understand, messy stuff."

"He had some problem with whitey in the police and now he hates their guts. From what I hear he's goin' back with the Uzi to settle a few scores, but.."

He considered his words carefully: "Seems to me that what I do here, he could do there, and what you want, to fuck up the system, could spread, who knows?"

He fell silent as the girl weighed his words. She glanced at her companion:

"We'll think about it, in the meantime you get him dirty - good and dirty - and then you bring him to us yourself, no-one else mind you, you do it."

Stick spread his hands and pulled a face. She took the hint:
"Oh don't worry, if he checks out O.K. you'll even get a bonus, we've got some good stuff arriving soon, uncut, raw, it'll make you a fortune!"

Stick grinned: "In the meantime what do I tell him about the merchandise?"

"Tell him a grand, and we'll take £750, O.K?"

He nodded, beaming. It wasn't the £250, after all, he made more than that each and every hour of the day, but it was the principle, the larcenous instinct that nothing was for nothing that had put him where he was today. That and the knowledge that he was confirming himself as the main man with these guys in the whole Toxteth area.

That meant a continuing and very safe source of drugs and guns at low prices which he could move on for vast profits and hook hundreds, no thousands, into his web of evil.

It never crossed Stick's mind that in the same way that he used and despised the people in his power, and would dispose of them without a second thought when their usefulness was at an end, this couple across the table looked upon him in the same light.

They weren't interested in drugs, and enlarging a circle of addicts, no, only in as much as it helped to disturb and disrupt the functioning of normal society.

Tie up more and more police in local troubles, encourage the young unemployed to see the authorities as their enemy, spread discontent, overload the courts and the police, do anything and everything to generate hate, envy, confusion and misery, and whilst the poison permeated society the smoke-screen would serve to hide the setting up of safe houses for bombers who would add further confusion to chaos, when the Cease-Fire finally ended, as it inevitably would - and eventually there would be no choice for the British public!

They would become so utterly sick of the state of things that they would demand that the authorities devote their attention to cleaning up England itself, and leave the Irish to their own affairs!

Of course, the General Council would be prepared to offer certain inducements at this stage, such as withdrawing active units entirely from all mainland activities, and - purely as a gesture of good faith - they would be prepared to reveal to the authorities (secretly naturally) full details of all their contacts and activities with the same pawns like Stick and his Jamaican gangster that they had used to bring about the unrest in the first place!

After Stick left, the girl lit a cigarette and blew a cloud of smoke across the table, as if to exorcise some latent image of the flamboyant black. She turned to the big Irishman beside her, finishing the dregs of his stout.

"What do you think?"

He lifted an eyebrow: "You're the boss Maureen, but if your man Stick's sure of him it should be O.K."

He continued as she looked away across the empty bar, as if unconvinced: "It would be a fine thing if we could get ourselves into London again, and this could be the way to do it."

Maureen sighed and finished her drink.

As if making up her mind she got to her feet and crushed out the remains of her cigarette in the chipped glass ashtray. "OK. We'll go along with it, but we'll take no chances, right!"

The big man inclined his head wryly as she strode away, and got up to follow: "God fuckin' help the black bastard if it's a set up." He thought as he made his way towards the door: "Cos if it is, she'll rip his fuckin' balls off!"

CHAPTER FORTY-FOUR

MALLORCA AIRPORT.

Kennedy sat in the noisy and crowded departure lounge, waiting for his flight to Marseilles. One day, he vowed to himself, he would refuse to travel anywhere, especially by air, unless it were first class. He had managed it on occasion, but in general it was deemed best that he lose himself in the crowds of tourist class travellers.

Juan munched his way through what was probably the worst hot-dog in the world. He obviously didn't know it, but the tiny refreshment bar at Mallorca airport was famed for the dryness of its bread rolls and the interesting fashion in which it had patented a process of turning fresh meat into shoe-leather.

Whoever it was that had first established this quaint custom would have been well pleased with the efforts of the current 'chef' to maintain his standards.

As he chewed patiently, Juan was watching the international departures barrier, to make sure that Kennedy didn't have any sudden change of plan.

Hunter, meanwhile was on the 'phone to Mercedes, giving her the number and arrival time of Kennedy's flight so that she could maintain contact with him when he arrived back in Marseilles. It would be too risky for them to travel on the same flight again with the Irishman, so he and Juan would return on the next one and go back to the Hotel and wait for her to call them.

CHAPTER FORTY-FIVE

'Henry's' was loud, but it did have an upstairs bar away from the crush of the packed dance floor, and in Moss-side, Manchester, it was considered to be one of the better night clubs to frequent.

Leaving his woman to get the drinks, a sweating, sharp hair-styled black man pushed his way through the gyrating dancers, through a door and into the relatively quiet coolness of the gents lavatory. Still swaying to the pulsating bass rhythm that could be felt in his belly even through the walls, he edged into the remaining space between two other figures using the urinals.

As his hands reached down to ease his penis through his zip, his head smashed sickeningly into the white glazed wall. The men on either side of him grabbed him by the arms and thrust him bodily into the tiles.

Time, space and reality suddenly went away as his senses scrambled.

Semi-conscious, he was numbly aware of the salty-tasting fluid dripping from his nose, and the wetness from the urinal channel soaking into his shoes.

Behind him Dennis Martin emerged from one of the stalls. He walked up to the rear of the protesting figure.

"Ah! What the fuck's goin' on Man? What..." With a sharp nudge, Martin sent the complaining man's head bouncing forward into the wall once more. As he did he noticed that the hair on the back of his close-cropped skull was shaved into zig-zag lightning patterns.

He didn't relish what he was about to do, but - he rationalised
- it was better than leaving it to Stick's regular enforcers who
would probably chop bits off him with a machete.

"Shut it!" He snarled, his voice thick and heavily accented:
"You need a lesson man, and I'm the teacher. You sell stuff
where you ain't no right to sell, understand? This is Stick's
territory, and he don't like it when arseclarts like you try to
take a piece! So, you got to learn a lesson!"

He drove a short fierce punch into the man's unprotected right
kidney, then another, and another. After one great bellow of
agony the shock overwhelmed the spread-eagled man. With
his back arching in spasms of lung-wrenching pain he dropped
to his knees in the running water. As he fell Martin smashed a
circular elbow strike into the back of his neck.

The men holding him grinned in delight as for the third and
final time the designer hair-styled head hammered into the
unyielding tiles. Like a squashed fly, he hung momentarily on
the wall, then slowly slithered down into a untidy heap as the
two men on either side of him released his pinioned arms; his
flaccid penis drooped comically from his open trousers.

One of the goons laughed in delight and nudged the exposed
member with the toe of his highly polished shoe.

"Just look at dat little ting now Bro." He flipped it with his
toecap. "It don't look too dangerous now." He bent over the
sobbing man:

"Just you think yo ass lucky we don't cut dis little ting off
and feed it to yo woman, yo hear!"

Hawking, he spat thickly into the fallen man's face then straightened up, crushing the dangling penis beneath his right foot as if extinguishing a cigarette butt.

The gobbet of phlegm worked its way down the tear and blood-streaked cheek as his mouth worked like a goldfish's, opening and closing soundlessly. The pain was beyond description, his paralysed lungs unable to provide the means of expressing the overwhelming rivulets of agony spreading throughout his body.

Grinning hugely and nodding at Martin in delighted satisfaction, the two gorillas clapped him enthusiastically on the back as they turned away from the squirming victim and walked out, leaving the blood and tears dripping from his swollen battered features to mingle with the flowing water in the urinal channel.

CHAPTER FORTY-SIX

MARSEILLES.

The tiny radio handset buzzed briefly. Hunter, half-asleep, rolled from the soft armchair and lifted it from the debris of cups, saucers and old sandwiches on the low coffee table.

"Yes." He coughed, easing the phlegm from his throat.

"It's on!" Mercedes' tinny but urgent tones penetrated the fog in Hunter's brain.

"Go on!"

"The target's on the move. He took a taxi to the Container depot, and Juan and I followed him. Now he's in the little Routiers café, and he's just been joined by a man in overalls, he looks like a driver. I think this is it. They've made contact!" The excitement in her voice was evident.

"O.K." Hunter considered briefly. "You stay there and wait for me. If they leave before I arrive get Juan to follow and keep in touch with the walkie-talkie. Where is this café?"

"It's called: 'La Hirondelle', and it's right by the main vehicle entrance, you can't miss it."

"Right. Go back and try to stay out of sight, don't go back inside, or they might notice you. Stay outside and wait for me. If they leave you can contact Juan when they come out. I should be there in ...about 20 minutes."

Outside it had been raining. The evening rush hour traffic had eased, and it was still too early for the cinema and theatre-goers to cause a problem, so Hunter made rapid progress through the wetness which had as much to do with humidity as rain, or so it seemed to him. The dankness of the atmosphere settled clammily on his black leather jacket as he splashed from his hired car through the puddles towards 'La Hirondelle'.

Noting the slim rain-coated figure in a doorway across the potholed road, Hunter ignored Mercedes and paused for a moment peering in through the steamy windows of the transport cafe.

Turning up the collar of his jacket, as if considering the Plat du Jour detailed on the menu in the window, he could make out Juan, sitting alone in a corner, tucking into what appeared to be a bowl of Spaghetti with apparent relish.

Across the room, Kennedy sat sipping from a large coffee cup. Leaning over the table in animated conversation with him sat a skinny runt of a figure enveloped in old blue overalls and an over-large, scruffy donkey-jacket. On his head sat a battered flat cap, the greasy curly hair fighting its way from under it straggled around his ears and down the back of his neck.

As if deciding not to fall prey to the temptations of the culinary delights on offer, Hunter casually turned his back and strolled across the street to join Mercedes in the doorway. "It looks as if you're right." He said softly. "I.....What?"

His sentence was cut short by her urgent nudge.

"Christ!"

It was like a Pop-eye cartoon come to life. Bluto himself had rounded the gates and was walking towards the cafe. Although walking hardly seemed the appropriate way, thought Hunter, to describe the progress of the gargantuan as he approached.

The man was massive! Hunter had seen smaller Sumo wrestlers! This one was not Japanese, however, no, probably an Arab from his looks. He watched as the figure turned sideways to negotiate the cafe entrance. Without a doubt, Hunter knew that 'Bluto' would walk over to Kennedy's table and sit down. He also knew with absolute certainty that this was the shipment's bodyguard, and protector. And he also knew that he was going to have to deal with him sooner or later!

Moments later the door opened again, and the skinny runt appeared. With a quick glance at the threatening sky, he turned towards the container depot.

Hunter thought quickly: "We'll follow him. Juan will stay with the Irishman, and with luck this one'll lead us to the shipment."

Hand in hand like lovers oblivious to the elements, they strolled apparently aimlessly, but always with the hurrying figure in sight. Through the open gates and past the lights of the dispatch office, then past the long lines of parked containers and their tractor units, some with little closed curtains as their drivers slept, some with all the comforts of home, even coloured televisions playing behind the screened windows.

Along row after row of the massive vehicles, moving always in the shadows thrown by the harsh security lights, they followed the scruffy figure until he stopped suddenly and hauled himself up into the cab of a huge M.A.N. diesel tractor and trailer combination.

"Fine." Hunter breathed into Mercedes' ear. "This looks right, but I'd better try and get a look to make sure it's not a decoy. You'd better give him something to think about while I'm getting in."

Inside the cab, Joseph Donahue busied himself with his night-time ablutions. He dragged the bottle of the Hirondelle's red wine from his voluminous jacket and set it between the pedals at the side of the make-shift bed arranged along the seats. He struggled out of the jacket and slung it carelessly along the back shelf. Kicking off his wet boots, he leaned over and from the glove compartment he extracted a well-thumbed Eros porno photo magazine. His imagination already full of bulging breasts and pouting lips sucking ecstatically on thick-veined penises, Joseph reached over to draw closed the curtains.

His heart stopped!

In the pool of light across the driveway between the rows of trucks moved a figure from his fantasies. Mercedes tilted her head to one side, and with half-closed eyes let the front of her coat fall open to reveal.....

Donahue's eyes focused with a start upon her two naked breasts, thrusting obscenely into the stark white light. As she swayed her hips enticingly she allowed the coat to drop open even more. Against the whiteness of her nakedness he could make out the dark triangle of her pubic hair.

It would have made no difference if an atom bomb were to be detonated in the next cab, Joseph Donahue would not have noticed.

He had almost forgotten to breathe as he watched mesmerised as Mercedes ran her long fingers lingeringly down her exposed belly, through the tiny bush and down along the slit of her vagina.

Twisting her head to one side, Mercedes leaned back against the rear wheel arch of the next tractor unit, and opened her legs a little wider, allowing easier access to her sliding, pulling, penetrating fingers.

Blood pounding in his ears, as if in a dream, Joseph reached down and eased his aching erection from his trousers. In time with the movements of Mercedes' hand he drew the foreskin backwards and forwards over the bulging tip.

Mrs Katherine Donahue, a large, loud woman, fat-thighed with shapeless no-nippled flour-sacks for breasts, with not a hint of an erogenous zone to her white flabby body, had never - not even in the early Guinness-happy days - never ever brought such iron to his penis. Fathering four children had been as unmemorable to Joseph as his taxi-fare conquests; tarts so drink-befuddled that even the obligatory groans of simulated passion only served to underline the supreme sordidness of their barter. A ride for a ride!

Had Donahue been less of a weasel, more of a man, then perhaps he would have climbed down from his cab and sunk himself deep into that enticing, hypnotic vision.

In the back of the trailer, Hunter was busy forcing the lid from a long wooden case bearing the legend "Agricultural Parts, Tractor. His knife blade bent alarmingly, but held. With a final creak of protest, the nails gave and the top slid back. "Bingo!"

Unless of course AK47's were an integral design feature of

tractors these days, thought Hunter. No decoy then, but the real thing. So now the only problem was how to make sure it never arrived at its destination, and how to deal with the driver and Kennedy, not to mention 'Bluto.'

He replaced the rough wooden lid and forced it home as quietly as possible, eager to get out and away before whatever Mercedes was doing to distract the driver's attention ceased to be effective.

He need not have worried, Donahue was at that peak stage of sexual arousal known to all men. Nothing on earth could have stopped the fierce and frantic movements of his hand as he jerkily climaxed over the unopened Eros.

Hunter was clicking home the final padlock when he froze. "And what's this then?"

Kennedy's inquisitive brogue cut through the silence like a wickedly honed open razor.

Hunter peered carefully around the rear of the container, hand slipping onto the re-assuring revolver butt. He didn't want to do it here, but if necessary....

Kennedy's tall silhouette towered over Mercedes. Her coat was tight shut, her face twisted up to the light, cheeks gripped between his powerful fingers.

"M'sieu, si vous voulez....il n'est pas cher...?" She smiled.

"Vamoose! Skedadle! Allez!" Kennedy's amused tones followed her as he thrust her away and into the safety of the darkness. "And that's a novel way of drumming up business!"

Holding his breath, Hunter feared that the sound of his

beating heart must surely be heard.

With a final shake of his head Kennedy swung himself up into the cab: "Now Joe, I hope you weren't tempted, you've to stay in the cab not follow your cock after some tart!" Beneath the chiding banter there was no mistaking the steely hardness.

Covering his confusion with bluster and his semen stained magazine with his cap, Donahue missed his chance of seeing Hunter in the rear-view mirror as he slipped noiselessly away.

Mercedes pulled her coat tightly about her, shivering, not simply from the cold and damp, but from the memory of those hard eyes and steely fingers gripping her chin. With a shudder, she thrust her balled-up underwear deeper into her pocket, then gasped as she felt a slight touch on her sleeve.

She spun, then sighed with relief as she looked into Hunter's twinkling eyes:

"Quite a show, sweetheart." His face split into a broad grin at her discomfiture: "I could hardly keep my mind on the job."

She kicked him sharply on the shin, in mock anger. "Well? What did you find?"

Hunter's expression sobered immediately: "It's the right one all right. I opened one of the cases, and it's full of rifles!"

"What now then?" She asked.

Hunter slipped her arm through his and began to move back towards the entrance.

"First, we'd better find Juan.."

"No need Señor Jim."Juan's voice came out of the shadows close by. "I followed the Irishman back to the trailer. Do you wish that I stay with him if he goes back to the hotel?"

Hunter nodded to him as he moved into the light: "No, Juan. There's no way he's going anywhere now without that shipment, so we'll concentrate on that. When it moves, he'll move."

He thought quickly, and turned to Juan again: "You stay in sight of the trailer; we'll go back to the hotel and try and come up with some way of making sure that it never gets delivered. Call in if there's any sign of movement."

Juan grinned, his teeth gleaming in the semi-darkness. "No problem."

Back in the comfort of the hotel room, Mercedes excused herself briefly, and made straight for the cleansing warmth of a hot shower, emerging from the bedroom some twenty minutes later, clad in a fresh denim shirt and jeans. Meanwhile Hunter had made do with towelling dry his damp hair and swallowing mouthfuls of steaming hot coffee. He lifted his head and smiled at her as he bent over the confusion of road maps spread over the carpet.

He spoke, his voice quiet and thoughtful, as if summing up an academic dilemma: "The problem is to stop them - well, to get them to stop, especially when they're going to be ready for trouble - and to do it somewhere where we can at least stand a chance of getting them over the border into Spain so that your boss can go to work on them."

Mercedes sat on the corner of the couch: "Is it necessary to take the whole shipment, can we not simply, well, I don't know.....destroy it somehow and...?"

"Just take the men, you mean? Ye-es."

He pulled a face as he stared thoughtfully at the maps, then continued: "But somehow I don't think that they'll be so easily parted from the shipment, and anyway we can't just lose crates of arms and ammunition, not just like that. And if we blow it up it would attract the attention of every living soul for miles around."

He chewed at his lower lip: "No. If there were just some way we could hijack the lot of them, shipment and all....but how to get them to stop without getting suspicious....what could do it?"

His voice trailed off as he mentally flicked through the possibilities: "Road-works perhaps? No." He answered himself: "Too suspicious."

Mercedes cut into his train of thought: "James, perhaps they would stop for an accident, if we could arrange..."

Hunter gave a brief shake of his head: "No. They might not stop, and anyway it would be practically impossible to stage, it's too elaborate, and would need the involvement of too many people." Restlessly he got to his feet and began to pace the room, heedless of the scattered maps at his feet, whilst Mercedes sipped from a mug of long-cold coffee, wondering if she might chance Hunter's sarcasm by lighting up a much needed Gouloise.

Her eyes rested warmly on Hunter as he walked up and down, lost in thought.

A powerful man, with much presence. A man to depend on, she mused, but not to cross. Not overly tall, his body perhaps just beginning to show its years. She noted the hint of grey just starting to lighten the sides of his thick brown hair - it would be better for cutting, she decided - and the almost Latinate darkness of his complexion.

A man's man, not one who would take easily to the mundaneness of ordinary life.....but perhaps with the right woman.....

Mercedes knew of his recent loss, it had been detailed in the file shown to her by Col. Rodriguez in Madrid, but she had also felt his almost animal need for relief, and his soft gentleness in the aftermath. Intuitively she had touched and recognised the loneliness which was held in secret at the centre of his maleness. Who knew: "Que sera, sera.."

Oblivious to the turn of his companion's thoughts, Hunter spun on his heel, eyes alight with excitement. "Police! What will everyone always stop for? The Police, of course!"

He punched the air with a clenched fist: "Now let's see the maps again."

On hands and knees they traced the various possible routes which could take the shipment across country to board a ship for the final leg across the Irish sea.

There were only two main routes, the quieter, Hunter noted with satisfaction, running fairy close to the Pyranees. If they could do it there then perhaps there was a chance after all of taking the shipment up through the mountains and over the border. Selecting the spot, both on the preferred route and on the other as a back-up, just in case, was simply a matter of logic. A quiet stretch of road, away from towns and villages, no side roads for possible ways of escape, it was all academic.

But how to set it up? There was no way they could get real Gendarme's uniforms or police cars, so it would have to be something that would stand up to inspection until it was too late. Workmen? No, not enough authority.

Suddenly the answer flashed into Hunter's brain, memories of a hot frustrating family holiday journey in Cornwall swam back, and he could see again the long lines of cars and caravans on the tiny country roads being further delayed by the bureaucratic logic that dictated that a sunny holiday weekend would be the perfect time to hold a traffic census! That was it, then, a census check point with police in the background, supervising, that would do it!

What would they need? Hunter's mind raced. "Traffic cones! "Easy."The streets of Marseilles, like those of any city anywhere abounded with traffic-jamming road-works and cones in abundance. It would be a simple matter to 'borrow' a few.

A fierce grin split his face as the plan came together. They would need overalls for the census taker, oh yes, and a clipboard. Probably Mercedes, he thought, she would disarm any possible suspicion; whilst he or Juan - in a blue shirt, dark plain tie, military style coat, big black boots yes.... he nodded in satisfaction, it should look O.K. from a distance at least, and by then it would be too late!

Of course, it all depended on timing. If Kennedy decided to move the shipment before the shops opened and they had bought the clothes, then..But even then, Hunter realised, they could still do it. As long as Juan stayed on their tail in the hired car, then he and Mercedes could still buy the clothes, hire a suitably official blue van, fill it with cones and catch up.

It would be necessary anyway, he realised, to overtake the

truck at some point in order to get enough distance ahead to set the trap.

Hunter looked at his watch. It was almost time for him to take a cab to the container depot and relieve Juan who was still on watch. In that case, he decided, it had better be Juan who played the policeman and bought the clothes.

He rolled over on his back and stretched his cramped muscles like a cat, confident and eager now that the plot was hatched. Ignoring the crumpled maps, he was clearing the debris from his mind. Beginning the focusing process which centred on the image of Kennedy, smiling, debonair Kennedy, good-looking sophisticated Kennedy, Murdering bastard Kennedy! Wife-killing Kennedy...!

The cold hate that suffused his thoughts like an icy douche of freezing water seemed like an old friend to Hunter, distancing him from any hint of mercy or self-recrimination.

Giving him freedom to kill.

Of course, it also cut him off from the freedom to live an ordinary life, like an ordinary person, subject to ordinary constraints and normal emotions. It never occurred to Hunter that all this could equally apply to Kennedy, and probably did.

Perhaps it was just as well, for to understand Kennedy might be to forgive him, and then where would he be?

Hunter shook his head sharply as if to free his mind of the intruding, unsettling thoughts. He clambered to his feet and reached for his coat, checking it for the reassuring weight of the automatic in the side pocket.

"I'll go and relieve Juan now, and fill him in with the details,

So, first thing in the morning you know what to do?"

Mercedes held out her hand, and Hunter grasped it, pulling her to her feet. She smiled and nodded, and leaning forward offered up her cheek, gripping his arm tightly as he placed a gentle kiss upon its softness.

"Take care James." She flapped her hands at him, shooing him out.

"Now go, I need to get my sleep." And have a cigarette! She thought longingly to herself, closing the door behind him.

CHAPTER FORTY-SEVEN

The late evening sun painted thick black shadows almost horizontally across the tree-lined Autoroute. Leaving behind the last in a line of innumerable small villages with their single main streets and shabby white plastered houses sheltering from the oppressive humidity behind cool wooden shutters, Donahue kept their speed at a constant 80 k.p.h.

It was refreshingly cool in the air-conditioned interior of the cab, and in normal circumstances Donahue would have been whistling tunelessly. A snarl from the unappreciative Algerian with the unpronounceable name and, as far as Donahue was concerned, very uncertain parentage, however, had cut off his version of Sinead O'Conner's latest offering in the bud.

"Ah. What would he know?" thought Joseph, "probably not used to listening to anything more refined than the sound of camel's mating, and," he sniggered to himself, "come to think of it, from the way he smells in this heat I wouldn't be surprised if he actually took the part of a male camel himself!"

The huge Algerian was dozing, his massive bulk wedged firmly between the diminutive driver and the elegant Kennedy, his hands, like two bunches of bananas, thought Donahue, almost hid the dull grey Uzi lying on his lap.

Kennedy himself sat, impervious to the smell that even the air-conditioning couldn't eliminate, and to the occasional attempts at conversation from the driver. Eyes constantly flickering from the traffic on the road ahead to that in the huge rear-view mirror, checking, always checking, never for one moment did Liam allow the soporific rhythmic strobe-like effect of the regular lines of trees along the roadside to lull him into inattention.

It had been hours since they had left the suburbs of Marseilles, and they were making good time; there was no reason for Kennedy to expect any trouble, no-one should know anything about him or the shipment, but he was a professional.

For some reason his mind jumped back to the Shadow V and Mountbatten.

A very professional job. Yes, but not on the part of his two idiot accomplices, who, leaving the scene, were captured at a road block set up by the local police in order to check vehicles for road tax. And the two had not even bothered to agree on a story to account for them being in the area! Not much chance of glory like that anymore if the general council had their way......still, they weren't the only ones who could make use of his talents!

Of all the thoughts in all the world, and whatever Gods ordain them, it was the supreme irony that one about a road block had to enter Kennedy's mind at that moment!

As the slight bend straightened, Kennedy and Donahue could see a line of red and white cones, narrowing down the road into one lane. In the distance he could see a Gendarme waving on a slowing car.

At the side of the road a dark blue van was parked. A slim figure in blue overalls, carrying a clip-board under one arm walked over to the gendarme and stood next to him.

"Ah. Now what?" exclaimed Donahue, easing off the accelerator and beginning to apply the brakes, as the truck approached the policeman who began to flag them down.

Kennedy was uneasy. The train of thought about roadblocks was reverberating in his head. He dug the dozing guard savagely in the ribs.

In an instant the shocked giant jerked into wakefulness, automatically snapping off the Uzi's safety catch. Kennedy eased his own weapon free from beneath his left armpit and cocked it. In the rear-view mirror he could see a dark Renault pull up behind them, the Raybans of the driver glinting in the reflected rays. It came to a halt, waiting its turn at the census ....or...

Kennedy's head snapped round as the uniformed figure moved to the driver's side, whilst the girl in the overalls clasping a clipboard to her chest approached him on the passenger's side.

"Votre papiers Messieux, deux minutes seulement, s'il vous plait!" The gendarme reached up to the driver's door handle.

The bad feeling in Kennedy's head worsened.

He looked down at the girl, just at the instant that she raised her head in a disarming smile.

That face! That smile!

Before Mercedes could say a word, Kennedy jerked up his gun and shot her through the right eye! Simultaneously, reaching across the numbed driver the Algerian blew out the off-side window in a deafening burst of fire, catching Juan directly in the face!

As if the universe were in slow-motion, time seemed to thicken and almost stop for Hunter.

From around the rear of the trailer he saw Mercedes fall backwards from the force of the shot. A fine pink spray seemed to hang in the still air as the bullet drilled through her brain, blowing away a brilliant chip of white bone from the back of her head! Her gun, concealed by the clipboard, fell with her.

As if forcing his way through treacle he moved along the side of the trailer towards her, keeping his gun aimed at the passenger's door.

Crouching down beneath the trailer, Hunter saw a figure drop from the driver's side. He snapped off a quick shot, the big Algerian cursed violently as the bullet smashed into his leg, dropping him in a heap at the roadside. Twisting round he loosed off a burst from the Uzi which tore splintering groves from the surface of the road inches from Hunter.

A second burst forced him to duck behind one of the wheels, just as another figure dropped lightly from the cab and ran like the wind towards the parked van. A final spray of bullets from the giant, followed by desperate metallic clicking and savage cursing told Hunter that 'Bluto' was out of ammunition.

Warily he chanced a quick peek around the wheel. He could see the injured bodyguard hopping and limping towards the van which suddenly lurched into life and began a desperate three-point turn. Waving and shouting, the guard almost reached the passenger's door before it gathered speed and roared away from him up the road.

Almost incoherent with fear, rage and pain, Bluto shouted imprecations at the vanishing Citroen, and clutching his injured thigh, staggered off towards the trees.

Hunter moved carefully and slowly around to the open truck door, weapon held high. Who was driving the van? Who had got away, Kennedy or the driver? Who was left, waiting, waiting for him?

His eyes flickered briefly over the still twitching body that once was his comrade. The top of Juan's head had been completely blown away by the shattering impact of the Algerian's bullets, one startled eye gazed back uncomprehendingly at Hunter from the bloody ruin.

It took several lifetimes to ease quietly along the side of the cab, and several aeons without breathing to nerve himself up to seize the door, hurl it further open and thrust the muzzle of the Walther PPK into the face of....a petrified, sobbing, trembling Joseph Donahue!

In a towering rage, Hunter hauled the abject, terrified figure down from the cab. Begging for mercy, Donahue wept hysterically.

Hunter was stuck! He couldn't leave him to run off, but he had to get after the fleeing bodyguard.

He grabbed the driver by the hair and viciously jerked him onto his knees by the front wheel. Keeping the gun aimed at the back of his head, Hunter forced the weeping man to lie face down next to the still bleeding corpse and place his left hand flat on the ground behind the wheel.

Clambering swiftly up into the cab, he momentarily disengaged the brakes and rolled the huge front wheel back onto Donahue's hand. Screaming in agony, as the small bones cracked and crunched, the driver leaned his head against the wheel in despair. His trousers rapidly staining from release of his bladder and the rivulets of Juan's blood, he was going nowhere.

Thrusting home a new clip as he ran, Hunter made for the grass verge where the hobbling bodyguard had disappeared.

He wasn't hard to track. From the amount and colour of blood on the road and the grass Hunter's bullet had obviously hit an artery. Cautiously, bent double, Hunter followed the beaten-down bushes and the dark red evidence of his marksmanship, every nerve taut in expectation of a surprise attack.

He needn't have bothered. Almost falling over the Algerian's outstretched legs, Hunter practically trod on him, lying in the undergrowth. The unfocussed gaze and the blue-grey pallor of his normally swarthy features told their own story. His eyes rolled as Hunter knelt beside him. Trembling with anger and frustration, he seized him by the throat. Jamming his gun into the dying man's face he spat out his rage:

"Where'll that Bastard go?"

He shook the Algerian's head fiercely from side to side in an attempt to pull him back from oblivion. A single frothy bubble of spittle was all the answer Hunter got. With a snarl of frustration he dropped the corpse's head back onto the grass and got to his feet.

Black despair mingled with a terrible anger as he stood over Mercedes' slim body, lying as if not dead, but only asleep. The beauty of her face unmarked on the side that lay upwards.

Only the darkening halo on the surface of the road told a different story. Numb and aching as the adrenaline left his system, Hunter climbed slowly up into the cab and released the air brakes. With a snort the massive vehicle rolled backwards, releasing the crushed hand of the driver. Wrenching the brakes back on, Hunter swung down and, ignoring the sobbing Donahue, stared down at the almost headless body of his former companion. Juan had not had a chance either. Whatever had tipped off the Irishman was not evident to Hunter. It was uncanny. It should have worked!

With a mental shrug, he straightened up and walked to the back of the trailer. He stood, leaning for a few moments against the tailgate, then he threw back his head and roared out his pain and anger to the heavens: "Whatever it takes, Irishman you Bastard!....and as long as it takes!"

Shuddering gulps of air squashed down the fearful overwhelming anguish, but the process ground away yet another micron of his humanity.

CHAPTER FORTY-EIGHT

Close to the Spanish border, the container lorry was parked in a quiet lay-by at the side of the road, by a telephone box. The driver, Donahue, now with his hand crudely bandaged, waited sullenly at the wheel whilst Hunter spoke to Colonel Rodriguez.

His voice was terse: "About ten, fifteen minutes, O.K?"

The Colonel's reply was equally brief, Hunter hung up and climbed back into the cab. He motioned Donahue to move off, and with a sharp hiss, Donahue released the air brakes and, trying to ignore the ache in his hand he manoeuvred the truck back onto the road.

In the distance Hunter could see the border crossing post approaching. He leaned across the cab and tapped Donahue on the knee with his gun. The driver nodded nervously, he was in pain. The throbbing of his crudely bandaged hand reminded him of Hunter's callousness each time he turned the wheel. He began to slow the vehicle.

A hundred metres from the barrier, just a little outside of the pools of light surrounding the post, Hunter turned to Donahue:

"Right, slow down and be ready!" "And don't forget….." he stared bleakly at the trembling man: "I will have you in sight at all times, so if you should be foolish enough to try to get away….."

He slid his automatic from its holster, he lifted it slowly and caressed the side of Donahue's face with the barrel. He snapped the slide back with a sudden jerk, jacking a round into the chamber. The metallic click sounded deafening in the frightened driver's ear.

There was no need for Hunter to verbalise the threat. Pitiful as Donahue's life undoubtedly was, he wanted to hang on to it for as long as possible, and he had no intention of pushing his luck with this fiend of a man!

Satisfied, Hunter leaned out of the blind-side cab window and took careful aim at the rear wheel. The sharp crack of the bullet was lost in the bursting of the tyre.

Donahue eased the container lorry to a stop, and sat there motionless behind the wheel as Hunter jumped down and made a show of irritation over the blow-out for the benefit of any frontier guard who might be watching.

Assuming a look of long-suffering resignation, Hunter hunched his shoulders a little and walked across to the glass-fronted Customs post.

The door opened before his knuckles could rap the glass. The uniformed figure of a customs officer stood there, wiping crumbs from a walrus moustache that Hunter had only seen the like of before on a torn old 'Kitchener needs you!' World War One poster that had adorned the wall behind the c.o.'s desk of his first training unit. His jaw worked slowly on some final morsel as he appraised Hunter with his head judiciously nodding up and down.

"You 'ave trouble, M'sieu?"

The heavily accented voice was full of self-congratulation as he selected the correct language with which to address Hunter.

"Oui. Je regret, M'sieu,.."

Hunter searched for the words, then threw up his hands in disgust:

"No. I'm sorry, I'm afraid my French is a little rusty."

The Walrus beamed expansively in the satisfaction of superiority.

"We have had a blow-out, a puncture, perhaps I may telephone for help?"

Chewing ruminatively, the officer moved back from the doorway, beckoning Hunter into the office. Returning to his newspaper strewn table bearing the remnants of bread sticks, wine and dirty plate, the Customs man waved a plump hand towards the wall phone.

" 'elp yourself, M'sieu." He gazed at Hunter thoughtfully; "Er, Perhaps you will need assistance with ze number?"

"No thank you." Hunter shook his head. "We have our own arrangements, and luckily there's a garage fairly close to here."

He moved over to the telephone and as the unfinished bottle of red wine reclaimed the official's attention he dialled the number given to him earlier by Col. Rodriguez when he had made his report.

Less than five kilometres away, on the Spanish side of the border in a tumble-down garage, the plan devised by Hunter and the Colonel following the disaster at the road block was in operation. At one end of the main work bay a large figure in greasy mechanic's overalls sat drumming his fingers irritably and incessantly on a tool covered wooden bench, filling every nook and crevice of the workshop with the pungent smell of cigar smoke.

Over in one corner, surrounded, almost hidden amongst the entrails of a battered Citroen van, the owner shot nervous glances at the large man perched precariously on two legs of wooden stool, flicking absently through the pages of an old and well-fingered soft-porn magazine.

A wide no-go area centred upon the colonel, similarly clad men glanced nervously in his direction, but skirted around him like minnows around a shark, the last one to encroach upon his territory to offer coffee retired with ears burning from the savage barks of invective!

The sudden jarring ring of the 'phone froze all movement in the room with the exception of the colonel, who leaned forward and snatched the receiver off the cradle. "Si!" He bellowed into the mouthpiece.

"Muy bien" The relaxation of the furrows on his forehead and easing of his shoulders spoke volumes in body language. He leaned back, almost defying gravity to do its worst, calm and unruffled once again. "Yes I speak English." He played along to Hunter's masquerade.

"That should be no problem, Señor." He listened while Hunter detailed his tale of woe. "We can be there in about 30 minutes, Señor, and we will soon have you mobile."

He hesitated briefly. "Ahh, is everything prepared for us, so we do not waste any of your valuable time?" He listened and nodded. "Muy bien, adios Señor."

With a shout to one of the blue-overalled figures, the Colonel crushed the stub of his cigar into an overloaded ashtray and leapt to his feet. Lithely for such a big man, he clambered up into the driving seat of a large battered tow-truck, gunning the engine into life with a shattering roar in the tinroofed garage. He forced it clumsily into gear and lurched off, barely allowing his companion time to climb aboard.

The owner breathed a sigh of relief as the quiet, firm-eyed group of young men silently and unhurriedly got into a dark metallic grey BMW and eased their way smoothly out of the pot-holed yard, in the clattering wake of the breakdown wagon.

It was now fully dark. Hunter stretched himself wearily, rubbing the gritty tiredness from his eyes. He glanced across the cab at the abject crumpled figure of Donahue, curled up in a fitful troubled sleep behind the wheel. The colonel won't have to lean on him very hard, he thought to himself, if ever anyone had chosen the wrong profession it was Joseph Donahue. He just wasn't cut out for this sort of stuff.

How right he was!

In Joseph's dreams now he was back home again, in Flannery's bar, downing another deep dark Guinness, touting for the odd taxi job to maintain his supply. Ah Dear God! even in his dreams he couldn't quite figure out how the illness of the wife's brother, a large roll of banknotes, a surreptitious meeting with shadow men, "generals" they were called, and the possession of a current HVC licence, had led him to this.

He would talk if pressed all right. He would talk if even asked nicely! But as to what he could say...

Hunter's head snapped up as he caught the flash of headlights approaching from the Spanish side of the border.

He watched as the breakdown truck pulled into the lights of the frontier post.

With a casual wave, the Spanish frontier guard waved the truck through, and on towards the French section.

Under the light, Hunter watched walrus moustache come out of his office, brush himself down once more, and go up to the driver.

A brief inspection of papers, and a cursory look around the sides and back of the lorry, and it was bumping its way towards them, leaving the plump figure to retrace his steps back into his office and the few crumbs possibly still fresh enough to sop up the dregs of what had been a very satisfactory bottle of wine. The faint feeling of sadness he always felt when contemplating the end of such a bottle was fleeting, mitigated by the knowledge that there were still three more bottles in the filing cabinet.

The truck drove up to the container lorry, and then past it, finally reversing up to the rear of it, effectively concealing the back of the trailer from the customs post. Two figures climbed down from the cab. Hunter jumped lightly down and walked to meet them. Gripping the Colonel's meaty hand, Hunter stared for a moment into his pain-shadowed eyes, almost shocked by the repressed emotion he saw there. Then, for the benefit of the customs officer, he made a show of calling attention to the offending tyre.

He marched off towards the rear of the wagon, with Rodriguez and his companion in his wake. As they reached the comparative concealment of the back of the two trucks, the big man spoke softly:

"Where are they?" The gentleness of his normally boisterous

tones and the sadness in his eyes spoke volumes.

"In the back." Hunter nodded to the rear doors of the container. Swallowing the sudden lump in his throat, he turned away sharply and began to unlock the heavy doors. He felt the colonel's heavy hand touch him on the shoulder. He turned. What could he say?

For a brief moment they stood, the older, larger, strong featured man and the younger, taller - almost boyish faced, sharing the intimacy of each other's grief.

Rodriguez abruptly turned away and began spouting a stream of orders in Spanish at his colleague, who had been unloading equipment from the breakdown truck. As Hunter swung open the container doors he could feel the lurch as the jack began to ease the flat tyre off the ground.

With a glance in the direction of the customs post, Hunter climbed up into the back and began to heave aside some of the heavy crates. Hidden from the view of the official, Rodriguez had undone some connecting bolts in the flat, deep base of the breakdown truck beneath the lifting crane to reveal an empty compartment.

Manhandling the last of the wooden cases aside, Hunter could see the plastic-wrapped bodies of Mercedes, Juan and the big bodyguard, lying there like so many rolls of carpet. Urgently he began to tug and slide them out of their hiding place and with the Colonel's help, into the secret compartment.

Hunter blanked his mind off as he eased the slim roll containing Mercedes' lifeless form into the narrow darkness. Juan was hardly more difficult, as if even in death he wanted to help as much as he could.

Hunter sneaked another look around the back of the trailer towards the customs post.

His heart nearly stopped!

Unnoticed by the mechanic working on the wheel, the portly shape of the customs official was looming up out of the shadows, apparently duty, or curiosity, or simply the desire to talk to somebody had briefly overcome his slothfulness.

Gesturing frantically to Rodriguez, Hunter dropped down and hastened over to intercept him. Rodriguez cursed silently and horribly, and turned back to the last of the bodies.

Tugging and heaving frantically, he hauled the corpse of the huge Algerian across the tailgate and straining, face purple with the effort, began to force it into the remaining space. He could hear Hunter attempting to delay the lugubrious official, but it seemed that he liked to walk whilst talking, and in spite of Hunter's efforts their voices came nearer.

In a cold sweat, Rodriguez pulled savagely at the body as part of the plastic sheeting worked loose and snagged upon a raised bolt. Furiously he heaved on the slippery material, it was stuck fast. With a snarl of anger he heaved again. With a jerk it tore free, the plastic peeling away on the protruding metal.

With only seconds to spare Rodriguez forced the body into place and slammed the secret tailgate into place.

Unnoticed, the blood from the dead bodyguard's gaping artery, kept away from the congealing air by the plastic sheet, began to run from the hole and drip down, through gaps in the trailer base, onto the gravel by the Colonel's shoes.

With a sigh of relief Rodriguez clipped in the final retaining pin and straightened up, just as Hunter and the guard came around the back of the truck.

"Vous êtes finis, M'seu?" The big dark eyes gazed interestedly around. The Colonel looked over at the bent figure releasing the tension on the jack. "Oui. Peut etre cinq minutes seulement, je pense." "Eh. Bien!" The walrus showed no signs of moving. He stared with all the fascination of those unfit and disinclined to manual labour at the mechanic straining to haul away the heavy jack.

Hunter caught the Colonel's eye and shrugged. Then he froze! Something moved where it should not!

He stared. A drip, no a series of drips, ran along the underside of the tow-truck until they reached the lowest point from where they dropped, forming a small black puddle at the Colonel's feet!

Seeing the querulous look on Hunter's face, the Colonel followed his meaningful gaze.

He gave a start, covered immediately with a slight cough to cover his involuntary response. As the official turned a sympathetic eye, Rodriguez leaned back against the tailboard, wiping the drips on the back of his overalls scuffing the ground with his feet as he coughed again, obliterating the telltale little puddle of blood.

Spraying spittle the Colonel bent forward in a paroxysm of coughing, forcing the startled official to retreat. With a faint air of distaste the walrus grunted and marched purposefully back to his sanctum.

"That's what you get for bothering to be polite." He thought as he crunched across the gravel, now I expect I'll catch a bloody disease." His equanimity returned as he recalled the newly opened bottle, left to breathe, awaiting his return.

"Madre de Dios!" muttered the Colonel, transferring another grease stain from his sleeve to his forehead as he watched the retreating figure.

"Be quick, we must go. He probably will not wish to be disturbed again so soon."

With a heave, Hunter, the Colonel and the mechanic hoisted the jack onto the back of the truck and clambered rapidly aboard their respective vehicles. Wasting no time both motors roared into life and Donahue eased off the air brakes with a squeal as he swung the giant lorry onto the road behind the pickup truck.

In seconds they were at the barrier. The door to the office shut with a noticeable slam behind the disgruntled official. Was he to get no peace at all? This was getting to be too much!

He marched up towards the container lorry, waving the Colonel and his bloody cargo through without a second glance. In a scattering of gravel the breakdown truck lurched forward and moments later gathered an escort as the grey BMW waiting just out of sight moved in behind it.

Checking the paperwork for the container lorry took no time at all, and in the cab Hunter leaned back easing the tight tension knots from his shoulders as he did so.

As they were waved through the Spanish side they could see the Colonel waiting at the side of the BMW. The breakdown truck was nowhere in sight, obviously it was now en route to somewhere quiet where its sorry cargo could be transferred to a more fitting conveyance. Hunter motioned Donahue to pull up behind the parked car.

Carefully, like an old man, Hunter climbed down, his eyes dark with exhaustion. He felt spent now in the aftermath of the operation.

As he dropped to the road, one of the blue overalled young men swung up on the driver's side and motioned Donahue to slide over into Hunter's place. Leaning across the cab he handcuffed Donahue by the wrist of his injured hand and clipped the other bracelet through the door arm rest. Satisfied, he slid back into the driver's seat and with a crunching of gears the truck and its container load of arms began its final journey towards Madrid.

The Colonel put an arm around Hunter's shoulder and urged him gently into the waiting car. There was much to discuss, and many drinks to down, and many more plans to make, but first ....but first came the welcome relief of sleep to knit up a very ragged sleeve of care as the motion of the car soothed the Irishman's frayed nerves and rocked him into temporary forgetfulness.

CHAPTER FORTY-NINE

The Cyprus registered freighter "*Clotilda*" was an old rust-bucket.

Broad in the beam and with leaky welds along its seams, it bludgeoned its way through the slight swell of the grey Irish Sea. Owned by a German shipping company, it had been a long, long time since the ancient tub had made a profit by carrying a legitimate cargo.

The owner of the line, Walter Schultz, had for years now been a proven and trustworthy ally to various political dissident factions, provided anyone with the money the means of transporting and smuggling contraband, be it in the form of gold, arms, drugs, whatever, he didn't care as long as there was a good profit in it.

Today, however, from the rust-specked bridge, he looked gloomily down at the lone figure on the foredeck, leaning into the wind and spray from the bow, as if searching for the first sign of the little fishing vessel which was due to rendezvous with them.

Walther didn't know what had gone wrong, but he knew something had! His contract had been to take on board a cargo of so-called Agricultural Machinery, and one passenger.

Well, he thought bitterly, there's the passenger, but at the Dock-side in Brest he had been curtly informed that there would be no container to load, and he would have to speak to his principals about the question of loss of bonus.

He was inclined to argue the point, but there had been something about the ice in the slim Irishman's eyes that persuaded him that he would be better served by at least keeping to his part of the arrangement.

After all, he mused, there was no doubt that there were many more shipments of 'Agricultural Machinery' yet to come out of Libya.

CHAPTER FIFTY

Martin spoke quickly into the handset, not that there was much danger of him being seen, he had certainly lost any follower who might have been assigned to watch him; his constant erratic backtracking and bus-hopping would have taken care of that. No, it was simply a matter of ingrained caution and training that had led him into the crowded city centre, and to this telephone box to make his report to Grey.

Actually, Martin was quite cheerful. Everything seemed to be going according to plan, and Stick had found his men's description of Martin's victim splashing around in the urinal hugely appropriate:

"Dat's just where shit belong Man! Down with the piss!" He had laughed until the tears streamed from his eyes: "A piece of shit sliding about in the piss, in a toilet!"

Later, when his mirth had subsided, he had taken Martin to one side and agreed to set up the purchase of the Uzi. "But you won't need no Crack, Man. Just the money will do. A whole lot of money. If you got it, then we can do business."

After some haggling, they had agreed a price. A price that Martin knew would include a kickback for Stick, but then, business was business.

Of course, Stick wanted Martin to hand over the cash and leave it to him to collect the weapon and deliver it to him later.

Of course, Martin wasn't prepared to let Stick or anyone else for that matter walk away with £1000 of his money.

Stick considered Martin thoughtfully, then grinned and clapped him on the shoulder. "That's the way, man, don't trust nobody!" Without the shades, his eyes were pale and piercing. Even as he laughed, Martin could sense that Stick was weighing what he knew of this quiet and dangerous man, assessing, judging.

The smile died away from his lips as he reached his decision.

With his arm still around Martin's shoulder, Stick pulled him closer, so that their heads were almost touching. When he spoke it was very quietly.

"I know all about you, Mr Martin."

Martin's heart almost stopped!

"You might be a hard man, and very handy with your fists, but you got to remember who I am!"

"I am the man with the power here." The black eyes bored into Martin's: "What ever I want I get, whatever I say goes!" Martin's back crawled with tension as the soft menacing voice continued:

"I've had you checked out, and I know all about your Pig background.." Martin's heart beat again..."and I've seen what you can do, for me and maybe against me....but!" The word hung in the air:

"But if you cross me, Man, you're dead! You fuck with me, and you will find your black ass in the graveyard. No-matter how good you are, you cut same as anyone, and bullets kill any man!"

Stick held his gaze for a few moments longer, then gave his shoulder a final squeeze and dropped his arm, smiling again.

"So, I'll set it up for you to meet the sellers personally, you just make sure you got the bread ready."

He turned to walk away, then turned back and added, as an afterthought: "I'll give a piece of advice, bro, don't even dream of fucking with these people; 'cos they don't give a shit about anything or anyone, and you're goin' to your own funeral if you try any funny business with them!"

"I just want the piece and some ammunition, no funny business from my end!"

Stick paused, then nodded as if satisfied by Martin's flat statement. "O.K., I'll contact you when it's set up, stay out of trouble!"

Martin watched as he slid his round shades from their case and slipped them on. Hefting his swordstick jauntily in one hand, he thrust the other deep into his trouser pocket and walked out of the gloom of the club into the bright sunshine As ever, he collected a train of large minders in his wake. Martin had felt an inward glow of satisfaction as he watched one of them limp painfully along behind.

Grey had listened quietly as Martin spoke, then, when he had finished, he gave him his instructions.

From now on Martin was to be under surveillance around the clock because it was highly unlikely that he would get the chance to make contact by 'phone again, when the meet was arranged, so Martin was to make sure that he collected a poste-restante parcel which would be awaiting collection at the local post office.

In it he would find a small leather briefcase containing £1000. Whenever Martin left his hotel carrying the case, the watchers would know that he was on his way to the rendezvous, and would follow him. He was to have no more direct contact, from now on he was to act as if he were on his own.

Martin replaced the receiver, thoughtfully. It was sensible, and even if he was still being watched by Stick's men they would know that he would never have been so foolish as to have kept the money in his room, so picking up a package from the post office would seem reasonable.

If only it contained a gun as well, he thought.

He didn't relish the prospect of going to meet these people without one, but as Grey had pointed out, why would he be going at all if he already had access to firearms? He couldn't take the chance that they would search him and find it.

CHAPTER FIFTY-ONE

IRELAND

Founded by Saint Finbarr, the city of Cork is a little like
Amsterdam, being a city of innumerable bridges over
tributaries of the river Lee upon which it stands.

Kennedy loved it, the hustle and bustle of a busy port
combined with the ancient deeply traditional nature of its
inhabitants had proved irresistible to him when life in the
North became too dangerous for a known IRA bomber.

Of course, the history of the county - known by many as the
'rebel county' because of its long involvement with the
struggle for Irish independence - also struck a chord in him.
For Liam, Cork epitomised everything that Ireland stood for.
Even the air smelled sweet after the tautly oppressive foreign
atmosphere of Belfast.

The eloquence of the county's people found recognition in
the myth of the Blarney stone, which if kissed, (something no
self-respecting Irishman would ever do, acknowledged Liam
to himself, entailing as it did hanging over the battlements of
nearby Blarney castle with your feet being held secure by
some fellow you'd never met before) would confer upon the
kisser the gift of persuasive oratory.

Then there was the vivacity of its inhabitants. Cork was a
place of culture and the arts, with its Opera House, the
University and its strong literary traditions, but it was also a
thriving centre for shopping and night-life, even if one end of
its main thoroughfare, St. Patrick's Street, was dominated by
the statue of the 19th century Capuchin Friar, Father Matthew,

who was famed for his crusade against the demon drink.

Luckily, the local Corkonians had countered by establishing two local Stout breweries, and a distillery for Paddy's whiskey!

So, when the time had come to leave the North, Kennedy had settled easily in the city that he had come to love. Perhaps it was simply co-incidence that Cork was also the clearing house for most illicit arms shipments into the country, its craggy inlet-dotted coastline affording countless secret landing places for small boats ferrying contraband cargo from passing freighters.

It was also the county favoured by a number of the most dangerous men in Ireland, the unholy trinity who controlled and directed both the political and the military campaigns of the IRA.

Thus it was that with a passing nod to the good Father Matthew, Liam set out for his appointment and strolled over the bridge to O'Leary's, the little pub situated on St. Patrick's Quay.

Inside, the Snug was gloomy, although by rights it should not have been so. The muffled cling of glasses and the music of the ceilidh could still be heard from the public bar, but the serving hatch was firmly shut and the door to the bar securely bolted. On a small table in the far corner were the remains of a tray of sandwiches, pies and bottles of Bushmills and the curiously named Sheep Dip, as well as the inevitable pint glasses of Arthur Guinness's contribution to Irish culture.

Everything had been prepared in advance; no-one would interrupt the council of war. The Snug in traditional Irish pubs was almost designed for such clandestine meetings, being originally a place where assignations with young ladies might take place away from public scrutiny. Now more dangerous intrigues were pursued behind the warmth and conviviality of the Pub's noisy facade.

Even though the evening was warm, the curtains were closed, only the light from the ancient table lamps illuminated the three shadowy figures grouped in deep discussion across the table from Kennedy. He could not prevent the image of the three wise monkeys from popping into his mind. Not that he would ever let them know that that was how he saw them.

Not that Kennedy was afraid. He sat in studied nonchalance, swinging one elegantly trousered leg in time to the muted dance music from the public bar.

Not afraid exactly, but uneasy nevertheless. Anyone would be uneasy in this company. The shadowy triumvirate opposite him were the three most powerful figures in the Provisional IRA, responsible not only for decisions regarding the political campaign against the North and the invaders as they considered the British, but also for direct terrorist action against them; fighting for freedom was how they saw it of course.

In their eyes they had assumed the mantle cast off by Michael Collins in accepting the partition of Ireland in 1921, which led directly to his execution at the hands of his former colleagues. They were the inheritors of the only legitimate parliament of Ireland and would not rest until all political ties with Britain were cut away.

To the hard-liners, in promoting partition 'The Big Fellow' had failed them, and he had paid the price, dying in a hail of bullets from the guns of the very people he had set out to lead.

Kennedy too had been involved in a failure, but not his failure. The loss of the arms shipment was a serious blow to the men across the table. but not an irredeemable one. Thanks to Colonel Gaddafi another shipment of 'tractor parts' would soon be leaving Tripoli. No, it was unfortunate, but no more.

That it was more unfortunate for the beautiful girl who's head he had blown off, did not occur to him. On the contrary. Liam did not know how he came to recognise her from the container depot in Marseilles, but somehow something in his subconscious had warned him; perhaps the Devil looking after his own, he thought with a rueful smile.

Kennedy was needed. His special expertise was to make up for a series of failures.

Shooting Protestants in the North was now deemed to be counterproductive, it only led to an escalating level of individual violence which had not weakened the occupying forces' resolve in the past, and probably would be no more successful in the future. Anyway, the general council's policy was that a cease-fire would now enable them to claim a political stance which would force the Brits to make concessions.

This was not a unanimous view, however, there had always been those, especially within the breakaway Irish National Liberation Army, who nursed a pathological hatred of anyone, man woman or child who even lived on Protestant ground, and who would not rest until Irish soil was poisoned with their life-blood. Nevertheless, the council had spoken: It was now considered bad policy to alienate the ordinary people of the North. After all, they reasoned, in a re-united Ireland they would all have to learn to live together.

No, better to give the impression of mature statesmen, rather than that of merciless killers!

But when the contact was made Kennedy knew his very special talents wouldn't go begging. As he sat there, his mind turned back to one of his earliest inventions, the bicycle bomb.

Over the years this had claimed many a victim, for who would have imagined that the innocent bike leaning against a wall in the path of a foot patrol would be packed with explosive!

That had helped establish him as a bomber of more than average ingenuity, and his Porno-magazine bomb had confirmed it. His eyes danced with delight as he thought about it.

The problem had been to make an anti-personnel device that would be irresistible. A time mechanism was no good, of course, he had to be sure that a target was in range. It had come to him in a flash, watching an illicit copy of Eros going the rounds in his local bar. All the men crowded round, laughingly jostling each other for sight of the explicit pictures.

Leave a porno magazine open on the floor, with just a thin length of black cotton stuck to the bottom. As soon as someone bent down and picked up the magazine "Bang!" the cotton line activated the detonator of the explosive device hidden close by.

Kennedy had carefully selected a title in the 'Colour Climax' series for the job. It appealed to his warped sense of humour that it would indeed be the biggest climax of the reader's life!

If only the council had concentrated on legitimate targets instead of ratifying those foolish sectarian killings that had only heightened the hatred of the North for the South.

In the end it had been these very shadow men across the table who had decided the change of policy and had sent active service units into Europe and onto the UK mainland. Even this had not seemed to work, however. The killing of British servicemen and their families on the Continent had not had the desired effect on mainland opinion.

The deaths of seven young guardsmen musicians in Regents Park had only hardened the resolution of the British public. Liam remembered the debriefing for that one well, it was a beautiful day in July 1982 and he had been serving his apprenticeship as assistant to Kevin O'Brady who had placed the first of the bombs in Hyde Park, set to explode just as the Blues and Royals of the Household Cavalry trotted proudly towards Horseguard's Parade along South Carriage Drive.

O'Brady had constructed a terrifying device of 25lbs of gelignite, which he surrounded with 30lbs of 4inch and 6inch nails, to cause maximum damage and injury. This he had placed in a parked car on the route, and detonated as the main body of the troop passed by.

The result was a horrendous explosion of tremendous force, which ripped the car apart and sprayed the surrounding area with a lethal hail of metal splinters, shrapnel and nails, killing and maiming soldiers, civilians and horses alike.

Kennedy's task had been to place the second device in a suitcase under the bandstand in nearby Regents Park to be detonated during an open-air concert by young bandsmen of the Royal Greenjackets. He could remember the tension he had felt, not because of the bombing, no, that had been excitement, but afterwards he had to explain to O'Brady and the others why he had not managed to pack his bomb with nails too. In fact, as the others grudgingly accepted, when he had sawed through the floorboards of the bandstand there had just not been enough space to fit the nails in as well as the explosive!

Kennedy had managed his job well, without attracting any attention he had disposed of the nails and saw by dumping them in the lake, and he had watched from a distance as his handiwork tore apart the bodies of the young musicians.

The success of this operation for the Provisionals had exacerbated the hatred between them and the breakaway INLA. The IRA regulars despised them. Blood-thirsty butchers, not professionals working for an achievable end, but psychopaths who murdered and maimed with no other end than to satisfy their bloodlust.

Mostly they were viewed by the Provos as no more than scum! Criminals who funded themselves by raiding banks and linking with any Middle Eastern despot who would supply them with money and arms.

Of course, the INLA didn't see it that way. To them the Provisionals were too soft! That was their argument. Total warfare against any target which would weaken the grip of the British Government on the North was their policy, and if the Provos got in the way, well, they too would pay the price!

Many had. For a while there had almost been open war between the two groups, but this bloody feud had settled down into an uneasy truce, with each trying to outdo the other in scale of atrocity, to win the backing of the majority who supported the aim of a united Ireland, whatever the cost.

Kennedy took a long drink, allowing the tension to melt away. He lit up a cigarette and blew a long stream of smoke over the table and up to the ceiling as he leaned back.

Across the room the dark trio were still intent upon their discussion.

Another swallow and Kennedy turned his thoughts back to the INLA and the problems that they had caused the official body. Every success of the Provos was matched by an attempt to win back credibility by carrying out some even more outrageous - and counterproductive - act.

They had murdered Airey Neave, a British MP, blowing him up with a car-bomb outside of the House of Commons, but Neave had been a war hero, one of the few who in World War II had escaped from the notorious German prisoner of war camp Colditz Castle. He had also been a close friend of the Prime Minister. The outcome was predictable. Public opinion was outraged by the killing, and the government pledged even tougher action against the terrorists!

Kennedy was not against killing! But it had to be productive, especially if on occasion there were to be a few unavoidable civilian casualties. Those INLA bastards couldn't care less!

In reply to the Regents Park and Hyde Park bombs they set off a gelignite bomb in the Droppin Well Inn at Ballykelly, deliberately designed to bring down the roof supports and kill anyone who might survive the initial explosion. Set to go off during a pre-Christmas Disco, they succeeded in killing eleven British soldiers, but the bomb also caused the deaths of four girls who had been at the dance.

This casual murder of innocent Irish civilians simply enraged the very people in whose name the act was carried out!

Kennedy hated them with a passion, each atrocity lessened the value of his own work, and heightened security even more, making legitimate target penetration more difficult.

He knew, however, that he had not been brought to this room for any minor task. He was here because he, Liam Kennedy, was the best. It wasn't difficult to work out that his masters had something special planned. He shivered suddenly, as if someone had walked over his grave.

He also was well aware that whatever the outcome of the so-called 'Cease-Fire' these men would never, never ever, relinquish their power! No-matter what the public face would show, he knew without shadow of a doubt that they owed their power and their status solely to fear; to the certainty of the murderous vengeance which would be wreaked upon anyone foolish enough to stand in their way.

This was a heady brew not easily forgone! If the superficial mantle of a type of legitimacy gained from the cover of "Freedom for Ireland" were to be removed, he could not imagine that these hard men would simply give up their guns and become one again, simple shopkeepers, accountants and teachers.

No, Kennedy knew as sure as night followed day, that in spite of the public image that they would erect, their efforts would simply go deeper underground, and that blackmail, beatings and terror would still be their weapons to ensure the continuation of the lives to which they had become accustomed.

The shadowy group broke up. The murmuring undertone of their voices ceased. Three pairs of eyes turned as one.

"Come." Through the sudden silence, the flat, quiet authoritative voice of the central figure stilled the thoughts swirling through his mind. He joined the Chief of Staff of the

IRA army council and two other senior members at the table.

The logic was spelled out: Sinn Fein's lack of success in gaining a voice at the peace talks together with the activities of the dissident hard-liners had brought the Cease-Fire teetering on the brink of collapse. The stupid insistence that the IRA should simply give up its stockpiles of weapons and explosive was the stumbling block that would bring down the whole charade.

In truth it had collapsed, it was over! Yes the factions still played out their foolish pretences across the conference table, but really it was over! The Provisional IRA had tried to establish a united Ireland by the bullet, and by the ballot box, but the intransigence of the British Government had led them to be seen to be defeated on both fronts.

The hostile murmurs of the dissidents in their ranks were growing in volume and vitriol, scathingly confounding the Provos as 'Yesterday's Men' lacking the will to fight for victory. The shootings and the bombings were starting again, and the tail was beginning to wag the dog!

Thus the council needed to regain the initiative and control of the dissenters. The only choice was either internecine warfare against the INLA, or a combined operation, a sudden atrocity of overwhelming audacity which would seize the initiative once again, and force public opinion into demanding the withdrawal of all troops from Northern Ireland.

Bluntly, harshly, and with no frills, the iron-hard voice with its flat Northern accent that years in the South had done nothing to soften continued coldly: He was to organise and carry out the assassination of the Prime Minister of England and as many of the cabinet as was possible in one go! If the Cease-Fire was to end, then they would be the ones to end it, and in no uncertain fashion!

How and when was up to him.

The INLA would be invited to share equally in the operation, in 'recognition' of their expertise and in an attempt to form a working collaboration between equals.

He would have a three-man mainland unit at his disposal, consisting of the INLA's top men, plus contact with one of their own quartermaster units for any necessary weaponry and explosives. He was to be in charge, and in him lay the opportunity to once and for all bring about the defeat of the invaders and at the same time confirm the Official General Council's control over the dissidents and hotheads!

There was in this act, however, a hidden agenda which would in one blow achieve all of their stated objectives, and, in addition, would destroy the credibility of the INLA dissidents for ever.....if only Kennedy were the man do carry it out?

Kennedy's heart leapt! "If he were the man?" He leaned forward as the details burned into his soul.

A moment more of silence, then a nod of dismissal and Kennedy slowly rose to his feet and – with a brief nod in return, made his way back into the hustle and clamour of the public bar.

His heart was pounding in his chest, as he ordered a Guinness and pushed his way through to a quieter corner. He had guessed, naturally. It was the obvious step to take. Even so, a sudden charge of adrenaline coursed through him at the thought.

The danger, yes, but the challenge!

It had been tried before, of course, but those video-recorder timers were just not sophisticated enough, he mused, remembering how the Grand Hotel in Brighton had looked after the explosion. The whole centre had been destroyed, but Margaret Thatcher had not been touched.

Then there was the last attempt, when an active unit had aimed mortars at Ten Downing Street itself, from the back of a parked van. Notoriously unreliable, however, and difficult to aim......still the attempt had embarrassed the Government, and those city centre mainland bombs were wreaking havoc in the City......but it wasn't enough!.

But now Kennedy was back, and the target agreed. With the new detonating devices from America...and the destruction of The Ritz had proved their effectiveness...or perhaps in another fashion, it mattered little.

The new factor, the difference this time that took away Kennedy's breath, was almost unbelievable! Incredibly there was to be collusion between the IRA and 'certain high officials' well-placed in the English government that would ease the way!

Kennedy, chief bomb-maker to the Provisional IRA was to engineer the death of the British Prime Minister.

The little twist that would also end the power of the INLA and confirm himself as the master of his trade brought an extra savage glee to his heart. The deviousness of the plan was so appealing. And even then he had no clue as to just how devious these men really were!

He sat there for a long time, lost in his own thoughts, oblivious of the barman clearing away the dirty crockery and glasses.

The silence in the blue smoke-hazed room ended as the door closed behind Kennedy. "Do you think he bought it?"

A moment's consideration and then.: "Of course. He's an arrogant young bastard.. "But he's as bloody dangerous as those INLA fuckers! We'll only put ourselves between a rock and a fuckin' hard place if we give him and his like free reign!"

The reply came quiet, hard and flat:

"We know the future lies in only one of two possible directions. The Brits aren't going to go away, and we cannot bomb them out of Ireland! So, two choices – either we establish a working truce and make sure we keep political power for ourselves, or.." – the pause seemed never-ending – He continued harshly:"Or we create such fucking mayhem that even the Brits wash their hands of us!"

"If we chose to talk, then we could lose the peace and any political power at any time, because of those INLA bastards who will continue to bomb and kill and tell everyone that we have let down the Irish people, and that they are now the only true upholders of freedom!"

"If we chose the latter course, then..." As the other two stared, the speaker slowly leaned forward over the little table.

"If we chose Armageddon, then even after that, even after the Brits have finally scuttled back to their rat-holes, even then we will still be faced with having to deal with those bastards who will claim it was only their continuing influence which forced us to use their tactics, the bomb and the bullet, and that, therefore, they would be – should be – in the driving seat for political power! He sat back into the shadows again.

"We have decided the only real answer is to get rid of the Brits and those INLA cunts at the same time, and that is exactly what we are now going to do!" "There will be no winners – only us!" "In one instant, we get rid of the invaders, we also get rid of our enemies here, and we also remove the only man outside this room who knows that we are working with the INLA and a rogue Brit." "And...our little...extra..." His lips tightened: "Will fix the bloody lot of them!"

"We get rid of all of them – and we will shake our heads, denounce the violence and look forward to working in peace and harmony with our erstwhile masters!"

After a moment, the three staff officers stood, and without a word, they turned, pulled open the door and exited into the noise and warmth of the tiny bar, collecting as they went the hulking figures of their minders.

CHAPTER FIFTY-TWO

The tiny hotel room smelled stale from the acrid smoke of countless cigarettes, and was littered with the remains of sandwiches and pots of strong coffee.

Stretching his neck wearily to ease the stiffness, Kennedy levered himself out of the armchair and, noticing the fug for the first time, tugged open a window, drinking in the clean night air. His eyes felt hot and prickly, and his back ached from being bent over a note-pad for the last four hours, as he jotted down, considered and then dismissed various ideas of how to penetrate the security of his new target.

"'When" and "Where" marched round and around in his brain. Not "How", that went without saying, he was the best bomb-maker in the IRA, and that meant in the world! So that was not a consideration.

No. Time and Place were the problems to solve. How to get close enough, but more than that, where to get close enough! And how to survive - oh yes! That too was a consideration! And not just from the security services. He knew his very success would engender the enmity of his breakaway 'colleagues!'

Well, he would have to give that some serious thought!

Sighing, Kennedy turned back from the window, lit yet another cigarette and dropped heavily onto the bed, stretching full-length on the candlewick spread. Pushing himself up on one elbow, he reached over and splashed a generous measure of Paddy's into a glass. He took a long swallow and lay back again.

The strong bite and aftertaste of the whisky took his mind
back to the first time he ever tasted it, he had been no more
than five or six, and curious, he had sneaked a pull from his
granddad's bottle filched from its place on the kitchen shelf.

He smiled to himself as he recalled the breath-stopping
gagging reaction! How in God's name had he come to like
such firewater?

After the Paras killed his father Sean at a Bogside roadblock,
and his mother's subsequent breakdown and death, Liam had
been put in the care of his grandparents, and he could even
now conjure up a picture of his Granddad Michael, a huge ruin
of a man, wearing the uniform of all old men, the collarless
shirt and ubiquitous stained waistcoat, sucking wetly on his
empty blackened, battered pipe through a still remarkably
bushy, yellow-stained walrus moustache.

He could see him now, silent, perched with elbow on knee
and chin in hand on the dry-stone wall in the little back
garden, just staring into yesterday with the continual flow of
his Grandma's voice flowing over and around him, but never
really touching him in his private world.

God but he must have been a strong man in his day! Liam
thought; never quite the same since that debacle at the
O'Connell Street Post Office, and his detainment by the
British.

It had been at Noon on Easter Monday 1916, when his
Granddad had set out with Michael Collins and the other
rebels, to 'liberate' the Dublin Post Office. They took the
building and ejected all the civilians. Later they opened fire on
a party of Lancers who attempted to dislodge them, killing

four, who had ventured too close, near the Nelson Pillar.

Proudly they fixed a Tricolour to the roof, tying it to one of the fallen Lancer's pikes, and one of the officers - Patrick Pearse - funny how he could still remember the name after all these years - proclaimed the establishment of the Republic. Liam remembered his Gran telling him of the carnival quality of the initial days; even that (and he was never sure of the truth of it) the action had been set for the previous day, but was cancelled, so, typically, they all went home and then they came back the next day!

Then his Gran herself had marched through the siege lines to ask his Granddad what time he was coming home for tea!

After the collapse of the uprising, Liam's Granddad was taken by the authorities along with Michael Collins and the other surviving rebels who were not executed on the spot and sent across the water to an English prison, the first of many sentences served for his country. The harsh conditions he endured whilst in jail eventually ruined his health and further fuelled his desire to free his nation from its oppressors.

Much later, the murder of Sean, his only son on Bloody Sunday, only confirmed him in his hatred of the British.

As he lay there, Liam recalled the heartfelt pride which stirred within him when his Granddad balanced him on his boney knee and spoke quietly of the deeds of his father Sean, setting him in the panoply of other Irish heroes past and present, like young Kevin Barry, just a student, helpless and savagely ill-treated by his English captors. Powerless and pain-wracked under torture he had steadfastly maintained his proud defiance:

"And what can your leaders do for you now?" His

tormentor's had shouted into his pain-filled face.

"Nothing!" Came the defiant retort, then the quiet reply that made Liam shiver: "But I can Die for them!"

Just as Liam's father had done at that fatal roadblock! How he came to hate all Proddy bastards!

He could still almost taste the simmering ever-present undercurrent of hatred and lurking violence that had permeated every aspect of daily life in his childhood Belfast. Even going to the cinema was fraught with danger if you happened to want to see a film playing in foreign territory. You had to remind yourself not to stand up and walk out as soon as the film finished, and the British National Anthem was played.

All the Proddies would stand there until it finished, but of course Liam was used to ignoring it and walking out, as did everyone else in the Catholic enclaves.

To make a mistake like that was to invite at best a violent beating on the way home, at worst....

As he lay there drifting, neither asleep nor awake, the whisky started to depress him. Just sometimes he could see his whole life as if from a distance, unemotionally, as it ran before him. He could see the patterns, the influences, the weaknesses, the enormous inevitability of it all. Trapped in a web of Irish history and myth, alone, an orphan, frail as a child, he could see it all clearly as choices arose and weakness won.

It was all mapped out, his progress from minor villain to top-bombmaker and assassin; what was the point of free-will if the choices were so limited?

Would he have had it any different? How could he possibly know now? Should he even hint at wanting to get out, the generals would have him killed without a second thought.

Liam knew from first-hand experience the penalties awaiting anyone who was even suspected of wavering in their support of the hard-line policies expounded by the hard-core of the Provisionals. Indeed, as a youngster on the outer fringes, he had been included in a kneecapping punishment of a twenty-three year old man, who was accused of nothing more than intervening in an argument between his sister and a fellow who turned out to be a convicted IRA man.

Kennedy was handed a mask and baseball bat and ordered to accompany three others to the man's home in Downpatrick and teach him a lesson! In the middle of the night they had kicked their way through the front door, and regardless of the noise, smashed in the windows. They knew that no-one on the estate was going to call the police.

His screaming mother had finally convinced them that her son was not at home, so Padraig, the leader had issued her with an ultimatum:

"If her boy didn't come to meet them the next day in one of the bars on the Falls road, then his girlfriend's face would be blasted apart with a shotgun!"

Like attending a dentist's appointment, the terrified man had come at the appointed time and was taken into the back alley behind the bar and ordered to lie face down on the ground. Kennedy had watched fascinated by the total power wielded by the force of the IRA's threats, as the man lay down on the wet strip of waste ground and quietly accepted the bullet through the back of each knee.

He recalled the queer mixture of stomach-churning fascinating horror and the almost erotic sensation in his groin as he watched the helpless victim squirming in agony, face down on the wet ground.

He remembered the irrelevant thought that crossed his mind as he stood there, that if he had used his brains the idiot would have taken off his trousers. As it was, his suit would be completely ruined.

Of course, that was only a minor punishment in the repertoire of these utterly ruthless killers, and Kennedy himself had eventually won their approval by becoming one of them. He was in no doubt as to what would be his fate should he ever reveal even a hint of disapproval!

And, he had to admit, he had also grown to enjoy the fruits of his labours; his status, the deference with which he was treated by those in the know, and his ability to afford his indulgences in hand-painted silk ties, Cerruti suits and expensive cars, even if this was frowned upon by the rank and file of his peers who went by 'The Green Book' the IRA training manual which preached against flamboyance and over-indulgence and exhorted politically more attractive concepts such as modesty and discretion.

Only the exceptional nature of Liam's skills had enabled him to obey these guidelines with a nod rather than by the letter. Never-the-less, he knew that there were always those who were jealous of his privileged position and would be secretly pleased at his downfall. But that would only happen if his position of supremacy were to slip.

The sharp burning of his fingers snapped him out of his reverie, swearing, he stubbed out the forgotten butt-end and sat up. Blowing on his smarting fingers, he swung his legs off the counterpane, got up and switched on the television.

Giving a final stretch, he picked up the scattered newspapers and sat down in the chair again, idly skimming the pages as the News Round-Up began.

Without really listening he began to be aware of the newscaster announcing details of a forthcoming Anglo-Irish summit meeting to be held in London between representatives of the North and the South, and the Minister for Northern Ireland, to discuss the setting up of an advisory committee for All-Ireland affairs.

Co-incidentally he had noticed something about it in the paper, and about one of the Southern Irish delegates being injured in a Skiing accident, but it hadn't registered as important.

He turned back to the report. Yes. There it was, complete with photograph of stoically smiling Eamon Kavanah being pushed across the airport tarmac in a wheelchair. "No change of Plan" the caption read under the picture. The delegate was to attend the conference, even though confined temporarily to a wheelchair.

Kennedy saw neither the newspaper nor the rest of the T.V. programme. He was far away.

Eventually he closed his eyes and leaned back with a slight smile of satisfaction easing the lines around his mouth.

Now there was just the other little matter to consider......

CHAPTER FIFTY-THREE

LONDON

The passenger arrivals terminal at Heathrow was crowded, as usual, but for once this worked to Kennedy's advantage as he studied the flow of people pouring through the gates of the Customs area, it meant that he could remain close to the gates, but still be inconspicuous.

He looked up at the bank of T.V. monitors relaying the latest flight information. The scheduled arrival from Cork had been on time, and the passengers should shortly be clearing Customs.

Suddenly, sooner than he had expected, he saw a little group of officials and porters clustered around a large figure in a wheelchair, easing him briskly through the hurrying throng.

He breathed a mental sigh of relief as the little convoy weaved its way out through the automatic doors. He ground out the stub of his cigarette under his foot and slipped totally un-noticed into the continuous stream of people making for busses, trains and taxis. Briskly, he made his way over to the parked hire car waiting on the double yellow lines with its bonnet raised and emergency flashers winking.

Slamming the bonnet shut, he reached across and peeled the "Gone for assistance" note from the windscreen, crumpling and dropping it in the floor-well as he slid behind the wheel and concentrated on imprinting in his mind details of the limousine loading up with the Irish diplomat and his luggage. Minutes later the long black car, with Kennedy following, was nudging its way into the streams of London-bound traffic, heading for....well, Kennedy smiled to himself in satisfaction, he would soon know.

CHAPTER FIFTY-FOUR

MANCHESTER

The interior of Stick's white BMW was as stereo- typical as the man himself, thought Martin, as they drove to the rendezvous, some idea of class, but over the top. Living up to the street explanation of the acronym 'BMW' as "Black Man's Wheels!" Contrasting black leather would have been nice, but Stick had selected white with a black trim, and the regular steering wheel had been exchanged for a small 'boy racer' version with thick white leather padding.

The dashboard was cluttered with high-tech gadgets that would have enabled a Harrier pilot to have navigated up Saddam Hussain's left nostril, and the stereo system, playing at the obligatory 1,000 decibels, was like a mini juke-box!

Martin's relief at stepping out of the car was balanced by the increasing knot of tension building up in his stomach. His ears still ringing from the deafening pounding from the Greatest Hits of Bob Marley and the Wailers, he waited, briefcase in hand, on the pavement as Stick pointed his electronic alarm at the car, and then came round to join him.

"You can't trust nobody, Man!" He said, oblivious of the irony as he glanced fiercely up and down the street as if to deter any potential car thief.

"Come on, they'll be waiting."

At that he strode off up the steps of the Two Star

Recommended Hotel.

"Recommended for what and by whom?" thought Martin facetiously as he hastened after him.

The foyer was deserted, there was not even anyone in attendance at the tiny reception desk, but Stick had no need of directions. He caught Martin by the elbow and steered him towards the solitary lift. "O.K. Man, you're on your own. Go to the second floor, room 214, knock twice, then once, then three times."

"And then?" Martin asked.

"Well, you do your deal Man, but you make your own way from then on, I'm not drivin' through the streets in daylight with no gun in my car! That's up to you!" Turning, Stick sauntered casually out into the street.

Taking a deep breath and trying to relax his shoulders, Martin entered the lift and punched the button for the second floor.

Across the street three pairs of eyes watched as Stick emerged from the hotel on his own, climbed into his car and drove off. The front passenger door of the dark blue Daimler which had been following him and Martin opened and an athletically built young man in a dark business suit got out and walked over to the Hotel.

In the lobby he crossed to the deserted reception desk and rang the bell. The disgruntled porter-receptionist cum telephone operator marched belligerently from the back room, wiping sandwich crumbs from his mouth with the back of his hand.

His manner changed abruptly to one of servile helpfulness at the sight of the Special Branch warrant card.

In the back of the car, Grey slid the window open a fraction for some fresh air and opened his copy of the Guardian.

Feeling a little absurd, Martin carried out his instructions, and knocked sharply twice, then once, then three times. After a moment, he heard the sound of the lock turning, and the door still on its security chain, slowly opened a little to reveal a very pretty young woman in her mid-twenties, slim, wearing a man's shirt and jeans.

A little disconcerted, Martin spoke: "Stick sent me." He couldn't help but smile to himself, recognising the cliché of just about every gangster movie he had ever seen! The smile froze on his lips as the girl flipped off the safety chain and moved back into the room, pulling open the door to reveal the twin black holes of the wrong end of a sawn-off 12-bore shotgun, pointing straight at his face.

"Come in." The twin barrels swung steadily, following him as he slowly entered the room.

His mind seemed to have an independent existence, as if somehow to refute the reality of what was staring him in the face. He could suddenly hear his karate teacher's voice reverberating through the years: "If you really want to win every fight, then get a shotgun!!"

Martin knew then, suddenly and surely, that this was one fight that he was not going to win! No technique on earth could evade the fatal scatter of lead shot at that range.

The large man holding the shotgun motioned Martin to sit at the table set in the centre of the room. As he did, a second man that Martin had not noticed moved from behind the door, closing and locking it. The big man moved to sit facing Martin across the table.

"So, you're from our Sticky friend eh?" His Irishness was thick in his voice. He smiled pleasantly. "Have you got the necessary?"

Martin's heart jumped in his chest. It was just a precaution then, they weren't on to him after all! He took a deep breath and forced his body to obey him. He reached forwards with the briefcase.

"Slowly!" The shotgun jerked back upwards as Martin carefully placed it on the table.

The girl came back into the room, carrying something wrapped in a grey cloth. Martin had been so mesmerised by the gun at his head that he had not even been aware of her leaving. She put the object down on the table, it made a metallic 'clunk' as she did so. Staring at him, the girl sat down next to her companion with the shotgun, and pushed the shrouded object across the table towards Martin.

Keeping one hand on top of the package, she inclined her head towards the briefcase.

Martin couldn't seem to break out of the cocoon of dread that permeated his very soul. He knew that this was going to turn out wrong! He knew!

The shotgun never wavered as he forced himself to lean forward and push the case towards the girl.

The double click of the briefcase locks almost made Martin jump out of his skin, sounding to him like the falling of hammers on cartridges!

With a little grunt of satisfaction, the girl shut the case. "Aren't you going to look?" She asked Martin. "Have you handled one before?"

He let out his pent-up breath as he reached over to pick it up:

"The fully automatic, ... in the army, but never one of these." He lifted the object and unwrapped it. It lay on the table, dully gleaming in its fine sheen of oil, grey and deadly, and beautiful in its deadliness. An Israeli UZI 9mm 20 shot pistol. Smaller all over than the submachine gun it resembled, but firing the same 9mm parabellum cartridge!

He picked it up slowly, turning and inspecting it as he did so.

He didn't see the flare in her eyes as he worked the cocking handle on top of the weapon and thumbed and released the safety catch on the left of the frame; slotting the grip into his right hand he squeezed in the rear safety catch. The lightness of the weapon gave the game away. He snicked on the safety and ejected the clip.

Empty!

The unmistakable double click of the cocking hammers of the sawn-off resounded deafeningly in the deathly silence of the room!

Martin looked up. The pretty face opposite him was distorted in fury. "You Bastard!!"

Martin knew he was lost!

"Stand up!""You fucking, fucking Bastard!" The girl

Maureen's twisted mouth sprayed spittle as rage gripped her.

"Army! I knew it! You were never in the fucking police at all were you? A fucking army spy!" Her voice shook with rage. "Put your hands on the table!"

 The man with the shotgun stood up and leant across the table placing both barrels against Martin's forehead. His chair scraping backwards as he rose.

 "Push your hands across the table." He snarled, and eased the pressure slightly as Martin bent nearly double across the table in front of him, his hands flat down on the top.

 In an instant the big man snatched away the shotgun from Martin's face and crashed the butt down with all his force on the back of his outstretched right hand. Sickeningly the small bones and ligaments burst, ripped and tore apart, in the same continuous motion he smashed the butt into Martin's mouth as his head jerked upwards to scream!

 As if viewing from a million miles away, the semi-conscious man was vaguely aware of the three moving around him, talking, swearing, and of the woman's overwhelming hatred, but he really felt nothing much at all, even when both men turned his back to the table and supported him by both arms as the girl, spitting in fury, drove her balled fists time and time again into the bloody mess of his face.

 The vehemence of Maureen's snarling questions made her almost incoherent; not that Martin could have formed an answer with his torn tongue and swollen lips.

 Panting from her exertions, the girl stood before the sagging figure, gripped him by the hair, and snarling she forced her face into his.

"You'll talk, you Bastard! You'll talk!"

Stepping back for a moment, she surveyed the wreckage of Martin's nose, and mouth.

She sneered viciously: "Well, your face won't pull the girls anymore, now let's make sure the rest of you won't!"

From his far away planet, Martin could feel the girl's fingers fiddling with his belt and the top of his jeans. He was aware of a cold feeling of nakedness as she pulled his Levis and briefs down to his ankles. Her eyes lit up with an terrible excitement as she reached down and gently gripped Martin's scrotum.

In spite of his semi-consciousness, his penis reacted to the cool feather-like touch of her fingers as she delicately bounced and rolled his balls, scraping her fingernails lightly over the roughness of the sac.

Maureen licked her lips briefly as her searching fingertips closed gently around the elusiveness of Martin's right testicle, lovingly working it to and fro. Leaning her face close up to his, she stared into his eyes. Without warning she savagely squeezed her fingers shut, violently snapping the spheroid up into Martin's body.

His body spasmed upright as the shockwave of pain exploded in his groin. Far gone as he was, the intensity knotted his stomach and paralysed his lungs.

Out in the street, Grey made his decision.

Refolding his newspaper, he leaned forward in the Daimler's back seat to the two men in the front. "He's been in there long enough, we're going in!"

In his sea of agony Martin was dimly conscious of a cold wetness spreading around his naked groin.

The girl placed the can of lighter fluid on the table and reached for a box of matches. "He'll talk!"

Feebly, like an exhausted, dying fly struggling in an inescapable web, Martin tried to pull himself away from the spluttering flame.

The big man gripped him from behind by both arms and forced him backwards over the table, the girl jammed her foot onto his jeans and pants, trapping them between his ankles, bending him like a bow, thrusting his exposed maleness defenceless in front of him.

The girl bent over Martin, drinking in the pain and terror in his eyes, tasting it, savouring her power. She brought the burning match closer and closer to his dripping penis.

Martin closed his eyes.

The door smashed from its hinges as Grey and his two companions kicked it open and burst into the room. Three silenced automatics froze the occupants into immobility.

The two men in dark suits were tight-lipped with rage at Martin's condition. Grey said nothing, as he motioned to one of them to attend to him. Only the cold blackness of his eyes offered any hint of his emotions. His face remained impassive as, at gunpoint, he directed the three terrorists to sit facing him in chairs placed side-by-side.

The girl, purple with fury, twisted and struggled as her arms were pinioned behind her back. All three were handcuffed, with the cuffs threaded through the chair backs, to keep them in their seats.

The two men were quieter.

Grey slowly walked over to the table in front of the trio, and perched himself, one leg swinging. He said nothing, his eyes were flat and unblinking. As if coming to a decision, he suddenly got to his feet and walked over to the group; he bent over the seated girl.

Very quietly he spoke: "There's something I must know, and you will tell me what it is - I need you to tell me where I can find the man you call the bombmaker."

Twisting on the chair, Maureen snarled out her defiance in a torrent of abuse and threats. Running at last to silence, she hawked and spat a gobbet of mucus at Grey, which hung from his unflinching cheek.

Grey looked at her, and quietly wiped away the phlegm.

Without a word he lifted his gun.

She laughed mockingly in his face: "Who do you think you're kid...."

The force of the silenced bullet jetted a fine crimson spray as it punched through her skull, slamming the girl and chair backwards across the room like an oversize skittle.

Without a word, Grey turned his attention to the horrified big man who had been bending Martin backwards over the table.

On the floor, the girls sprawling legs were twitching and jerking, drumming in a grotesque parody of a tap-dance.

"There's something I must know, and you will tell me what it is..."

Later, Grey was sitting in an easy chair in the corner of the hotel room, idly tapping his fingers on one knee as his call to Bainbridge was put through:

"Hector?" "Charles." He listened for a moment:

"No, insecure line but probably safe." "Yes, we got there just in time for Martin's sake, but too late for us I'm afraid."

He listened for a moment, then continued: "Two out of three, now in interrogation, one lost, but they've already revealed that the Semtex was left at a dead-letter pick-up some ten days ago........of course we'll check, but it will no doubt be gone by now."

He listened for a moment whilst Bainbridge spoke. "No. There'll be no problem there, Special branch are liaising and their cleaning firm is on the way to mop up."

"There is one thing, however." He lowered his voice: "It seems that a special sniper's rifle was ordered to be left with the explosive......yes, special....apparently it's collapsible into basically a set of tubes, so it'll be difficult to spot."

"We don't know what it's for as yet." He continued in reply to Bainbridge's worried query. "We suppose as a back-up, but we can't be sure, and we don't know how many rounds of ammunition, nor do we know the target, but whatever or whoever it is must be important to risk anything obvious in the current climate. He really aims to make sure of this one!"

As they talked, Grey watched as his two companions

prepared for the arrival of the aptly named "cleaning firm", specialists in removing all traces of potentially embarrassing activities.

Never ones to be caught short in a situation, they would be bringing with them their own roll of carpet and driving a brightly and clearly marked 'Carpet and Upholstery Cleaning Services' van.

He glanced briefly at the stiffening body of the girl, now lying un-cuffed from the chair, with her sprawling limbs tidily straightened, so that rigor mortis would not prevent the corpse from being rolled neatly in the carpet for removal to the van. The two surviving Irishmen were sitting quietly, still handcuffed to the chairbacks in the centre of the room, heads down, refusing to catch the eyes of either Grey or the two young men for fear of inviting further, perhaps deadly, attention.

"Look Hector, we must collate all our information on this one, can you set aside some time for a meeting when I get back to Town? You can, good. I'll call Century House and see if we've anything helpful on file, and I'll have any GCHQ and Intelligence gossip channelled through my desk, and perhaps you can have a word with your chaps?"

He was hanging up as the room bell rang twice, one of his men went to the door and peered through the security viewer. Satisfied, he turned to Grey:

"It's the cleaners, Sir."

Grey nodded, and he turned back to the door and unlocked it,

CHAPTER FIFTY-FIVE

LONDON.

The Hyde Park Hilton was not the hotel that Kennedy would
have chosen for himself, it was far too public and busy a
place, but he really had no alternative, once the Irish diplomat
had booked into one of the executive suites. He could have
gone elsewhere, but the risks of carrying explosives through
the streets were too great. It was far simpler to be in the same
hotel, especially with what he had in mind!

Kennedy checked that the door to his room was locked and
that the 'Do not disturb' sign hung from the knob. Satisfied, he
turned to the bed and began to tear open the two large
cardboard containers which lay there. They looked for all the
world like two giant-size Pizza cartons. Pulling back the top
flaps, he slid the contents out onto the bed. There they lay
gleaming, two replacement wheelchair wheels, the same make
as those on the diplomat's chair.

He bent over and selected two small tyre levers from his
repair kit, and began easing the tyres from their rims.

This done, he moved over to the dressing table and carefully
picked up what appeared to be a long tube of playdough
wrapped in thin plastic polyfilm. He carefully separated the
tube into one long and one small length, pushing the smaller to
one side for the moment.

Holding a tyre in one hand, Kennedy gently pressed the long
worm of Semtex into the hollow inner-tube space with the
other, until the tyre was completely encircled with it.

He repeated the process with the other tyre, and then, very carefully, for until now the Semtex had been relatively safe, he pressed a small short-burst electronic detonator into each, making sure it was firmly embedded. Next he picked up a large tube of bathroom sealant, and a packet of strong peppermint sweets.

Moving with an ease born of long experience, he went into the bathroom, tore off the wrapping and emptied the packet of mints into the bath. Standing on one leg, he swung the other over the edge of the bath and pressed his weight down on the little white sweets, grinding them down into a powder with the sole of his shoe. He collected up the crushed residue and poured half into the recesses of both tyres, finally topping the whole thing with a layer of the bathroom sealant.

He struggled to refit the inner tubes into the smaller space, and then inflated them. When this was accomplished he sealed every gap between each tyre and rim with a layer of superglue. "That should take care of the sniffer dogs." He thought, satisfied that the distinctive marzipan smell of the plastic explosive was now thoroughly disguised from even the best trained canine nose.

Of course he knew that these precautions would not hide the presence of high explosive from the Hydrogenous Explosives Detector, one of the Ministry of Defence's latest anti-terrorist devices which fired a beam of radioactive particles through any solid object and which reacted to the atomic structure of the explosive.

He was confident, however, that any sweeps made with this apparatus would be made when the building was empty, and, as at that time according to his plan there would be no explosive present, would therefore pronounce the area clean.

Now he turned his attention to the little 'Extra' as arranged in the tiny public house backroom, for his INLA 'friends.'

A carton of Marlboro cigarettes. Carefully slitting the cellophane wrapping with a razor blade, Kennedy extracted a pack from the middle. He strode over to the waste paper bin by the coffee maker and dumped the contents into it. He went back and sat on the bed, carefully packing the remaining semtex into the empty box, finally pressing home another of the special detonators.

He eased the pack back into its original place in the carton and carefully resealed the cellophane with a dab of super glue.

A nice gesture of friendship for his co-conspirators. He grinned. It was also a nice little additional failsafe to the prepared 'hidden agenda'.

In less than an hour, it was done. Now all that remained was to make the switch, but first he had a 'phone call to make.

Taking his time, Kennedy fastidiously cleared up all evidence of his activities. He carefully shredded and flushed away the leftover Semtex wrapping and washed all traces of the crushed sweets out of the bath. Then, satisfied that everything was in order, he sat on the bed and picked up the 'phone. Swinging his feet up onto the bed, he eased a cigarette from its packet whilst he dialled the memorised number with the other hand. He lit his cigarette and relaxed for a moment listening to the ringing tone until he heard a click. He spoke into the silence.

At the other end of the phone, in a tiny Bayswater flatlet Michael Farrell, leader of the three-man active service unit, listened carefully to his instructions.

CHAPTER FIFTY-SIX

"He's not really badly hurt, Hunter, superficial cuts and bruises, thank God! What he'd be like if we hadn't got to him when we did, well...."

Grey was in his shirtsleeves.

This rather shocked Hunter, who had never seen him even slightly unbend before. Given the circumstances, however, he could understand it. They had been in Grey's office more or less permanently for the last two days, with people coming and going, fax and computer data pouring in, constant telephone calls, everything aimed at the one task - to try and determine Kennedy's next target.

Now even Dennis Martin, face and mouth still swollen and sore from his beating, his injured hand bandaged, had been called in to help.

Hunter had voiced his doubts quietly to Grey as Martin busied himself stiffly with the coffee pot in the corner.

"He's better off getting involved, not just sitting about moping." Grey had stated bluntly.

Martin handed a steaming mug to Hunter, and winked cheerfully at the look of concern on his face.

"Right. Let's start again shall we." Grey's brisk tone brought them back to business. He sat back in his desk chair, motioning the others to sit also.

"Let's run over what we know, and what we may deduce:"

"Firstly, we know that Kennedy's their best man, so they won't waste him." He ticked off one finger.

"Secondly, it's bound to be a bomb as first choice, but there's also the gun to consider." He ticked off another.

"Thirdly, we know that he's smarting a little from Hunter's interference over the arms shipment, so he'll be looking to get his own back with something big."

"Fourthly, CIA intelligence in Southern Ireland are getting hints that something is about to go off which will radically affect North-South relations, they seem convinced that the Official IRA are being forced by their own malcontents into some display of power which will seriously affect the possibility of any renewal of the cease-fire"

"Fifth, the P.M. is worried over the security at Number Ten."

"Sixth, SAS undercover agents have tapped some 'phone conversations which indicate that the Sinn Fein publicity section has been alerted for something special in the near future, something which will swing the balance of power back from the breakaway factions and so we can assume that whatever it is, it's going to be soon."

"Seventh." He spun his chair angrily, until he looked out of the bay window:

"Damn it, but there is no seventh!"

"Well sir," Hunter said, breaking the silence: "If I were him there'd really only be one target worth considering if it meant the resumption of the armed struggle, and that's got to be the Prime Minister!"

He continued, warming to his subject as the other two stared at him.

"Can't you see, they've tried just about everything else, and it's been no use, so they need to do something which, once and for all, will make us wash our hands with them for good!"

He got up and began to pace the room as the words poured out as fast as his thoughts. "They can't just go back to bombing shops; for a start, they kill innocent women and children, and worse still from their point of view, American tourists, which would totally undo all the propaganda successes that Sinn Fein achieved over there. They can't bomb army parades any more, because killing young musicians, not to mention horses, only makes people angry, as does murdering war heroes like Airey Neave."

He was in full flow now.

"They can't murder Royalty, they saw that when they blew up Mountbatten's boat. That gains them nothing but hatred, and public opinion would demand extremely punitive measures in retaliation if they pursued that course."

"Bombing motorways and airports only gets up the back of all the ordinary people whose travel plans get delayed, so, what are we left with?" He clenched a fist excitedly.

"It's got to be the Prime Minister! That way they could expect public revulsion, yes, but not as if it were the Queen, and if properly orchestrated by the Sinn Fein media and others it might just force a reaction vote through the House to withdraw the troops from Northern Ireland, and then.." He broke off, ..

"And then they've won!"

Grey sat bolt upright. "You could well be right," He said slowly, shocked rigid that Hunter had, in a few mental leaps, arrived at the centre of the plot!

Thoughtfully Hunter continued: "They've gone that route before with Mrs Thatcher at the Grand Hotel in Brighton, and there's also been that botched mortar attempt on Number Ten itself, even if it was by a breakaway group."

"Mind you," he continued: "That could well be another reason for the Provisionals to go for the P.M., just to show that they can make a better job of it!"

Martin stood up and joined Hunter at the desk. "I think Jim's right, Sir, it's got to be, it all adds up!"

Grey reached for the intercom switch. "Mrs Hemmings... Yes, get Sir Hector on the 'phone for me will you, thank you."

He sat back. "Yes. I think you're right." He said slowly: "Now, God help us, all we've got to do is figure out how, where and when!"

CHAPTER FIFTY-SEVEN

It had been so easy for Kennedy to obtain a duplicate electronic key to Kavanah's room that it was almost criminal! He simply took one of his own plastic keys back to the night receptionist and complained that it no longer operated the lock.

Profuse apologies were immediately forthcoming, as he waited for it to be reprogrammed - with the diplomat's number naturally. "We change the programming regularly, for security" explained the helpful receptionist, charmed by Kennedy's easy smile: "But sometimes it doesn't seem to take."

"Well, you've been well and truly taken!" chuckled Kennedy to himself as he walked away to take the elevator back to his own room.

Three A.M., was the deadest part of night, the time well known to doctors when sleep is deepest and body functions at their lowest ebb. Kennedy stealthily pushed the key into the lock of the executive suite and quietly opened the door.

He quickly flashed the beam from his little torch around the room. Reassured, he let himself in, and carefully put the two packages under his arm down on the floor.

He tiptoed silently over the thick carpet to the door of the darkened bedroom. Holding his breath, he grasped the knob and eased it open.

With a mental sigh of relief he saw the wheelchair at the foot of the bed. The stertorous breathing from the huddled shape beneath the sheets made his task easier. He stepped carefully, timing each footfall to coincide with the snores. Praying that the wheels were well oiled, quietly he pulled the chair back into the lounge and closed the door.

Quickly but not rushing the task, he took a canvas roll of tools from one pocket and unfolded it on the floor, from this he selected a small spanner. From another pocket he took out a can of aerosol penetrating fluid. Giving the retaining nuts a quick spray, he began to undo them. They came free with no difficulty at all.

In minutes he had removed the wheels and slipped on the new ones, packed with Semtex, and re-tightened the fastening nuts firmly.

Careful to ensure that he left nothing behind, he replaced the spanner and the spraycan, rolled up the tools and pushed them back into his pocket.

Gently he eased the bedroom door open again, and began to wheel the chair back to its place at the foot of the bed. The snores continued unabated, and he was almost at the bed when one of the new wheels gave a horrifying squeal!

The snores stopped, as did Kennedy's breathing as he froze rigid, like a statue. With a grunt, the sleeping Kavanah snorted and turned over. Kennedy stood there, not daring to move a muscle. Then, thankfully, after an interminable silence, with a spluttering and a clearing of the throat, the raucous snoring started once more, and he was able to nudge the chair into position and silently steal out of the room.

Collecting the original wheels, Kennedy carefully surveyed the room, nothing must be left to indicate his presence.

Satisfied, he tiptoed out of the apartment, pulling the door shut behind him.

CHAPTER FIFTY-EIGHT

The tour guide was shepherding her little group of camera-laden Japanese and American tourists on the last section of the tour of the Mansion House and its magnificent collections of paintings, porcelain, silverware and statuary. It had been a long day, and she was eager to escape and enjoy the last of the afternoon sunshine.

Thankfully, this was her last group tour for a while.

Margaret Baines' mind was already running on to her forthcoming visit to her old maiden aunt Vivian, and the blessed relief of being able to relax amongst the flowers in her tiny Hampshire cottage garden, such a welcome change from the drabness of her own tiny Hampstead basement apartment.

These irregular security clampdowns were sometimes a nuisance, but on the other hand, it did mean that she could get away for a few days now and again. What was it this time? She wasn't too sure, something about an Anglo-Irish summit banquet the memo had said. Anyway, with an effort she wrenched her mind back to the present; on with the last lap.

Pre-occupied as she was, she wasn't aware of losing one of her flock as they passed the Gentleman's Toilets. Even had she seen the tall figure limp away into the white tiled sanctuary she would not have thought it either remarkable or novel, the needs of the bladder were well known to her, one extra cup of tea with her elevenses and she was in and out of the loo all day!

Inside the empty echoing white porcelain-walled chambers, Kennedy locked himself into one of the tiny cubicles and sat down.

Satisfied that he was alone, he unbuttoned his jacket, and carefully withdrew a long cling-film wrapped metal tube from the waistband of his trousers. He propped the cause of his stiff leg in the corner and took two smaller similarly wrapped metal sections from his inside jacket pocket. Finally, from another trouser pocket he pulled out a small plastic bag that clinked as he placed it on the floor by his feet.

Taking a small roll of adhesive tape from his jacket, he taped the two smaller metal sections to the long pipe. Bending down, he retrieved the plastic bag and held it up, checking the contents one last time.

The five long rifle bullets weighed heavily in his hand, and through the opaque plastic he could make out the small screw-in trigger mechanism, spring and telescopic sight that would complete the transformation of the pieces into a high powered single-shot murder weapon.

With another piece of tape he secured the bag to the other parts, and standing on the lavatory seat, he slid the entire package into the water-filled cistern.

Climbing down, he tore off a few sheets of toilet paper, wiped his hands on them and flushed them away. Then, remembering to limp, he made his way out of the toilets and up to the entrance lobby, to join the last of the tourists as they made their final souvenir purchases at the small kiosk.

"It's a funny sort of security", he mused, thinking of his earlier purchase, "that publishes detailed layout plans of sensitive buildings in the form of tourist guides!"

CHAPTER FIFTY-NINE

The soft American voice in Grey's ear on the scrambled line from the Embassy was quite confident of the credibility of the mole's information.

Southern Ireland was one of the main European shipping centres for all kinds of goods to the United States, and on a reciprocal basis it was one of the busiest staging places for American goods and equipment into Europe. A number of international companies had recognised this, and taking advantage of relatively cheap labour and generous government grants, had established a small enclave of European-American businesses and factories in the country.

Thus it was not at all remarkable that American accents together with German, Dutch, Scandinavian and French, were to be heard mingling with the native Irish in the bars, clubs and restaurants of a number of the main Southern Ireland industrial centres.

It had been a positive boon to the fund-raisers of the IRA when they were able to convert visiting Irish Americans to their cause, especially when they turned out to be so useful in laundering the cash raised by NORAID activities in the States through their businesses and into the IRA coffers.

Patrick James Lawson Jnr. was a large raw-boned Bostonian. He was second generation Irish. He was also a tried and tested conduit for both money and classified computer equipment from the States into Southern Ireland.

Publically a tireless supporter of St. Patrick's Day parades, for more than twelve years he had never stinted in his work for the cause, proving his worth until he was included without second thought in the list of influential supporters privy to the decisions of the political and decision-making conferences of the higher echelons of the Provisional IRA. It was to Patrick Lawson that they turned whenever the question of American public opinion was considered, or whenever a particular piece of hardware was required.

During the Cease-Fire he had been given the task of whipping up popular feeling in the United States against the forthcoming Anglo-Irish summit, which was to be depicted as yet another nail in the coffin of a united Ireland, ground under the heel of a foreign oppressor, sold out by weak or crooked officials from both sides of the border.

In confidence he had been privy to the whisper. This was the big one! This was the one which would break the alliance for ever! This time the bastards would learn once and for all that the yoke of servitude to a foreign power was to be broken! And those pushy INLA bastards! - they too would once and for all be put in their place!

Of course, he didn't put it in quite those terms in his report back to the Agency Central Bureau.

James Patrick Lawson Jnr. was also a CIA mole!

It was from information passed on by him that the SAS had been dispatched to Gibraltar to wipe out the three-man (or more properly the two-man and one woman) unit preparing to carry out bombing operations on the island.

It was also Lawson who had provided details of the time and strength of the planned attack on the police station at

Loughall, which had ended in the deaths of eight of the Provisional's most trusty soldiers in a bloody ambush set by the forewarned security forces.

Grey replaced the handset, thoughtfully.

Although he had agreed that there was only one course of action open to end for once and for all this endless procession of tragedies, he was not privy to the innermost secrets. He would be informed when the time was right and only then would he subtly steer events in their desired course. Until then he was forced to act as his position demanded. Any other course would – in retrospect – invite suspicion.

He forced away a moment of creeping doubt and concentrated on the task as if engaged in a momentous game of chess.

The answer jelled into focus in his seething brain.

It had to be at the Mansion House! That was the only place where it could be guaranteed that the Prime Minister and members of the cabinet would be together with the entire summit group. It would also give maximum publicity to any terrorist attack. Especially, considered Grey, if the attempt were timed to coincide with the televised address by the P.M. and the delegates following the concluding banquet!

He picked up the 'phone again.

It didn't take long to alert the security services. One call to Hereford had the 22 Regiment SAS anti-terrorist squads scrambling into their dark blue unmarked vans, and another brought into action a pre-designated security co-ordinating team drawn from MI5, Special Branch and Home Office personel.

Within the hour the team was operating from a mobile unit in a side-street next to the Mansion House, overseeing the bomb detection dog and electronic survey sections sweeping the building for concealed explosives.

Naturally, security was at a high level anyway, in anticipation of the conference and banquet. No movement in or out of the building was possible without a special pass, and Special Branch officers were stationed at each entrance to search everyone who entered.

Within hours the surrounding building tops were searched and declared clear, and snipers from the special police D11 unit placed in advantageous positions covering the entire area. As an extra precaution, portable metal detectors were installed at each entrance to prevent the possibility of any fire-arms being smuggled into the building.

Inside the mobile centre, Hunter and Grey were receiving the reports from the various units, summarised by the duty co-ordinator.

Hunter was exhausted. He and Martin had been over the building again and again. Even when the dog found nothing, they had ordered a complete re-sweep. "It could just be that for once we've acted in time James," Grey sat behind a tiny desk littered with telephones and piles of reports.

"There's not much escapes the dog, and now we've got the electronic sweeping teams in as well. If there is anything there we'll find it!"

Hunter raised his eyebrows quizzically: "Dog, sir"?

"Cut backs , James, always bloody cut backs!" Grey shook his head

"Yes Sir" Hunter's voice was weary and dull. He pulled back his shoulders to ease the crick from his neck. "It's just that....well, I'm not so sure...."

He broke off as Dennis Martin clambered up into the cabin and moved passed the seated controllers to join them. "Nothing sir." He flashed a tired grin at Hunter. "The dog found nothing and the electronic boys found nothing; not a trace of explosive in the entire building!"

He nodded in satisfaction as he reached over and poured a coffee from the thermos on the desk. "That bastard'll never get anything past us now, so he's too bloody late!" He lifted the paper cup and toasted them happily.

Hunter listened with half an ear as Martin and Grey went over the precautions yet again. It could be right, he mused, but deep down inside he still felt uneasy. He had expected more than this, but what could they have missed? Still, he couldn't quite shake off that little tendril of doubt that niggled in his brain.

CHAPTER SIXTY

Next morning dawned bright and sunny, in the early quietness Grey could hear the birds singing. He sat for a moment in the back of the Daimler outside the Mansion House. On a day like this, how could grown men be scurrying about with their heads filled with thoughts of death and destruction? Sometimes he despaired. Not so that anyone would be allowed to see, of course, but inside he was always aware of the huge gulf between the world as he wished it to be, and the world as it really was.

But how else could it be, if men like him lost heart and gave up the struggle, then who else would stop the men with guns?

He gazed out of the side window. In the distance he could see Hunter talking animatedly with the SAS major in charge of the squad from Hereford.

Grey knew that Hunter had probably been up most of the night checking and re-checking the building. Grey also knew that he was ultimately responsible for turning him into the killer that he now was.

Has he been right? Was this paradox inevitable, that to catch a killer you had to subvert a good man into becoming a killer? He sighed and closed his eyes, leaning his head back, feeling the coolness of the leather against his neck.

He thought for a moment of Priscilla, of how it had been when he was young and the future looked so challenging for newly married couple.

Not being able to have children had hurt. It had hurt Priscilla even more when tests revealed that there was no treatment that could have helped her. It had changed things, even though he had tried to deny it, the future had not seemed so sure.

Work had helped. Even more when the cancer eating away at Priscilla's bowels took her away from him for ever.

He sighed deeply, remembering and feeling again the overwhelming sense of futility that had almost destroyed him. Fate, he thought, seemed to have contrived to have brought him to where he now was. Helpless again, in the face of inevitability.

In the end he had devoted his life to destroying cancer. Not the kind that surgeons excised, but those cancerous sub-humans who threatened to contaminate the lives of every innocent man woman and child that they came into contact with.

"The greater good…all for the greater good!"

It was true, but somehow it wasn't the palliative it should have been. Throwing his lot in with Sir Ambrose, and Hector Bainbridge made him feel dirty and ashamed, no-matter that it would be for the public good! He felt debased. He re-called a quote from Richard II: "For God's sake let us sit upon the ground and tell sad stories of the death of Kings." And now he too was ready to usurp and murder. Not a King, perhaps, but a Prime Minister! As if that made any difference.

"The greater good!" His head sank lower.

He was stuck, whichever way he moved. He was determined to end the horror of murderous men, and to do so he was turning a good man into one.

At the same time he was helping to engineer an act of violence as despicable as any of his enemies, and betray not only his country's leader, and his conscience, but also the good men working for him. All in the name of the greater good!

He removed his glasses and rubbed his tired eyes. This was no good. There was work to be done, time to make sure that the health of the nation was protected. He suddenly broke into a broad grin. Didn't that make him a kind of prophylactic? A gigantic human condom?

Feeling somewhat better, he swung open the car door and strode purposefully across to join Hunter and the Major.

CHAPTER SIXTY-ONE

The little ex-British Telecom telephone engineer's van swayed on its worn shock absorbers with the weight of the last of the three men as he climbed in the back and slammed the door shut.

All three wore regulation overalls, and yellow hard-hats lay on the floor of the van next to bags of tools, large reels of cable and steel boxes packed with gelignite and bags of six inch nails.

All three were INLA, 'co-operating' - for the time being - with the official IRA, and liking it not one little bit. In fact, if they hadn't certain special instructions concerning their temporary commander, well....even the most successful operations sometimes carried a high price tag!

The Bayswater traffic was light, making the journey to the Mansion House an easy one. This early in the afternoon there were no restricted areas as there would be when the VIPs began to arrive for the banquet. Approximately one mile from the building the van pulled into a quiet side-street and stopped by a red telephone box.

With no sense of urgency, the three climbed out of the van and opening the back, pulled out the tool boxes, a small collapsible striped canvas awning and two 'Danger' boards. Unhurriedly they erected the awning next to the telephone box, fixed an 'Out of Order' sticker on the door of the box, and laid a out a variety of tools. Then, with one occasionally busying himself with a headset and pair of pliers, they spent the rest of the afternoon as any typical workmen, eating sandwiches, drinking tea and reading the racing pages.

The bottle of Bushmills with which they laced the tea was somewhat incongruous in such a setting, as was the carton of American cigarettes, but no-one could actually see inside the canvas hut and, like typical workmen, they disappeared into the background.

CHAPTER SIXTY-TWO

"Go home James, you can't do any more here now, so go and get some rest while you can."

If Hunter hadn't been so desperately tired, he would have wondered again at the other side of Charles Grey that this crisis had revealed. As it was he nodded wearily and allowed himself to be ushered out of the mobile control room and into his commander's waiting car. Thankfully, he sank into the yielding leather.

With his eyes closed, Hunter could hear Grey issuing instructions to the dark-suited Special Branch driver: "Take him home, see him to bed, then make sure he's back here for 8pm tonight."

God he was tired! How long had it been since he slept last? Hunter couldn't think straight. The motion of the car rocked him gently as it sped through the traffic, and although he knew that he would feel like death when he arrived at his apartment and would have to get out, within minutes he was fast asleep.

The three fake-Telecom engineers spent the time that Hunter was sleeping in various ways. Sometimes in the van, occasionally sitting in plain view on the tool boxes, sometimes "working" behind the awning. At 5.45pm however, they began to pack away their newspapers and tools, and stowed the signs and toolboxes back into the van. Then they folded up and loaded the awning. When everything was packed, the driver got into the front, whilst his two companions climbed into the back, clutching the remains of Kennedy's little gesture – a bottle of Bushmills and the opened carton of Marlboro.

Michael Farrell did not enjoy being so exposed, but he had had his instructions from Kennedy, and it did make sense.

It was always possible that Special Branch had discovered the safe house where they had been staying, and were simply waiting for the right moment to move in. Best be out as soon as possible. Also, by getting so close to the target as early as possible they would avoid the possibility of running into heavy traffic, and, of course, the vehicle security checks which would later on be set up around the Mansion House.

That was what Kennedy had said anyway. Farrell leaned out of the open van window and spat expressively into the gutter.

"Some chance!" He thought. He and the others had been like mice since moving in some six weeks before. There was no chance that their cover had been blown. Still, he admitted, although he personally didn't like mixing with the PROVOS, Kennedy was the boss on this job, and he had determined that once the plan was in operation they must be close to the target, with no chance of interception.

His lips tightened in a grim smile as he briefly contemplated the manner in which his appreciation of his leader was eventually to be shown.

He looked over his shoulder to the two men working steadily away in the back. "How's it going?"

"Not long now, the last one's going in, so just you make sure you don't go over any fuckin' bumps now"

Farrell grunted and turned back, looking at his watch. It was 6pm. Nearly time to move.

He ran the plan over again in his mind.

Once the detonators were set into the nail and gelignite packed steel toolboxes, he was to drive to the telephone box at the front of the Mansion House and, whilst pretending to check it, plant the bombs in it where they would be set to explode as the Prime Minister arrived for the banquet.

Simple. Yes but also obvious!

Farrell sniffed. he had to hand it to that bastard, he was a devious one!

Kennedy had explained that he didn't mind if the bombs were discovered. Of course, there was always a chance that they wouldn't be, and that they would explode as planned and that would be that. If, as was more likely, they were found and defused, then the security forces would be cock-a-hoop with their success, and thus less alert to Kennedy's penetration, and the real attempt - whatever that might be - for, naturally, Kennedy wasn't about to tell him.

"Clever bastard!"

The tap on his shoulder told Farrell that all was ready. He reached forward and turned the ignition key, starting the van, and, careful not to hit any raised manholes or obstruction on the road, he began to drive the final mile to the Mansion House.

CHAPTER SIXTY-THREE

Special Branch do not advertise their telephone number, but Kennedy knew that a call to the duty officer at West End Central Police Station, if containing the correct key words agreed with the IRA to facilitate area clearance in the face of genuine bomb threats, would certainly reach the right ears within minutes.

At the very moment that the final detonator was attached, he made the call as ordered by General Command that was to alert the SAS and D11 sniper sections that three bombs were due to be planted at the Mansion House, and that the bombers were driving a fake British Telecom van.

Clearly he spoke the correct code words that were to seal the fates of Farrell and his two accomplices, and in one fell swoop remove the INLA's best mainland unit!

All calls in to West End Central Police Station are recorded as a matter of course, and in less than two minutes the duty officer was playing the tape over the secure 'phone to Special Branch officers. In no more than five minutes all units in the area of the Mansion house had been alerted to clear the streets and watch out for a British Telecom van, and the duty co-ordinator was briefing Grey, Martin and the SAS major in charge of the black-clad sniper teams.

In less than seven minutes from Kennedy's call, the three men in the van were as good as dead.

At six-thirty precisely, the first reported sighting of a suspicious Telecom van in the immediate area was heard over the loudspeaker in the mobile control unit. Within seconds reports were coming in from rooftop observers, plotting its progress.

"Sir." The Major saluted Grey."They'll be passing within range of our first fire zone any moment now. Permission to shoot?"

Every head in the room turned towards Grey.

Grey was in a quandary. This was not the arrangement at all! One clinical shot one target was the agreement, not another indiscriminate slaughter of innocent people!

And what if this was another diabolical plot to make it appear that the British security forces were trigger-happy killers! What if the van driver was a totally innocent victim of an IRA trick? He couldn't just order the SAS to open fire without at least finding out.

But who could he order to do the finding out? If there were terrorists in the van, then it would be suicidal, but if there weren't, and he simply had them shot, then it would be murder!

"Shit, shit shit….."

Abruptly Grey got to his feet. Ordering Martin to stay in the control unit, he hurried outside and ran quickly over to his car. The radio in his hand crackled and spluttered as fresh information about the movements of the Telecom van was relayed from the rooftops. It would be there in less than two minutes.

There was no time to delegate. Grey wrenched open the door of his Daimler and pulled out the startled driver.

"Wait over there out of the way!" He shouted, tossing the handset onto the passenger's seat. He leapt behind the wheel and started the motor. Jerking the gear lever to 'Drive', he slammed his foot down hard on the accelerator and aimed the speeding car down the road in the direction of the oncoming van.

The voice on the radio beside him crackled into life: "Target should be turning into sight any moment now, just at the top of the road."

Grey's heart pounded madly in his chest. There it was, coming around the corner, driving at a leisurely pace, straight towards him.

This was it! he thought, snatching up the radio with his left hand and fingering the transmit button.

"If they go past me shoot them!" He yelled his instructions into the radio, then threw it down as he grabbed the wheel and yanked it hard over with both hands, skidding and sliding the powerful car sideways directly in the path of the oncoming vehicle.

Swearing violently, Farrell savagely wrenched at the steering wheel of the van, tossing his companions into a heap as it threatened to overturn. With a bang the front wheels mounted the kerb as he fought to maintain control.

For brief agonising moments it looked as though he were going to succeed, then with a sickening crump the front of the sliding Daimler smashed into the rear of the van, spinning it over and over in a spray of glass and shattered metal.

"Holy Shit!" The voice came tinnily from the radio somewhere in the bottom of the halted Daimler.

Bruised and shaken, Grey blessed the armoured strength of the car, and bent over to retrieve it.

Shaking the cobwebs from his brain, he pressed the transmit button again: "Nobody approach. If there is a bomb it might go off, so stay clear. I'm going to check."

"But sir.." the tremor in the voice was apparent."Sir, don't! Please wait! We'll have the army bomb disposal remote vehicle check it out, its too dangerous…"

Angrily Grey jabbed the button again. He had to know the truth. "If there is no bomb then some poor bastard might just be bleeding to death there!"He tossed the handset onto the back seat to curtail further discussion and jerking free the stuck driver's door he clambered awkwardly out.

Swaying slightly, he took a deep breath and walked slowly over to the upturned van. The only sound in the street was that of his breathing and the crunching of broken glass under his feet. The only movement that of the one of the van's rear wheels as it spun slowly in the air.

Cautiously he approached the back of the van.

Then he knew; for scattered all around were hundreds of six-inch nails! Either they hadn't trusted him, or they were playing doubly safe! Whatever the consequences, he couldn't let this happen.

Sliding his hand under his armpit, Grey eased his automatic from its holster and pulled back the slide, jacking a bullet up into the chamber, and clicked off the safety catch. Slowly, very slowly, holding his breath, he peered in through the shattered back windows.

Amidst the shambles he could tell that he would have no trouble from the two occupants. The awkward, unnatural angle of the neck of one made it obvious that it was broken, and the head of the second, well, it wasn't really recognisable as a head anymore, just a crushed and bloody pulp underneath what appeared to be a heavy steel toolbox.

His feet crunched on the broken glass as he carefully moved around to the front of the van, to check on the driver. Holding his gun two handed in front of him, he kept it trained on the unmoving body that lay sprawled half out of the smashed windscreen. He was a mess! Limp and with no obvious signs of life, blood dripped from a tremendous wound on his head.

Clicking on the safety and easing down the hammer, Grey allowed himself a long ragged breath. He slid the automatic back under his arm and checked the driver's pulse. It was weak, but it was there. He began to ease him bodily through the remains of the windscreen and onto the glass strewn pavement.

Pulling out a handkerchief, he began to wipe away the blood in order to find the wound and staunch it.

Suddenly, he wasn't sure how it happened, but he found himself lying down on the pavement, looking up hazily at wavering buildings and a universe that contained no straight lines at all!

He felt numb, far away somehow.

A black swaying shadow loomed over him, and through swirling mists he was vaguely aware of looking up at the muzzle of a big black revolver.

That was the last moment of awareness that this life had to

offer Grey. In the next instant, the gun that the injured Farrell had first used to club Grey to the ground blew a hole right between his eyes!

Hauling himself erect, the staggering, betrayed Farrell lifted his head to scream his anger and defiance to the skies. Not a sound left his lips, however. All he did was a marionette dance of death as four rifle bullets ripped and tore his chest to shreds, smashing his body into the side of the van bouncing it back into a heap next to the still figure of Grey on the blood-spattered and wreckage-strewn road.

Then the world exploded into confusion and blackness, as a long way away from the scene, Kennedy pressed the detonator trigger.

CHAPTER SIXTY-FOUR

Apart from the occasional crackle as routine reports came in, the mobile command unit was quiet.

Within 30 minutes of the incident, forensics had measured and photographed the scene, Grey's body had been removed along with those of the three dead terrorists. Traffic control had cordoned off the remains of the van behind large screens, workmen cleared away shattered glass from nearby windows and uniformed constables began to take up their stations along the route of the motorcade bringing the dignitaries and politicians to the banquet.

Hunter sat behind the tiny desk where, not that long before, Grey had sat, issuing instructions.

He stared blankly out of the small window at the activity outside. None of it registered, however. He wasn't thinking, he wasn't even aware of anything. Like a Yogi or Buddhist monk in profound meditation, he simply sat.

When the 'phone call had come, waking him from a deep sleep, it had not been to inform him of the arrival of his car, as he had expected, but to shock him into wakefulness with the news of Grey's death.

The journey back to the Mansion House had been a blank to him. He had no recollection at all of making it. He had arrived in time to see the bodies being bagged and lifted into the waiting ambulance. Numbly he watched as it drove away at speed, as if its contents would somehow benefit by getting to their destination sooner rather than later.

Martin had taken charge of the immediate arrangements, and he had steered Hunter into the command centre, sat him down and thrust a mug of hot coffee into his unresisting hand.

The high degree of external security had been maintained, the snipers remained on the rooftops, and the checks on the press and TV reporters entering the building to cover the ceremonies were as thorough as before. Those were Martin's orders, but it was difficult to deny the sense of satisfaction that had followed the termination of the bomb threat. Grey's death had been a bitter blow, but the general feeling was that the attempt on the Mansion House had failed.

"Ah Hunter!" The plummy tones of Sir Hector impinged on Hunter's awareness, and he looked up as the tall elegant figure, resplendent in evening dress pushed his way passed the seated controllers and over to the desk.

"Dreadful business, absolutely dreadful!" Bainbridge spun round angrily gesturing. "All this, and he had to go and do it himself!"

"Bloody fool!"

He took a breath and regained his composure. He turned back to Hunter.

"Right!" He was back to normal again.

"You will take charge until further notice, Grey's number two will be here shortly, but until he arrives you will have full authority. Martin here..." He waved a hand in his direction..."He'll liaise with me, and between us we'll see this sorry mess through."

He stared at Hunter, noting the grim lines around his mouth.

He continued gently: "At least we've the satisfaction of knowing that he managed to stop those bastards."

Hunter suddenly felt cold. His spine prickled as he spoke slowly:

"Did he sir?" Like a shower of ice-cold water, realisation hit him.

"What do you mean?" snapped Bainbridge sharply." Of course he did!"

Hunter slowly got to his feet, how could he explain his uneasiness? "I'm not sure, but somehow it just seems too easy." He chewed his lip.

"First of all we get information about the target, which we all agree on, then we get an anonymous telephone call giving exact details of how and when the bombs are to be placed."

He thrust his hands deep in his pockets, and continued: "It's just not like Kennedy to get caught out like this..." His voice trailed off into silence as realisation dawned.

"That's it!" He grabbed Bainbridge's arm exultantly: "Don't you see, he didn't get caught at all!"

He cut off Sir Hector's protest. "I saw the bodies. I suppose I was so upset at seeing Mr. Grey like that, and it didn't really register, but I'm willing to bet that the man I followed in Marseilles and Majorca wasn't in that van!"

"But at least one of them was completely unrecognisable after that explosion. His head was crushed to a pulp!" Martin's voice cut in over Sir Hector's shoulder,

"I know, Dennis!" Hunter exclaimed excitedly. "But I'll stake my life that he wasn't in that van. The scheming bastard probably set them up himself to distract us from the real attempt!"

Bainbridge looked shocked. He turned to Martin: "Well, could this be true?" "Could he do that?"

Martin was dumbfounded. He looked first at Hunter and then at Sir Hector, then he replied, weighing every word.

"We've run fingerprint tests on the bodies, but so far we've come up with a blank. Even then, we don't have Kennedy's on file, but if we do manage to trace records on all three of the others, then Jim's right, and our man's still at large."

His eyes mirrored his concern: "The trouble is, that'll take time, and we've got the problem to deal with here and now." He fell silent for a moment, gnawing his bottom lip as he considering the problem. After a moment he came to a decision.

He looked gravely at Bainbridge: "I think we'd better assume that Jim's right, Sir."

The quiet order of the control room became a memory as Hunter and Martin hurried to issue fresh orders to all units.

It was a little after 7.30pm and the VIPs were due to begin arriving at eight. Less than 30 minutes. Hunter spoke urgently to a uniformed controller:

"Get the bloody dog back in again. I want a complete sweep, everywhere, dining room, kitchens, foyer, ante-rooms, gallery, everywhere including the toilets. Get moving!"

He grabbed Martin's arm: "Dennis, get the electronic snoopers to follow the dog, and get a move on, we've not much time."

He turned to the tall figure of Sir Hector: "If we don't find anything, Sir, I think we should call it off!"

Sir Hector was aghast: "Call it off! We can't do that, man, the P.M. would have a seizure. Think of the publicity. This is supposed to be the high point of the Anglo-Irish summit, we can't just 'call it off' like that. Not if we don't find anything!" Nor could Sir Hector falter at this stage, the die was cast, and – to mix a metaphor – the pieces were in play.

Hunter gave him a long hard look. He wasn't going to do any good standing here trying to change his mind.

Briskly, he brushed passed him. "You see the P.M. when he comes, I'll be inside, and I'll report when I can." Beckoning Martin to come with him, he hurried over to the security cordon at the front of the building.

Sir Hector Bainbridge's hands began to tremble violently and he stuffed them deep in his pockets!

"Christ! How was this thing going to turn out?" His brain seethed, momentarily his urbane equanimity was lost He hadn't bargained on losing Grey, and now Hunter wanted him to stop the PM from attending! Then all would be lost, all this.....horror...would be for nothing!

What was it Lady Macbeth said? "I am in blood stepped so far that, should I wade no more returning were as tedious as go o'er!"

He drew a deep and ragged breath; it was true! He could not back out now, he was in blood up to his bloody neck

CHAPTER SIXTY-FIVE

Hunter and Martin were too late, naturally.

Kennedy, complete with camera and equipment bag had been inside the building for at least twenty minutes. His Press badge gained him admittance along with about thirty others who were covering the event, together with BBC and Satellite T.V. outside broadcast units.

The door security had been very thorough, even the lense had been removed from his camera body and checked, and the contents of his bag turned out and individually examined. This had held no fear for Kennedy, there was nothing that would give any cause for concern, certainly nothing remotely like a bomb.

The short-burst transmitter was simply another piece of electronic flash equipment, and aroused no attention at all.

Nothing to do now, he thought, but to follow the rest of the throng of newspaper and television cameramen and reporters through to the Press refreshment rooms set aside for them, and have a cup of coffee. With a friendly nod to the security officer, he shouldered his camera and equipment bag and walked jauntily off.

CHAPTER SIXTY-SIX

The large black limousine pulled up outside Number 10 Downing Street, promptly at 7.45pm.

Inside, in one of the little ante-rooms off the P.M.'s private drawing room, Chief Inspector Douglas was giving a brief summary of the Mansion House situation to the Prime Minister as he prepared to leave.

The picture of unflappable calmness that the nation was normally presented with on T.V. and in the House was beginning to show signs of wear. Brushing off the ministrations of a fussing PPS, the slight edge in the Prime Minister's voice was sharply apparent.

He turned to the Home Secretary, waiting patiently by the door. "What do you think, Ambrose, is it safe?"

"Well, Prime Minister, I gather that Sir Hector feels that it's a fuss about nothing, he's assured me that they've intercepted the bombers and dealt with the problem."

He smiled reassuringly: "And, after all, he is going to be there too, so I don't believe we've much to worry about, and it would be just a little awkward cancelling your speech at such short notice."

"Hmm. Right, we'd better go then." The P.M. sounded unconvinced, but, what choice did he have, especially in the last few month's of the life of Parliament, and the bloody opposition looking to exploit any signs of weakness in his political armour!

Inspector Douglas coughed politely.

"The car's outside Sir, and I've arranged for an extra man to travel with you in it, and Sir Hector has ordered a full security cordon to be maintained around the whole area."

Wolseley nodded briefly to Douglas, and ushered the P.M. briskly out of the door, passed the waiting photographers and TV Outside Broadcast news teams and into the waiting car.

CHAPTER SIXTY-SEVEN

Back in the mobile control room, Hunter was biting his lip with frustration. The dog had covered the whole building again, from top to bottom, with no results; the electronics team had also gone over the same ground but absolutely nothing in any way suspicious had registered.

Now the VIPs were beginning to arrive, Sir Hector was greeting the summit members in the Lord Mayor's parlour, the P.M. and the Home Secretary were on their way, and Hunter was still convinced that they were on the brink of a catastrophe.

"I know I'm right, Dennis! But where has he planted it? He wouldn't delegate something like this to anyone else. No, he set those poor sods up. This is his supreme moment."

He paced up and down in the cramped space in a mood of black frustration.

Martin was pouring over lists of dignitaries and their wives and the plans of the seating arrangements, the desk was covered with papers. He sat back in disgust. Gesturing at the plans, he looked up:

"Look Jim, There's nothing out of the ordinary, nothing at all. I've even checked the originals against the updated set from Sir Hector's office and apart from a wheelchair ramp up to the dais for that Irish delegate who had that skiing accident everything is identical."

His words exploded into Hunter's brain!

"When did he give you another plan?" He demanded.

"This afternoon, when you were at home sleeping." Martin continued defensively: "But there's no additions to the first one, all the same people are going to be present."

"For Christ's sake, man!" Hunter snarled: "You've just told me one difference!"

"You mean the ramp? But Jim, its just a few wooden planks that's all!" He was shouting after Hunter's disappearing back, as he raced out of the command centre and across to the Mansion House entrance.

Swearing, Martin ran after him, holding his security pass high.

Pushing their way through the confusion of liveried ushers, waiters, security officers and reporters filling the corridors, Hunter actually brushed past Kennedy, as he made his way towards the main banqueting hall. He never gave him a second glance as he flashed his pass to the doormen and strode up to the dais. Martin caught up with him as he seized the end of the wooden ramp and strained to lift it up.

"Give me a hand" He grunted with the effort, as between them they levered it up and overturned it with a crash.

"Fuck!" Hunter sat disconsolately on the upturned ramp. It was empty!

CHAPTER SIXTY-EIGHT

The only tense moment that Kennedy had experienced before he went back to the refreshment room was as he watched Kavanah and his Trojan Horse wheel their way through the security checks. He felt a glow of satisfaction seeing the sniffer dog ignoring the chair completely as the Southern Irish delegate was manoeuvred by his aides through the crush into the private reception areas.

Two more hours, then the banquet would be over and the speeches underway. First the Home Secretary, to welcome the delegates officially; then Philip Monroe, chairman of the working committee, to thank HMG for its continued support through difficult times, and finally, the Prime Minister in person, to take the credit for it all!

Well, thought Kennedy gleefully, this will be one speech that will certainly go with a bang!

CHAPTER SIXTY-NINE

Hunter was desperate! The banquet was almost over, the main course already served. Perhaps thirty minutes before the speeches were due to begin, and in his bones he knew without a doubt that something terrible was going to happen.

Martin had helped him to replace the ramp, and had then gone to give a situation update to Bainbridge, leaving Hunter even more frustrated than before.

The liveried ushers ceremoniously pushed open the huge doors to the splendid chandeliered banqueting hall and the VIPs and their guests filed in and took their seats. Then the red-coated and bewigged master of ceremonies banged his gavel three times and announced the arrival of the top-table dignitaries and finally the Prime Minister, who shook hands with the various delegates, and then sat down in the central place of honour.

From his vantage point in one corner of the banqueting hall Hunter had a good view of the top table. He couldn't figure it out. No sign of anything out of the ordinary, nothing, even the wheelchair ramp was clean.

He glanced at Martin as he weaved his way through the hurrying plate-laden waiters towards him.

"Well Jim." He shrugged apologetically:

"Sir Hector's of the opinion that nothing's going to happen now, and he doesn't want us upsetting any of the VIPs, especially in a few minutes, when the speeches start, so that's it."

He shrugged. "He's probably right, after all the only alterations to any of the plans have been because of the wheelchair and the ramp, otherwise everything is as ....."

He stopped short at the look on Hunter's face.

"Of course! It's not the ramp Dennis, it's the fucking wheelchair!"

Martin's face mirrored his shock. "Come on Jim! Surely you don't think..."

Again Hunter cut him off. "It's got to be, there's nowhere else, and of course we never found anything, there was nothing to find until the delegates arrived, they brought the bloody bomb in with them!"

The vehemence and certainty of his logic struck Martin like a blow to the pit of the stomach.

"But what.." Martin's question was lost in the air as Hunter marched briskly straight across the marble floor, in and out of the groups of waiters, and directly up to the top table.

"Just a minute Sir.."

Hunter felt strong fingers clamp firmly around his elbow.

"Oh sorry Sir, I didn't recognise you from behind." The white-wigged and liveried close protection bodyguard released his arm and stepped back.

Hunter moved quickly behind the row of diners, passed the Home Secretary, along behind the Prime Minister who was deep in conversation with the head of the Southern Irish delegation, and passed Sir Hector, who stared at him with a horrified expression on his face as Hunter squeezed in between him and the wheelchair of Eamon Kavanah.

"What the bloody hell's going on, Hunter?" He demanded fiercely.

"Sorry sir, no time!" Hunter turned to the astonished Irishman.

"I'm sorry to bother you, sir, but I'm afraid I need your chair!" Kavanah's jaw dropped, revealing the remains of an unchewed mouthful.

"I'm afraid there's been an accident." Hunter thought quickly, his brain racing for a suitable excuse: "A heart attack, sir, we desperately need a wheelchair for a few moments, sorry!"

"A heart attack! For God's sake Hunter, why do you need a wheelchair?"

Sir Hector was livid with suppressed anger. "I'm so sorry about this Eamon." He swallowed his rage and smiled disarmingly at the astonished delegate, as Hunter and Martin manoeuvred his bulk onto the chair that Martin had seized from the master of ceremonies, behind the top table.

After a moment, Kavanagh remembered to close his mouth. He chewed mechanically not really sure what had happened.

He swallowed: "Think nothing of it, Sir Hector, obviously some poor fella is in desperate need!"

In the corridor between the private reception room and the banqueting hall, Hunter and Martin were frantically tearing at the imitation leather upholstery, slicing in to it with a pocket knife and ripping it apart.

Nothing! The ruined fabric revealed only sponge rubber, nothing else! Hunter kicked the chair in frustration.

His eyes locked onto the tubing of the frame itself.

In a frenzy he pulled, bent, twisted and yanked at it until with Dennis's help all that remained of the wheelchair was a pile of scrap metal and rubber, and the wheels. That's it, he thought hopelessly, as he slumped down beside the ruins. Not a bloody thing.

Dennis looked at him sympathetically. Disconsolately Hunter wondered how he was going to explain the destruction of his wheelchair to the Irishman.

"I suppose we could give him the wheels, Jim!" Martin's sorry attempt to lighten the mood penetrated Hunter's black thoughts and wormed its way down to join the niggling unease that he had felt for so long.

With a start, he snatched up his knife again and grabbed one of the wheels. In an instant he plunged the blade into the rubber and sliced open the tyre.

Martin gasped as he looked over Hunter's shoulder. There it was after all. A long plastic-film-wrapped snake of Semtex plastic explosive.

The two men worked frantically, Hunter sliced open all the tyres, exposing the explosive hidden in the two large ones, then between them, they carefully extracted the dough-like tubes from their hiding places, laying them gently down on the floor in two long strips.

Then Martin, holding his breath, took hold of the detonators between finger and thumb and with a prayer eased them out of the explosive.

With a sigh of relief, they both sat there, briefly savouring their satisfaction.

Inside the banquet hall, the coffee and cigars had been served, the port made its rounds, and the microphones placed in position in preparation for the speeches. In the press room an equerry announced haughtily that it was time for the photographers, reporters and T.V. crews to take up their appointed positions.

Kennedy joined in the scrum of bodies clambering to collect equipment and went with the main body along the corridors and through the massive ornate wooden doors into the roped-off section adjoining the main hall.

As the others poured in, however, Kennedy stopped in the corridor, bending over his gadget bag as if in search of something.

After a moment he extracted a small electronic flash unit which he clipped to the Canon's hot shoe. He waited, listening. From the corridor he could plainly hear the speeches and the applause that punctuated them.

The splendidly uniformed doorman looked quizzically at the lone cameraman not in the hall with the others, perhaps he had some problem with his equipment, he thought, seeing how he kept fiddling with his flash unit.

There was no way that Kennedy wanted to be in that room, He knew what 12lbs of Plastic explosive would do to anyone in range of the blast, and he was content to keep the thickness of the old stone walls between himself and the explosion. He could feel himself sweating slightly as the voice of the master of ceremonies rapped his gavel and announced the Prime Minister.

Kennedy waited a few seconds to allow the applause to die down. Then he was sure. There was no mistaking that dry crisp voice.

He reached for the test button on the side of the flashgun, the button that was in fact wired to the short-burst transmitter circuit board, took a deep breath, and pressed it.

Shocked, Kennedy jabbed it again. Still nothing! He could hear the Prime Minister extolling the praises of the work of the summit committee. He stabbed at it repeatedly.

Sweating and flustered, Kennedy started nervously at the touch on his arm.

"Are you all right, sir?" Solicited the doorman, concerned by the appearance of the obviously shaken reporter. "You don't look very well."

Ashen faced, Kennedy swallowed hard: "Oh. It's nothing, just a bad stomach ache." He smiled away the worried expression on the man's face. "Ulcer, you know!"

The doorman nodded sympathetically as Kennedy gathered his reeling thoughts and walked into the banquet room.

Jesus, Joseph and Mary! Where was the fucking wheelchair! Kennedy could see Kavanagh quite clearly clapping enthusiastically at the end of the table, but he was sitting on a normal dining chair, not in his wheelchair!

There was a madness inside Kennedy's head. To get this close and to fail was unthinkable. He didn't know what had gone wrong, but there was no way that he was going to leave this building as long as the Prime Minister still lived! Burning temper and ice-cold rage battled and fought for supremacy inside his seething brain. He, Liam Kennedy, was not about to lose!

He turned and pushed passed the doorman who watched him as he almost ran into the nearby gents toilet.

Inside the stall, Kennedy retrieved the dripping package from where he had hidden it in the cistern, and frantically tore off and discarded the wet plastic coverings. Hastily he assembled the rifle and fitted the silencer. He knew that he didn't have much longer, for the speeches would soon be over, and the opportunity for a clear shot lost.

Biting his lip with frustration, he pressed home one round into the single-shot chamber, thrust the bag with the remaining bullets into his pocket and ran back into the corridor.

Hunter's radio bleeped. "Yes." He lifted it to his ear.

"I'm sorry to bother you sir." The apologetic tones of the doorman came loud and clear: "But command patched me through to you. I might be wrong of course but one of the reporters was acting kind of funny, and....." He hesitated.

"Yes! What, man, what?" Hunter barked.

"Well, he said he had a bad stomach, and he ran into the gents toilet, and then he ran out again a few moments later, and...I know its probably stupid, sir, but I think he was carrying a gun!"

Hunter and Martin looked at each other dumbstruck with horror.

Moments later, with weapons drawn Hunter and Martin burst into the gents lavatory.

In haste they kicked open all the cubicle doors, but there was no sign of him, only scraps of torn wet plastic lying on the floor in one of the stalls. "The bastard's here, and it's not finished yet, we've got to stop him! Come on!" Hunter ran into the corridor with Martin on his heels.

"It's too late for a full security alarm, he'll be lost in the stampede, we've just got to get to him first!"

Martin caught Hunter's shoulder: "Jim, he'll have to be able to see the P.M. to get a good shot at him. He must've gone back in!"

Jerking to a halt by the entrance doors Hunter grabbed the doorman. "Did he come this way?" He demanded urgently. The doorman shrugged apologetically.

"I didn't see, sir. When I saw him come out of the Gents lavatory again I went to call you."

Hunter swore to himself and followed Martin into the chamber. They began scanning the audience. There was no sign of Kennedy. They looked at each other in dismay. Where on earth could he be? He must be somewhere where he could get a good view of his target, but where?

Hunter lifted his gaze to the galleries. Too exposed, any figure up there would be immediately apparent to the close protection squad, who would be onto him within seconds.

As his eyes travelled upwards, it suddenly dawned on him that the ceiling had a large central glass dome, from which it would be possible see everything.

Martin followed his gaze, the same thought rising in his brain.

"It's the ceiling, Jim. The fucking ceiling!"

They ran into the corridor towards the stairs. As they began to climb, Hunter contacted the mobile controller on the radio.

Breathlessly, Hunter ordered him to reach Sir Hector immediately, and tell him to warn the P.M. that he was in danger from someone in the ceiling galleries.

"Yes sir, but are you sure it's him?" The controller was doubtful, "And we have already got a man posted at the top of the gallery stairs to keep everyone out."

"Just bloody well tell him, will you!"

Stuffing the radio back into his pocket, Hunter raced up the steps, pulling his automatic from its hiding place under his armpit and levered a round into the chamber. Close to the top of the stairs, he suddenly stopped and thrust out an arm, holding Martin back.

He lifted a finger to his lips and pointed upwards.

Something rounded was just visible, projecting upwards over the top step. Crouching, guns ready, the two men inched their way further up the stairs.

As they neared the top, the object turned into the toecap of a boot, then the boot itself, and finally, into one of the sprawling legs of the dead guard.

"Fuck!" Hunter's curse was quiet but intense. Hastily he reached down to feel for the pulse in the man's neck. There wasn't one. There was, however, a ragged hole where one side of his head should have been.

Carefully avoiding the dark spreading pool of blood and matter that oozed thickly from the body, they began to move down the corridor.

Hunter reached over to check the first door, motioning Martin to move on to the next. Time was too short for regulation tactics, their only chance was to check the rooms in a leapfrog fashion.

Inside the end room, Kennedy wiped the sweat from his eyes and tried to control the trembling of his hands. That bloody guard! He had run straight into him. Luckily even from the hip Kennedy's aim was true, and the single, silenced, bullet had torn into the man's skull before he could raise the alarm.

Fumbling with the rifle, he cursed the bad luck that had slowed him down.

From the banquet hall below, the Prime Minister seemed to be coming to the end of his speech.

His fingers scrabbled to press another round into the breech. He had to hurry, but his fingers were too big!

Cursing savagely, at last his feverish fumbling thrust the bullet home and he jerked the rifle into the firing position, one hand frantically twisting the focusing ring of the telescopic site.

Panting as if he had run a marathon, Kennedy bit hard upon his bottom lip and forced his trembling hands to obey him. The hazy silhouette of the Prime Minister's head swam into view through the dirty, semi-opaque glass, then sharpened as he adjusted the image and centred the cross-hairs on the familiar horn-rimmed spectacles.

Out in the corridor, Hunter knew that there was nowhere left for the assassin to be, except in the next room. He motioned to Martin to follow, took a deep breath and with a yell kicked savagely at the door, splintering it from its hinges. As it sprung open he hurled himself bodily in, centring his aim on the figure he saw crouching there in the gloom.

Fate – if Fate is was – nudged the scales that weighed the balance of human endeavour.

Success, failure – joy, heartbreak – good, bad – in that frozen eternity Hunter had time for only one emotion which in an instant echoed vast aeons of human anguish:

"What was the point" His agonised soul screamed, as his right knee – so reliable and almost forgotten – gave way beneath him.

As he slipped, desperately trying to jerk his pistol back on target, the last thing he saw was the silencer, enormous in his wide-eyed vision, jerk slightly upwards as it fired.

There was no pain, perhaps a split second of surprise, then Hunter was hurled backwards by a tremendous slam in the head, as Kennedy's silenced bullet smacked viciously along the side of his temple.

Fate laughed and nudged again.

Hunter's unconscious body spun around like a child's top, his finger spasmed on the trigger sending an arc of deadly lead around the room. The first shot punched into Martin's clavicle and scapula, breaking his arm. The second round entered his leg just above the right knee, exploding his thigh into crimson porridge and severing the femoral artery, arcing a stream of blood high into the air. His helpless body careened into the wall then, slowly, like a puppet with its strings cut, it slid down into a ragged heap into a sitting position.

The room swam and danced in waves of frightful agony as the shock coursed through Martin's crippled body. Blood pulsed hugely from his chest and thigh.

Still alive, the pain robbed him of the power to even breathe. Dimly he was aware of the looming figure bending over him as he ineffectually tried to force his unresponsive muscles to lift the heavy weapon hanging limply from his fingers.

Kennedy's boot lashed out and sent the pistol spinning across the room.

In a paroxysm of fear and rage he kicked again at the stricken man, driving his foot directly into Martin's face. Again he drove his boot into the red mask with such force that the skin tore away revealing in a horrid parody of a smile the white, shining, teeth and jawbone.

The force of the kick smashed the back of Martin's skull into the wall with a sickening force, and all consciousness slipped away, but he knew – as the blackness enveloped him – that he had failed.

Savagely Kennedy tore himself away, almost slipping in the red gore as he did so. There was still time! He was the consummate professional – "Get a grip!" He ordered his rebellious body!

Dragging air deep down into his lungs, shaking with relief and terror he forced his hands to obey him as he forced another shell into the rifle and quickly raised the sights once more. Fighting to control his trembling, he dragged his sleeve roughly across his sweat-wet forehead and squinted once again through the sights. Just a little squeeze, that's all it takes, he thought triumphantly, exulting in his moment of glory!

Savagely he bit into his bottom lip and held his breath in his heaving chest in a desperate bid to stop the rifle bobbing and swaying.

There! Now! Just one chance..one shot..

As the figure of the Prime Minister steadied in the crosshairs, he squeezed the trigger.

"Fuck!"

He knew he had missed.

The Prime Minister, in the act of leaning forward to pick up his notes from the Podium, felt the thrum of the bullet zip audibly past his ear, smashing shards of oak splinters from the Heraldic device behind him.

Pandemonium erupted in the room below him.

Kennedy tossed aside his weapon and stepped carefully over the widening pool of blood issuing from the two inert bodies. Dragging out a handkerchief, he feverishly mopped away the sheen of sweat and blood droplets from his face, and within seconds he had vaulted the body of the dead security guard and was hastening down the stairs and into the milling throng below.

The only outward sign of his activities was the wetness at the bottom of his right trouser leg, and the gore on his shoe which he quickly wiped off on the back of his other leg.

The uproar in the hall was tremendous.   In the shouting, tumultuous panic that had erupted in the main chamber it was easy for him to make his way unchallenged through the corridors seething with a heaving cacophony of frightened diners and newsmen clamouring for information.

People were running in all directions, and if Kennedy was sweating and wild-eyed, then he was not alone! Within minutes he was out into the coolness of the night air.

Total confusion reigned, punctuated by the banshee wailing of ambulance and police sirens.

Exultingly, feverishly, savouring the sweetness of escape, he walked briskly but not too quickly through the back alleys until he reached the car Farrell had earlier driven to the quiet residential Mews. He forced his still trembling body back under control, and with a swift glance around, he pulled his copy of the key from his pocket. Swiftly he unlocked the driver's door and slid behind the wheel.

For a moment he sat there, panting, cuffing away the sweat from his brow, re-living the intensity of the experience.

"Fuck, fuck, fuck, fuck" He silently chanted a mantra-like litany of curses, as he tried to slow his breathing and control the adrenaline shakes.   "Next time!" He promised.

With a grim half smile, half grimace, he turned the ignition key.

Farrell's INLA bomb wired to the ignition was not as sophisticated as one of Kennedy's own. The subsequent explosion ripped mainly through the engine compartment of the car, and Kennedy's world vanished into a sudden haze of sound, orange light and a ripping sensation in his legs, then blackness and numbing, shocking, silence!

EPILOGUE

BBC 9 O'CLOCK NEWS

"..........In a prepared statement issued from Number Ten Downing Street today, the Prime Minister denounced the terroristic activities , which intelligence sources have attributed to a break-away splinter-group from the IRA, the Irish National Liberation Army. He stated that the failed attempt to assassinate him and members of Her Majesty's Government would not sway the elected members of a Democracy from the path of peace recently begun with the responsible leaders of the IRA and that he looks forward to a time when such savage and barbaric acts would be a thing of the past......."

The announcer concluded: "Police will not comment on the theory that the car bomb which exploded in street adjoining the Mansion House was somehow connected to the atrocity, but that there was strong evidence of someone receiving injuries in the blast, and state that local hospitals and medical centres have been asked to report anyone with suspicious injuries requiring treatment."

"Shit!"

In his pristine hospital bed, Hunter withdrew his attention from the TV set on the wall bracket opposite his bed, closed his swollen eyes, turned his aching head further into the crisp white pillow and drifted back into sleep.

Interlude

About the author:

Born of Welsh parents in 1944, Vince lived his early years in West Sussex.

At the age of 9 or so he began a life-long immersion in the Japanese Martial Arts.

He attended Grammar school and because of his rebellious attitude was eventually 'asked to leave.'

At 15 he packed a bag and a guitar and left to join a Rock Band, living for a while in London ad travelling anywhere he would be paid..

In his twenties, after a forgotten number of years in the band (hazy daze indeed) Vince entered Nottingham University to study English. He graduated and began a post graduate PhD in Old Norse Studies. He eventually taught for a while in university, but left to enter the world of business.

His career encompassed Video production, Photography, Auctioneering, Developing a home for the elderly, and writing a number of best-selling books on Karate.

Whilst at University he gained his "Gold" for representing his country in International Karate championships, and continued his martial studies under a famous Japanese master. He also represented England in British and European championships and was, at one time, appointed chairman of all the martial arts in England on a Government sponsored committee.

He continued to hone his writing skills with more well-received books and featured for a number of years as a columnist in a monthly national magazine. He also played many small parts in a number of TV series, and he is an Equity Actors member.

Now, after two marriages and three children, he is working harder than ever, having re-located the HQ of his world-wide karate group – Kissaki-Kai Karate-Do – to the USA after 9/11.

He is now a world-acknowledged expert on the inner meanings of the defensive techniques in karate, and also devotes much of his time to teaching Officer Protection classes to Police throughout the world.

Indeed, the Belgium Police Force rate his contributions so highly that they have re-written their training manual to incorporate much of what Vince teaches.

Continuing his love affair with Rock music, Vince continues to sing and pound the piano, on the principle of "Who's going to stop me?"

He is in a long term relationship with his best friend and partner, Eva, who, as well as holding two degrees is also a martial artist in her own right.

He can be reached at:
info@kissaki-kai.com

For those interested in the Martial Arts, go to:
www.kissakikarate.com

Or check out 'Kissaki-kai" on Youtube.